The
Golf Widows'
Club

EMILY HARVALE

Emily Harvale lives in East Sussex, in the UK.
You can contact her via her website, Twitter, Facebook or
Pinterest

Author contacts :
www.emilyharvale.com
www.twitter.com/emilyharvale
www.facebook.com/emilyharvalewriter
www.facebook.com/emilyharvale
www.emilyharvale.com/blog
www.pinterest.com/emilyharvale

Also by this author:

Highland Fling

Lizzie Marshall's Wedding

Acknowledgements:

Thanks, as always, to my wonderful friends for their support and friendship, particularly Julie Bateman, James Campbell, Rachel Taylor, Eileen Mills and Sherry Thomas.

Special thanks to Karina of Miss Nyss www.missnyss.com for the gorgeous cover. Karina is a very talented lady and I get very excited waiting to see the beautiful covers she produces.

Grateful thanks to Christina Harkness for editing this novel and for remaining professional and friendly no matter how many times I said, 'But I like exclamation marks!', or some such equally ludicrous comment. Her input is much appreciated.

Many thanks to David of DC Creation, not just for building my wonderful website and designing my newsletter but also for all the other clever things he does. He is always at the end of a phone or email when technology gets the better of me and never gets annoyed when I say, 'David, what's this button for?' for the thousandth time or 'David, could you just ...?' I don't know what I'd do without him. www.dccreation.com

Thanks to James Andrews, Head Professional at Sedlescombe Golf Club. www.sedlescombegolfclub.co.uk

Thanks to my Twitter followers and friends, Facebook friends and fans of my Facebook author page. It's great to chat with you.

And to you, whoever you are and wherever you may be, for buying this book – Thank You.

Best Wishes

Emily ×

ISBN 978-1482770551

Print edition published worldwide 2013
E-edition published worldwide 2013

Editor Christina Harkness

Cover design by Miss Nyss

This book is dedicated to Phoebe

CHAPTER ONE

'You've done what?'Jenna Baker stared at her father in disbelief.

'Don't glare at me like that, pumpkin,' Edward Baker said. 'You wanted a job – I got you one. You start on Monday. Frankly, I thought you'd be pleased. You didn't seem to be having a great deal of success on your own.'

Jenna watched him cut into the roast beef on his plate and realised he was disappointed; he'd clearly thought it would be a pleasant surprise. She knew he meant well but being a personal assistant to the Chairman and President of Green Miles Golf Club was not a position she'd imagined herself occupying.

'I'm an estate agent, Dad, not a personal assistant.'

'You *were* an estate agent, pumpkin. Now you're unemployed,' Edward said. 'You've got to be realistic. The property market's in the doldrums so you may as well forget a future as the next Kirstie Albright and –'

'Kirstie Allsopp, Dad. Her name's Kirstie Allsopp.'

'What? Oh, Albright, Allsopp. What difference does it make? My point is, you needed to find something to tide you over until the market picks up – and God knows when that'll be. You've been looking for five weeks and found nothing. I just happened to mention it to Roddy and he came up with the offer. Seems perfect to me. I don't know why you're so upset. I thought you'd thank me. What other options do you have? Well? Do you have any?'

Jenna sucked in a long breath and tried to keep her cool. Since she'd been made redundant from 'Perfect Homes' just over a month ago, she hadn't been able to find a single job, not even part-time and she was starting to feel desperate. She knew there were thousands of people who'd been out of work for months, some, for years, so five weeks didn't seem long in the scheme of things, but she also knew that the longer she was unemployed, the harder it would be to find work and in a small seaside town like Claremont, jobs were rarer than hens' teeth.

'No,' she reluctantly admitted. 'It's just ... well, I don't know the first thing about being someone's personal assistant and ... I'm not sure I'd enjoy working for Roderick Miles.'

'Enjoy working for Roderick Miles!' her mother, Fiona said, grabbing her wine glass and gulping down a large mouthful of Merlot as if it were holy water and would save her soul from the mere mention of that name. 'No one enjoys working for Roderick Miles, darling and how your father can even suggest such a thing is beyond me. He may as well send you into the jaws of a volcano!'

'Don't be so dramatic, dear – and volcanoes don't have jaws,' Edward said.

'It's an expression, Edward, as you well know, and an apt one in this case.'

Edward sighed loudly. 'Why you still have such a low opinion of Roddy, I'll never understand.'

'You know perfectly well, why!'

'Well, yes, but I thought you'd ...' Edward began, then clearly thought better of it. 'Well ... he's a good friend and a superb businessman – at least, he was. Jenna could have learnt a lot from him, but as it happens, she won't be working for Roddy, she'll be working for his son.'

'Was? Do you mean he's dead?' Fiona asked with the slightest hint of a smile on her lips.

Edward nearly choked on the chunk of roast potato he'd just popped into his mouth.

'Dead! Of course he's not dead! I just told you, I spoke to him today. He's retiring and he's handing the club over to his son, Robert. God alone knows why though. The boy's only about nineteen and he'll have no idea how to run the place. Bound to go downhill. Total nightmare. I suppose it'll come down to me and the other more experienced members, to show him the ropes.'

Jenna and her mother exchanged confused glances and Edward refilled his wine glass, shaking his head as he did so.

'Did you say, Robert, Dad? He's handing the club over to his son Robert.'

'Yes. He's going to make an announcement at the dinner dance on Saturday.'

'Well, Robert's not nineteen! He's older than I am. He must be around thirty-three, no, thirty-four,' Jenna said.

'Thirty-four! Good heavens. Last time I saw him, he was about twelve, I think. Yes, we went to his birthday party. It was at the club. You remember. Damn silly idea that was – having a child's birthday party at a golf club. No wonder Roddy divorced the mother. Full of silly ideas, she was. Wanted Roddy to turn one of the rooms into a family room, I seem to recall. A family room! I ask you. At *our* golf club! Good thing he got shot of her or heaven knows what sort of state Green Miles would be in now. Are you telling me that was more than twenty years ago? No! I don't believe it.'

'It was about eighteen years ago and Robert wasn't twelve, he was sixteen. It was his sixteenth birthday party,' Jenna replied.

'Oh, that's right! Amelia and Roderick had a terrible row. You must remember that, Edward. What was it about? I can't recall, exactly,' Fiona asked.

Jenna and Edward shook their heads. The only thing Jenna remembered about that day was what Robert did.

'Oh well, never mind. It probably had something to do with another woman, and actually, darling, I think you'll find it was Amelia who left Roderick, not the other way around. Not long after that party, if I remember correctly. Probably had enough of his womanising. Either that or she was tired of being a golf widow. Roderick spent every waking hour at that blasted club, from what I've heard.' She lowered her voice just enough so that only Jenna could hear her. 'Sometimes, I wish I'd taken a leaf out of her book.'

Jenna grinned, knowing her mother was joking.

'What was that, Fi? Couldn't hear you. Do speak up, dear. She left Roddy you say. Oh yes, I remember now. He was rather cut up about it as I recall. Always knew the woman was a damned fool. That confirmed it. Anyway, neither here nor there. Well rid, in my opinion.'

'I thought Amelia took the son to live in America,' Fiona said. 'They moved there some years ago, I'm sure of it. Didn't she remarry? Wasn't he American?'

Jenna nodded. 'That's what I thought. Amelia was American though, originally, on her father's side, I think. Anyway, the last I heard, she and Robert were in the States. New York, I believe.'

'America. Boy's been there has he? Even worse than I thought. Won't have the slightest notion how an English club runs. Clearly got a lot to learn. Must speak to Roddy before he leaves. Good thing you're the boy's personal assistant, pumpkin. I can tell him exactly what to do and you can keep an eye on him to make sure he gets it right.'

'Dad! I'll do nothing of the sort, and you can't tell him what to do. You're not in the RAF now, you know. He's the owner of Green Miles – or he will be on Saturday. You'd better not call him a boy, either, or you'll get off to a really bad start ... and whilst we're on that subject, *please* don't call me pumpkin at the club.'

'I always call you pumpkin,' Edward said, a confused look on his face.

'I know you do and that's why I'm saying this. I'm thirty years old and if I'm going to be working there, I'd rather you called me Jenna.'

'You're not seriously going to take the job, darling!'

4

Fiona announced.

'I don't think I've got much choice, Mum. I need to pay my mortgage. I've been looking and there's nothing out there, Dad's right about that. It'll just be until the market picks up or I can find something more suitable and ... wait a minute. Robert does know about this, doesn't he? I mean, you said he'll be taking over on Saturday but he has agreed to me being his personal assistant. This isn't just something you and Roderick Miles have decided and will come as a complete surprise to everyone else involved, is it?'

Edward shrugged. 'Does it matter? Roddy suggested it and the boy will go along with it, you can be sure of that. He'll probably be grateful that his father has sorted everything out for him and he can just turn up and start learning from those of us with more experience. I don't agree with Roddy going off and leaving him though. Should stay and settle the boy in. Make sure it's all running smoothly before he goes off gallivanting. Not really good enough. I will agree with you there, Fi.'

'How kind of you dear, but I don't believe I said any such thing. Where is Roderick gallivanting off to, anyway?' Fiona asked.

'What? Oh, he's off on that new yacht of his. Be gone for a couple of months. I think he's lost his mind. Told him so. Says he's in love. Needs to get away. Love! Love, I ask you. Still, there it is.'

Fiona smirked. 'I assume you mean he's in love with a woman and not his yacht, darling. I knew a woman would be involved in this sudden decision. Tell me, how old is she this time?'

Edward pushed his empty plate aside and glanced at his daughter then at his wife. 'I don't think that's any of our business, dear.'

'Oh don't be such an old stuffed shirt, Edward! She's younger than Jenna isn't she? That's why you're embarrassed. The dirty old sod.'

'Fiona! Really!'

'Er ... excuse me, Dad but Mum's right. He *is* a dirty old sod. That's why I didn't want to work for him. I've heard rumours about him and the female staff –'

'Jenna!' Edward coughed to clear his throat. 'I'd rather not discuss rumours, thank you pumpkin. Roddy is a dear friend and I don't feel comfortable speaking of him in such a manner. I'll admit, he does have a bit of a wandering eye and I'll also accept that his recent ... female friends ... have all been a few years younger –'

'A few years! Darling, the last one was at least thirty years his junior. I'd bet anything that this one's in her twenties! It makes me cringe just thinking about it. The man's sixty, for heaven's sake!'

'He's lonely! You can't blame a man for wanting a bit of female company. Perhaps if that wife of his hadn't abandoned him, he wouldn't need to chase women.'

'Ah! You admit it then, that he chases women. It's odd though, dear. Just a moment ago you were saying it was a good thing he was rid of his wife. Are you now saying he's lost without her?'

'No! You're twisting my words. I'm saying ... oh, it doesn't matter. If he wants to go out with young women, that's his privilege. If you left me, I'd probably do the same.'

Fiona sniggered. 'Don't be ridiculous, darling, you know you'd do no such thing. It takes a certain type of man to behave like that, and believe me, Edward, you are *certainly not* the type.'

Edward looked put out.

Jenna grinned at her father. 'Mum meant that in a good way, Dad.'

'Of course I did,' Fiona said, winking at her husband. 'You don't know how glad I am that you don't make a fool of yourself over young women like he does. I wonder if the son's turned out the same. I don't remember much about him, except that he was very tall for his age ... and very good-looking.'

'And you criticise Roddy!' Edward said. 'Looking for a boy toy, are you dear?'

Jenna giggled. 'It's a toy boy Dad, and Mum wouldn't do that any more than you would. You're right though Mum, Robert was good-looking. All the girls had a crush on him.'

'Oh! Did that include you, pumpkin?' Edward said.

Jenna felt herself blushing. She hadn't thought about Robert Miles for years. Well, that wasn't quite true she admitted to herself; she had thought about him a few times. Okay, she'd thought about him a lot, but boys like Robert Miles were difficult to forget, and now he was a man ... and she was going to be his personal assistant.

Suddenly, being a personal assistant to the new Chairman and President of Green Miles Golf Club didn't seem so bad after all.

'Yes,' she said, her voice just above a whisper, 'that included me.' Then she let her mind wander back in time.

At sixteen, Robert seemed so grown up, so confident, so masculine – in contrast to the spotty youths at her school. Jenna was only twelve at the time of his party and she and Robert had never spoken before that day. Robert went to an all-boys prep school then an all-boys public school whilst Jenna was educated at the local state schools and when Robert did come home, for the holidays, he mixed in an entirely different circle.

It always seemed a little odd to Jenna that Roderick and Edward never socialised outside the golf club, bearing in mind their lifelong friendship, until her mother told her what Roderick had done, many years ago, on Fiona and Edward's wedding day. Her mother had hardly spoken to Roderick since.

Jenna had met Robert before though, two years before his party, when she was ten, and she realised that love at first sight was real. She'd stood only feet away from him as their fathers chatted one day, at a local petrol station, and she'd stared at him from under her lashes for ten whole minutes.

She could still remember it. It was a hot, summer day; one of those days when the entire world seems to slow down almost to a stop and even the air is still. She got out of her father's brand new Ford Mondeo car, to get an ice cream and Robert ... well, Robert just seemed to be shadowing his father – standing beside him as he filled his car, walking beside him as he went to pay and staring up at him as he chatted to her father.

That was why she was able to look at him for ten minutes; he didn't even notice her. But why would he? Even as a fourteen-year-old boy, Robert Miles was gorgeous. He could have been a pop star, a film star, a god. He was tall for his age and had an athletic frame which the gangly boys at her school would have killed for. His eyes were like midnight blue pools any girl would want to dive into, framed by long dark lashes that even her mother couldn't achieve with an eyelash curler and volumising mascara. His thick, almost black hair looked like dark chocolate and as soft as a kitten's fur and when a breath of wind came from nowhere and lifted his tousled fringe from his tanned, forehead, Jenna was unable to stop a long, deep, soulful sigh escaping from somewhere near her heart.

Unfortunately, her father interpreted her sigh as one of boredom, not of adoration, and finally remembered that she was with him. Equally unfortunate, was the fact that her ice cream had melted down her hand – and the front of her dress, and her father said he'd better get her cleaned up before she got back into his new car.

She could still picture the look on Robert's face, as if

8

he'd only just noticed her, and those huge blue pools washed over her red, chubby face, her long, straight brown hair, her now stained, pink dress, right down to her flip-flops, where she was sure her toes curled up with embarrassment. She saw his lips curve up at one side but his eyes were full of sympathy, as if he knew exactly how stupid and insignificant she felt. And then ... he was gone, following his father back to their Jaguar.

She saw him a few times after that, in Claremont, during the holidays but only from a distance and he never glanced in her direction. For Robert Miles, Jenna Baker didn't seem to exist – until the day of his sixteenth birthday party. And that was another day, Jenna knew, she would remember for the rest of her life.

CHAPTER TWO

Roderick Miles hadn't seen his son Robert since the day, three weeks ago, when he'd told him Green Miles Golf Club would be his, and he was less sure of Robert's thoughts and intentions now than he had been then.

They met in New York, for lunch, on Robert's thirty-fourth birthday and although they hadn't seen one another for a few months, Roddy thought Robert knew what he had planned. Roddy had inherited the club from his father, as his father had from his. It had passed down through the generations since the original owner, Theodore Miles's time, and it was always Roddy's intention to follow this tradition and pass it on to his son.

He thought Robert understood that but the look of surprise he saw in his son's eyes was genuine and when Robert said he'd have to think about it, Roddy knew better than to push the point.

Fortunately, Robert didn't take long to think about it. The next day he called his father and agreed to take over the club, provided Roddy promised not to interfere in any way. This was a condition Roddy was happy to comply with but, just in case he felt the urge to offer advice, he decided to take his new girlfriend sailing for a few months. Things hadn't always been easy between him and Robert and he felt that this would prove to his son that he had complete faith in him. That should help to rebuild bridges between them, bridges he was only too aware, had been left unrepaired for far too long.

Robert Miles sat opposite his father, separated by an antique, solid oak desk. The desk had been in the same position in front of the window, since their ancestor, Theodore Miles had purchased the Manor House and five hundred acre estate of Claremont in 1813 and turned most of it into a golf club.

They were sitting in what had been Eleanor Claremont's bedroom, the room Theodore immediately turned into his office on the day he took possession. Some said that like the purchase of the estate, it was out of spite; others, that the room simply had one of the best views of the former estate and therefore, the best views of the fairways and greens. It was a story Robert had heard so many times that he knew it by heart.

Robert sat relaxed in a similarly old, chestnut-brown, wing chair, his elbows resting on the arms and his agile fingers dangling over the ends. Despite his casual air, he was dressed formally in a charcoal grey, tailor-made suit, white cotton shirt and midnight blue tie.

'All I'm saying is that it might have been nice to have let me choose my own personal assistant,' he said, meeting his father's gaze. 'I'm perfectly happy to be thrown in at the deep end and sink or swim by my own efforts but I'd rather have someone alongside me who is at least familiar with the water.'

'Well, the girl needed a job and when Irene told me she was pregnant and that her doctor said she shouldn't work because of some health issues or some such thing, it seemed the perfect way to kill two birds with one stone, so to speak. Of course, if you'd rather find someone else yourself, I'll explain that to Edward. I'm sure he'll understand, but surely it's better to have someone with connections to the club? Edward is the club captain, you know. It won't harm you to have him on your side and that daughter of his is a good girl; quite bright, I believe. Recently made redundant. Oh ... I've told you that already haven't I?'

Robert nodded. 'Twice. I can see the reasoning behind it. I'm merely saying there may be someone better qualified for the position than a former estate agent, even though she is the daughter of the club captain. I assume, as you didn't refer to him as the men's captain that you still don't allow women members. Women have had equal rights for some time now. Haven't you heard?'

Roddy opened his mouth to speak just as Robert's mobile rang.

Robert took it from his jacket pocket, glanced at the screen and sighed. He then pressed a button and replaced it in his pocket.

'Never mind,' he said, his attention now returned to Roddy. 'We'll see how it goes. If it doesn't work out, I'll look for a replacement. You did say that ... Irene is happy to make herself available, via the telephone and email, to answer any queries I may have, if needed.'

Roddy nodded.

'Well that's something, I suppose. Miss Baker can liaise with her and hopefully get to grips with everything fairly quickly. She's starting today?'

Roddy nodded again. 'Edward's bringing her in at eight o'clock. I suggested we all have a spot of breakfast together.'

Robert fixed his gaze on Roddy's face. He knew that handing the club over was difficult for his father, even though it was 'tradition'. It had been his life, for as long as Robert could remember. Roddy had left the RAF to run it when his own father had passed it on to him, on his thirtieth birthday and he spent most of his time there – or at least, he had when Robert and his mother had lived with him. Robert assumed that hadn't changed, even though he knew Roddy had now, finally, taken up sailing; something Robert's mother had wanted Roddy to do when they were together.

'You are sure about this, aren't you?' Robert asked.

'About the girl? Oh I see. You mean about transferring the club to you. Yes, Robert, I'm one hundred per cent sure. Anyway, it's a bit late for me to change my mind now, isn't it? The papers are signed and sealed. Besides, it's always been my intention to hand it over to you, just as my father did to me and his father did to him. It's a tradition ... and one I hope you'll continue, by handing it on to your son.'

Robert smirked. 'Well, that's assuming I have a son – or any children, for that matter.'

'Not have children? What do you mean, not have children? Of course, you'll have children. Unless ... is there a reason why that may be in doubt? Oh! Do ... do you have a problem ... in that area?'

Robert could see his father's concern. 'Not as far as I'm aware but I'd need a wife to have a child – and that's the problem.'

'Nonsense! People are leaving it later and later to get married these days and thirty-four is still young, in my book. Besides, you don't have to be married – although, I agree, that is preferable. I'm somewhat old-fashioned on that score but ... Oh! Are ... are you telling me you're … not interested in women?'

Roddy sounded horrified and Robert didn't answer for several seconds. He'd been surprised by the comment but he smiled sardonically at his father's obvious embarrassment as he saw the red flush creep across Roddy's cheeks.

'Would that be a problem?'

Roddy's eyebrows almost hit the ceiling. 'Good God! I ... I mean. No! N... not ... not in the least. Your ... your personal choices are ... are yours.'

Robert noticed that his father's eyes seemed to look everywhere but at him and when the grandfather clock near the door loudly announced the hour with eight resounding strikes, Roddy appeared to be genuinely relieved.

'Good God! Is that the time?' he announced. 'We'd better head down to the restaurant to meet Edward. Don't want to keep him and his daughter waiting.' He immediately leapt from his chair as if the seat were on fire.

Robert let out a short sigh. He knew he should have told his father that he hadn't meant that he was gay – as Roddy now clearly thought he was – but that he seemed to have trouble picking women, but he decided not to. He had started to hope, over recent weeks, that his father may have changed – just a little, but clearly he hadn't. He still expected Robert to be what he perceived as 'the perfect son' and that meant being a clone of the Miles' men throughout the generations. Tough, no-nonsense, military men, turned ruthless businessmen, golf addicts and womanisers.

Robert had already broken the mould by not going into the forces, but, by starting his own hotel business as soon as he left university, he knew he had redeemed himself slightly, in his father's eyes. Not that he did it for his father. The days of trying to do things to please him had long since gone. It might do Roddy good to think that his son had once again, broken the Miles' mould, if only for a few days. It would also be interesting to see if Roddy would now treat him differently.

'I'm so pleased you feel that way ... *Dad*,' Robert said, getting up from the chair.

Roddy was dashing towards the door but stopped and turned, meeting his son's eyes.

'That's the first time you've called me 'Dad' since ... well, since just after your mother took you to America, I think.'

Roddy clearly failed to detect the hint of sarcasm; he'd merely heard the word 'Dad'.

'Well, you weren't around to hear it, were you?'

His father visibly flinched and turned back towards the door. 'No, son. I wasn't,' he said, marching into the hall.

Robert sighed and followed him as he'd done so many times as a boy, eager for his father's approval. That at least had changed, Robert thought, heading downstairs to the restaurant. Whether Roddy approved of him or not, no longer mattered to him. The only thing that mattered now, was making sure Green Miles Golf Club would not be the reason any other children rarely saw their fathers.

Jenna was feeling more than a little nervous. Starting a new job – any new job – was bad enough but starting a new job in a position in which you had no experience was far worse, and knowing that her new boss was the man she'd been secretly in love with since she was ten years old, was verging on terrifying.

She knew she was being overly dramatic. She wasn't really in love with Robert Miles. How could she be? She didn't know him. She may have thought she was, once, but that was a long time ago and she had eventually realised it was more of an infatuation, a crush really. The sort of thing you would feel for a pop star or a film star when you would stick their posters on your bedroom wall, and gaze up at them dreamily every night before going to sleep, knowing they were unattainable. That's how it had been with Robert – but without the poster.

Well, Jenna thought, that's all part of growing up and when you do grow up, you take the posters down and start dating real, live men. That makes you realise that what you thought was love, was just a crush and that a person like Robert Miles is only someone you dream about.

'Morning, Roddy,' Edward said as he saw Roddy striding into the coffee bar area of the club restaurant. 'We've just ordered coffee. Pumpkin was running late and didn't get a chance to have any before I picked her up.'

'Thanks, Dad,' Jenna said through clenched teeth, slapping her father on the arm with the back of her fingertips.

She sucked in a breath and screwed her eyes tightly closed for a split second, in the vain hope that she could

15

magically make herself disappear. When she opened them, she looked directly into the deep, dark eyes of a tall, athletic-looking man whom she knew was Robert Miles, and she felt the same feeling she had had as a chubby ten-year-old, in a pink dress, stained with ice cream. Thankfully, this time, she was able to stop the sigh escaping.

'You must be Miss Baker,' Robert said, leaning forward to shake her hand.

Jenna waited for the bolt of electricity as their hands met, but there was none. His grip was firm and business-like and his skin was smooth and cool to the touch. No sparks, no magic, nothing, just two adults shaking hands. She couldn't decide if she were pleased or disappointed.

She didn't expect him to feel anything, of course; he had never really been aware of her existence – apart from on that one occasion at his birthday party, and the ice cream spectacle – but she'd expected some reaction from her body. The last time he'd touched her, she'd been positive she'd heard an entire orchestra playing the finale of Tchaikovsky's 1812 overture, including the brass band, cathedral bells and cannon fire, but then a girl's first kiss is always something special even if you are only twelve and your heart is broken fifteen minutes later.

'I'm very pleased to meet you,' Robert said. 'Please call me Robert and may I call you Jenna?'

He let go of her hand and Jenna realised, with some embarrassment that she'd been staring at him.

'Er. Yes of course.'

'Just don't call her pumpkin,' Edward said, grinning broadly, 'or she may well slap you.'

'We've actually met before,' Jenna said, immediately regretting the words as soon as they were out of her mouth but unable to think of anything else quickly enough to steer the conversation away from why her father insisted on calling her pumpkin.

Robert's brows knit together. He was clearly struggling to recall the meeting.

'Really? I feel sure I would have remembered that,' he said, smiling.

Jenna felt herself blush under the warmth of his smile. 'It was a long time ago, at your sixteenth birthday party. I didn't expect you to remember.'

She thought she saw a shadow pass across his face. He glanced down at his tie, which was the same midnight blue as his eyes, and straightened it, although it was already perfectly in place.

'That was a long time ago,' he added. 'To be honest, I don't remember much at all about that party.' He glanced briefly at his father then back at Jenna. 'I ... I got pretty drunk, I'm ashamed to say. I hope I didn't do anything I shouldn't have.'

Jenna looked away, unable to control the irrational sense of sadness she felt creeping over her. She knew the kiss had meant nothing to him at the time but to hear him say he couldn't even remember it and that he'd been drunk anyway, somehow shattered the crystal palace into which she'd placed that precious moment and treasured it for all these years.

'No,' she said, hoping her voice sounded calmer than she felt, and didn't reflect her disappointment. 'Nothing at all – as far as I was concerned, anyway.'

She immediately forced herself to smile her sexiest smile, one she and her best friend, Daisy had seen in so many films and spent most of their teenage years, and their twenties, perfecting, in front of the full length mirror in Daisy's bedroom.

'Well,' Roddy said, shaking Jenna's hand and squeezing it, 'I'm Roderick, Robert's father, but of course, you know that. I'm so pleased you're joining our little team – well, Robert's little team, I should say. He's in charge now. Edward, you've met Robert before, of course.'

Edward nodded. 'Yes, of course. How are you, my boy? Haven't seen you in years. Not since that birthday party, I believe. Shame your mother took you off ... to the States, my wife tells me. You used to be here all the time, as a young lad –'

'Hardly at all actually, Mr Baker. I was usually left at home ... with my mother.'

'Really? I seem to remember you always running around. Believe I even hit you with one of my balls, once. Dreadful day that was. Should have been a birdie. Instead it hit you and bounced into Devil's Hole. Took me six strokes to get it out! Aptly named, that bunker, let me tell you. Probably just as well you stayed at home. A golf course is no place for a child.'

Jenna saw Robert's eyes narrow but he smiled broadly, exposing perfect white teeth.

'I see you and my father agree on several points, Mr Baker. I also remember that day – but not for the same reason. It's good to see you again. I have big plans for improvements at Green Miles. It'll be very interesting to see what you make of them.'

'Edward. Call me Edward, my boy. Big plans, eh? Not sure there's much you can do to improve the place, is there Roddy? Runs perfectly as it is. Still, I'll be only too pleased to help you out. I told pum ... Jenna only yesterday how important it is to have experienced people to guide you.'

'My sentiments exactly, Edward. I was saying the same thing to my father, just a few minutes ago.'

Jenna had the strangest feeling that things weren't going well, though she couldn't put her finger on why not, exactly. She was just grateful that the coffee had finally arrived; she needed it. She'd had a really bad night, hardly sleeping at all then this morning, she'd fallen into a deep sleep and when she finally woke up, she realised she hadn't set the alarm. Not having a job to get up for during the last five weeks, she'd turned it off and hadn't thought to set it again when she got home from her parents' house yesterday evening.

She barely had time to shower, dry her hair and throw on her clothes. It was a good thing that she kept her suits and work blouses cleaned and pressed, in case she got an interview, otherwise she'd have been in a real state of panic. A few strokes of her mascara brush and a quick smudge of lipstick were all she had time for, before her father honked his car horn, something she'd specifically asked him *not* to do at seven forty-five in the morning. She'd grabbed her handbag and raced to the car, knowing that patience was not one of the virtues her father possessed and that he'd honk the horn every few minutes until she appeared on the doorstep.

Coffee and some toast at the very least, were seriously required if she had any hope of getting through the morning. She was more than a little relieved when Robert seemed to read her mind.

'Let's sit down and order breakfast, shall we? It's going to be a busy day for Jenna and me and I'm sure you and Edward are eager to get on the golf course ... Dad.'

Jenna was surprised by the almost derisory tone in Robert's voice but neither Roddy nor her father, seemed to notice it, although Roddy was looking at Robert, a little sadly, she thought.

'Yes. Thought we'd leave you to it, son and get a round in before the weather turns. Torrential rain is forecast for this afternoon.'

Robert raised his eyebrows. 'I didn't realise the weather stopped play. I seem to recall you played come rain, hail or gales. You even played in the snow, more than once.'

Roddy chuckled. 'I did, Robert! You're right. Mind you, I was much younger then. These old bones don't perform quite as well as they used to, you know. My entire

19

body starts complaining if I'm out in rough weather for too long these days. I can't keep up with the youngsters now, my boy.'

'Then perhaps two months on a yacht with a twenty-one year-old woman is not your wisest move,' Robert said, but Roddy and Edward had already headed towards the restaurant, reminiscing about 'snow golf'.

Jenna stepped forward and Robert seemed startled, as if he'd forgotten she was there.

'Sorry. After you,' he said, holding out his arm to indicate that she should go ahead of him.

She smiled up at him but he didn't seem to notice; he was staring at his father – and he seemed to be scowling.

CHAPTER THREE

'I remember playing one time in a blizzard,' Edward said as they all sat at a table near the window, overlooking the first tee. 'It snowed in the morning then stopped. There was only a light covering and it was one of the inter-club competitions. Got half way round and down it came. Could hardly see a thing ... Ah, there you are, Beth. I'll have the 'Full English Breakfast', please.'

Beth, the waitress, smiled. She was holding a pad in one hand and a rubber-topped pencil in the other but she didn't write anything down.

'You know what I want, sweetie,' Roddy said, winking at her.

'I always know what you want,' Beth said, winking back.

She must be all of twenty, Jenna thought and she was certain she heard Robert groan quietly across the table from her,

'Eggs and bacon for me, please, and some toast,' Robert said. 'Wholemeal if you've got it. The menu just says 'toast' – and butter. Thanks. What will you have, Jenna?'

'She'll have the Full English Breakfast, won't you pump ... Jenna?' Edward said.

'Actually no, Dad. May I have egg on toast please? Poached egg, also on wholemeal. Thanks,' Jenna said.

Beth still didn't write anything down.

'Sure,' Beth said, grinning. 'Tea or more coffee? Would you all like orange juice?'

'Tea and coffee,' Robert said, 'and orange juice, please. Will you bring it in a jug so we can help ourselves?'

'Sure.'

Beth tucked her pad and pencil back into her apron

pocket and sauntered off towards the kitchen.

'Let me guess,' Robert said to Edward, 'you continued playing.'

'What? Oh yes, the blizzard. Of course we did. Bit of snow shouldn't stop play. Old Smithers from Fernhills wanted to call a halt – and if I'm completely honest, if it had been anyone else, we would have agreed but that bunch from Fernhills had cheated in a previous round of the competition and that's just not done. Unforgivable. Golf is a game of etiquette. Honour, trust, good manners and thought for other players are paramount – but I don't need to tell you that. They let themselves down badly but we couldn't prove it.'

'What did they do?' Jenna asked.

'They had to play on, of course, or forfeit.'

'No. I meant, how did they cheat?'

'What? Oh. We discovered, quite by chance, they'd used a smaller ball but when we challenged them, regulation balls were the only ones found. Smaller balls can't be used in competitions, only the regulation 1.680 inches, are allowed. I've told you that before, pumpkin.'

'It must have slipped my mind,' Jenna said. She wished she hadn't asked. 'So who won on the day of the blizzard?'

'We did. I finished in eighty. You made seventy-eight, Roddy. Not one of our finest days. Still, we won the competition. That's what matters.'

'Of course it is,' Robert said.

'Damn fools at Fernhills tried to complain,' Roddy grumbled. 'Said it was unfair because of the weather! Weren't having that, were we Edward? Told them golf's not just a fair-weather game but we'd be happy to beat them again in perfect conditions, if they liked. They conceded.'

'You must be very proud,' Robert said.

This time both Roddy and Edward gave Robert a

curious look.

'You play with orange balls in the snow, don't you?' Jenna said, hoping to diffuse what could turn into an explosive moment. 'Do you remember, Dad? I painted one of your balls once the colours of the rainbow.'

'I'd like to have seen that,' Beth said, grinning cheekily at Edward and winking as she brought a jug of orange juice over to the table.

Edward grinned back at her. 'You cheeky little minx,' he said, apparently forgetting his daughter was sitting next to him.

Jenna blushed with embarrassment, realising what she'd said. She wasn't a prude by any means but this was her *dad* for heaven's sake.

'I meant his golf ball,' she snapped, giving Beth what she hoped was an icy stare and completely forgetting that she would now be working with her.

Edward had the decency to look a little embarrassed and he coughed a few times, lowering his eyes towards the table.

'Do you know when the first coloured ball was used and by whom?' Robert asked. Then to Beth, 'Thank you, Beth. Please bring the tea and coffee as soon as it's ready.'

It was clearly a dismissal and Beth was obviously bright enough to recognise that.

'I'll bring it right over, Mr Miles,' she replied, without the slightest hint of sarcasm.

'It was in the late 1920s I believe,' Roddy said. 'No idea by whom, though. I know Wilson brought out a bright orange ball and a bright yellow one too. Gave them strange names, I seem to remember reading. Cost a fortune at the time. Didn't catch on. Some other company brought one out about fifty years after but it wasn't until the early 1980s that coloured balls really took off.'

'Took off! That's a good one, Roddy,' Edward said, chuckling. 'I'm with Roddy. I'd say late 1920s but again,

23

no idea by whom.'

Jenna shrugged. 'I know nothing about golf, but I'd say 1895.' She glanced at Robert and her heart did a little flip.

The corners of his mouth had spread into a broad smile and his dark eyes twinkled like little constellations in the night sky. When he spoke, his voice was almost a caress.

'Isn't it a bit rash to admit you know nothing about golf when you're employed as a personal assistant to the owner of a golf club?'

'Oh!' Jenna felt herself flush crimson. 'Er ... well, I know a bit about golf ... from Dad ... and I'm a fast learner and –'

'It's not a problem,' Robert interrupted. 'I was teasing you. What made you say 1895?'

'Er ... because that was the year Marconi made the first successful radio transmission, wasn't it? I was reading about it the other day and I know that's got nothing to do with golf but it just popped into my head!'

Robert smiled again and once more Jenna's heart flipped.

'I think it was – and you're the closest. It was actually believed to be Rudyard Kipling, around 1893, though some say it was a year or two earlier. He was living in Vermont at the time and apparently painted a white ball, red, to make it more visible when he was playing golf in the snow. That's the story anyway.'

'Wow!' Jenna said, truly impressed. 'He and his family returned to England and eventually settled in Burwash, not far from here – but of course, you know where Burwash is. So, not just a brilliant writer, then. I love his books, especially the 'Just So Stories'. I know most people would say 'The Jungle Books' but I prefer the 'Just So Stories'.'

She was waffling, she knew. She always waffled when she was nervous. Why did Robert make her feel so nervous? she thought.

'Rudyard Kipling!' Roddy exclaimed. 'Where did you

hear that?'

Robert didn't take his eyes from Jenna's face. She could feel herself getting more and more flustered. She prayed she wouldn't start giggling, something else she usually did when she felt nervous or flustered.

'I read it, many years ago,' Robert said. 'I read rather a lot when I was young. I seemed to have a great deal of time on my hands.'

Roddy shifted uncomfortably in his chair and Robert finally turned his head away from Jenna and gazed out the window towards the green. No one spoke for several minutes.

Jenna followed Robert's gaze. The restaurant overlooked the first tee and fairway and the morning dew still covered the green. The sun had risen almost three hours earlier, and it promised to be a bright, if slightly chilly, May morning, but the first rays of sunlight were only just peeping over the trees to the east, and the clubhouse and this part of the course were still in shadow. Roddy had said rain was forecast for the afternoon but this morning, there wasn't a cloud in the sky.

Jenna knew a bit about Green Miles Golf Club and its history but not as much as she should, she realised. She knew that the clubhouse was a former Manor house which had been rebuilt several times over the centuries, since the first dwelling was erected around the year 1067. Nothing remained of that, but each house since, had been built or extended on the same plot, on high ground, on a ridge overlooking a valley with the tiny village situated in the centre of it.

The village was sheltered by hills on three sides and exposed to the sea to the south. After the Battle of Hastings in 1066 it was renamed Clermont after its new feudal Lord, Baron De Clermont, who was given village and several hundred acres of land by William The Conqueror. Jenna remembered that from her history lessons. The village had since expanded into a small town and at some point, the spelling had changed.

The Green Miles Golf Club brochure which she'd hastily read online last night, stated that Theodore Miles had purchased the estate of Claremont and turned the house and part of the grounds into a golf club in 1813. It also said that Green Miles was a Parkland Course, with copses, lakes and streams running through it, much of which had remained unchanged from the days when it formed the grounds and gardens of Claremont Manor. There were woodlands to the left and right boundaries, and many of the trees were hundreds of years old. Some were lost during the Great Storm of 1987 but replanting had taken place and they were almost back to their pre-storm days.

She also knew that the course itself was designed to fit in with the landscape and only minor alterations to the lay of the land had been necessary to make the course at Green Miles Golf Club one of the best in the country, although in 1813, there weren't nearly as many golf clubs as there were now, in 2013. According to her father, it was still one of the most prestigious clubs in the country.

From different parts of the golf course, the brochure had said, one could see either Claremont or the new house and gardens Theodore Miles had built for himself and his wife, back in 1813, or the English Channel. The vistas were breathtaking, not that she thought many of the members actually took much notice of them; all they saw, if her father was anything to go by, were the fairways, the greens and the many hazards which lie between the tee box and the pin with the flag on it.

Jenna watched a blackbird hop across the tee-off area and she marvelled at how peaceful it was. A slight breeze tickled the leaves of the trees and she thought that it finally felt like spring. It had been cold and wet from the end of March until just a few days ago and now tulips and bluebells were blooming amongst the remaining daffodils carpeting the woodland areas around the course. Birds were twittering in the trees and bushes and at last, it seemed that the season of new life and new love, was finally in full swing. She glanced across at Robert from under her lashes. New love, she thought. If only.

Beth's voice broke the silence. 'Two Full English Breakfasts, one egg, bacon, wholemeal toast and butter, one poached egg on wholemeal toast. Anything else I can get you?'

Jenna heard Robert sigh deeply as he turned to face his father who, along with Edward, had also been gazing out the window. She wondered what Robert had been thinking.

'That's all for now, thanks, sweetie,' Roddy said, grinning up at Beth.

'So, Dad,' Robert said. 'Tell us about your new adventure. Where are you and the, no doubt, delightful, Miss Starr headed? And when do I get to meet her?'

Roddy seemed startled but he soon recovered. 'Oh. Er ... you'll meet her at the dinner dance on Saturday. Then we're heading off on Monday and –'

'Yoo-hoo! Roddy!' a high-pitched voice called out from the direction of the kitchen.

Roddy's head shot round and his faced flushed scarlet as a young, buxom blonde tottered towards them, balancing precariously on the highest heels Jenna had ever seen. Her skin-tight, leather skirt barely covered her modesty and her equally tight fitting leopard print top was so low that it left little to the imagination. Her long, bare legs were the colour of Jenna's coffee and her teeth were whiter than the crisp, white linen tablecloths covering the restaurant tables.

Jenna could feel her jaw drop and a quick glance in Robert's direction showed her that he too, looked stunned.

'Don't tell me,' Robert said, watching the woman

27

approach, 'this is the, definitely delightful, Miss Starr – and right on cue.'

'What? Oh ... er ... yes. I ... what the devil are you doing here?' Roddy announced, sounding less than pleased.

'I just popped in to see Beth, babe. We're going shopping when she gets off. She told me you were here and I just couldn't *wait* to meet Bobbie.'

She hunched up her shoulders towards her ears and pulled a face somewhere between that of an excited child and someone desperate to use the lavatory.

Roddy struggled to his feet and the woman flung her arms around him, her bracelets and bangles jingling like tiny church bells out of tune. She planted a noisy, lingering kiss on Roddy's lips.

Jenna saw Robert's eyes narrow for a split second. Then he was all smiles. He stood up and stepped forward to greet the woman, holding out his hand towards her but with a flapping of her arms and a loud jingling of the abundant jewellery, she launched herself at him, kissing him first on one cheek and then the other.

'I've heard so much about you, Bobbie,' she shrieked, 'I feel as if I've known you all my life! Roddy! You didn't tell me he was almost as gorgeous as you, you old devil!'

'Won't you join us, Miss Starr,' Robert said when she finally released him. He pulled a chair away from another table, placing it at the end of the table between Roddy and Edward before offering it to her.

'Call me Sherree, Bobbie. That's S-H-E-R-R-E-E.'

'Of course it is,' Robert said. 'It's lovely to meet you. May I introduce Jenna Baker and her father Edward, whom you no doubt know already? I believe you worked here ... for a short time.'

'Yes,' she said. 'I was a waitress, right here in the restaurant when I met Roddy. Lovely to see you, Eddie. Nice to meet you, Jen.'

She plopped onto the chair with more jingling, hunching of her shoulders and strange facial expressions.

'Dad was just about to tell us about your trip. Are you a keen sailor?' Robert asked.

'Ooh! I'm ever so excited! I've never been sailing before!' Sherree shrieked.

'Really,' Robert said. 'Are you sure you'll like it?'

He returned to his seat but Jenna noticed his eyes remained fixed on the *lovely* Sherree.

'Ooh! I'm sure I will! It always looks so romantic, doesn't it? On the telly, I mean. And my mum said Princess Diana did it. And I know Cheryl Cole has. I can't wait!'

'Well,' Robert said without even a hint of sarcasm, 'I think I can safely say, it'll be the experience of your life. Would you like some breakfast?'

'Ooh! No thanks. I only have coffee in the mornings. Got to watch my figure. As my mum says, "If you don't watch your figure, no one else will want to watch it!" I put on a pound last week! It's all the lovely places Roddy takes me to, isn't it, babe?'

Roddy cleared his throat. 'Yes, well ...'

'So what's the itinerary?' Robert asked.

Sherree pulled an exceptionally strange face and stuck out her lower lip.

'Where are you going ... sailing?'

'Ooh! The Canary Islands first. My dad lives there and we're going to spend a few days with him. Then, Casablanca, because that's one of my gran's favourite films and I want to bring her back something with Casablanca written on it. Roddy says it's on the coast of North Africa in some ocean or other but I know it's in the Med. He's such a tease.'

She planted another of her kisses on Roddy's cheek, followed by the hunched shoulders and contorted facial expressions.

'I believe it is in the Atlantic Ocean,' Robert said, 'but it does sound as though it should be in the Mediterranean, you're right. Anywhere else?'

'Ooh yes! After that, we're going to Monte Carlo. Ooh, Monte Carlo. It even sounds glamorous, doesn't it? Then Roddy says, the Greek Islands, Turkey, maybe Egypt. I'd love to sail down the Nile, like Cleopatra.'

'It sounds ... truly amazing,' Robert said.

'Yes ... well,' said Roddy, standing up again. 'Why don't you go and tell Beth she can leave early and you two go off shopping. I'll see you later. Robert's got a lot to do and unless we get on with breakfast, Edward and I will be late to tee-off. Run along now.'

Sherree jumped to her feet, jingling as she did so. She kissed Roddy and tottered round to Robert, who had also risen from his chair. She kissed him, this time on the lips, clearly much to his surprise then she tottered towards Edward, who, having also stood up, visibly backed away and held out his hand. She was having none of that and said so, planting an extremely noisy, 'smacker' on his flushed cheek. With another hunch of her shoulders and a final, decidedly odd expression, she waved at Jenna then tottered away towards the kitchen with four pairs of eyes watching her go.

'So ... that is Miss Sherree Starr,' Robert said.

Jenna wasn't sure whether he was pleased to have met Sherree or not but she couldn't help but notice that he waited until she was out of sight before turning his attention back to his father. She found herself wishing that she possessed at least one or two of Sherree's scarcely hidden charms. There probably wasn't a man alive on the planet who didn't like a woman with long legs and large breasts. At five feet three with a size 34 bust, Jenna possessed neither.

What was strange, she thought, was that for someone supposedly 'in love' as her father had said Roddy was,

Roddy seemed rather too eager to get rid of Sherree. Was he embarrassed by his own proclivity to fall for younger women? Or was it because Robert was here?

'Well, I don't suppose you'd understand,' Roddy said, resuming his seat and cutting into his sausage. 'She makes me feel young again and she's very good company, when you get to know her.'

'I'm sure she is ... and I do understand, Dad, believe me,' Robert said. 'I can see precisely why you'd want to spend several weeks on a yacht with the lovely Sherree. She clearly has a lot to offer a man.'

CHAPTER FOUR

'Enjoy your day, pumpkin ... I mean, Jenna,' Edward said.

'Thanks Dad, and you.'

They had finished breakfast and the four of them strolled through the coffee bar area out into the main hall where one door led outside to the first tee and the driving ranges; another led to the pro shop and the club professional's office and another to the changing rooms. A wide, oak staircase led up towards the Chairman and President's office, club secretary's office and what was now, Jenna's office, together with many other rooms, some of which were used for storage but several others remained empty and unused.

Roddy and Edward headed towards the changing rooms and Robert and Jenna stood at the foot of the stairs.

'Why does your father call you pumpkin?' Robert said, dragging his eyes away from his father's back and turning towards Jenna. 'I noticed he did it a couple of times and ... it seemed to ... irritate you, especially when he advised us not to do so. Is it a sore point?'

Jenna sighed. She might as well get it over and done with, she thought. She'd known he couldn't possibly have missed her father using the term, especially just now.

'It's not a sore point exactly and I don't mind it at home, although I'd hoped it would fade as I grew up, but Dad can't seem to help himself.'

'Is it ... something embarrassing?'

Jenna could see he looked a little concerned.

'What, because I was a chubby little girl you mean?' she said, laughing. 'No – although I was a chubby little girl, so that could be part of the reason, I suppose. It's because when I was very young, Mum and Dad bought me a Cinderella doll and the pumpkin carriage to go with her. Apparently, I was more interested in the carriage than I was in Cinderella and when they later took me to Disneyland Paris, I kept jumping up and down and shouting 'pumpkin' every time I saw the pumpkin carriage in the parades. I don't know if you've ever been to Disneyland but believe me, there are a lot of parades so I did a great deal of jumping up and down and shouting 'pumpkin'. Dad started calling me pumpkin and, unfortunately, it stuck. I often wish they'd never bought me that Cinderella doll and carriage.'

Robert's smile lit up his eyes. 'That's a lovely story. Did they buy you Prince Charming too ... or are you still looking for him?'

Jenna hesitated. Was Robert talking about a doll, or was he asking, in a roundabout way, if she were single?

'No. They just bought me Cinders and the carriage. I suppose that's why I've always felt that the most important thing for any girl to have ... is a fast car to get her to where she wants to go. You said you have big plans for Green Miles,' Jenna said, changing the subject.

'Right,' Robert said, stepping onto the first stair. 'Is your father as addicted to golf and this club, as my father is?'

Jenna fell into step beside him. 'Er ... Dad definitely enjoys playing but to be honest, I'm not sure whether it's the game or the club which is more important to him and ... I'm not sure whether he'll want to spend more or less time here when your father ... leaves. Why do you ask?'

She had a strange feeling that Robert's plans would, somehow, affect her father and his next words confirmed her concerns.

'I'm not sure that your father will like my plans. There may be some ... shall we say ... heated discussions and I think it's only fair that I tell you this now. As my personal assistant, you'll be right in the middle of it and I don't want there to be any tension or ... bad feeling between us.'

She saw him glance at her from the corner of his eye as

she turned her head towards him.

'How ... heated?' she asked.

They reached the first floor and Robert stopped, turning to face her. 'I want to transform Green Miles Golf Club from the closed, elitist club it currently is – and has been since its inception – into a family friendly, everyone welcome, open house, sort of place. I want to get the wives involved. Have lessons for the kids. Open the club to women. Have events here other than just golf. I haven't decided exactly. It's been such a long time since I was here that I wanted to see it again before I made any concrete plans but one thing I am sure of, I want it to be completely different from the club it is now. To be brutally honest, I want it to be the sort of place my father thinks he would detest.'

'Wow!' Jenna replied, without a tinge of enthusiasm. 'Pretty heated, then.'

'Your father will hate that too, I'm guessing.'

Jenna nodded. 'I think I can safely say that most, if not all, of the current members will hate that. You may well find they'll rally against such changes – and Dad will probably lead them into battle. Does your father know this is what you have planned?'

Robert shrugged.

'When are you going to tell him? I ... I assume you *are* going to tell him.'

'Would you think me a complete coward if I didn't?'Robert said, grinning.

Jenna wasn't sure if he was serious. She didn't want to think of him as a coward. 'Are you worried he may ... disinherit you?'

'He'll probably disown me. Mind you, I hardly see him anyway, so I guess that wouldn't make much difference. Luckily for me, I have my own money – nowhere near as much as Dad, but enough to live on, so I don't need his. He's already signed the documents transferring the club to me so he can't take that back, but I'm not a complete coward. I did tell him that if he gave me the club, I would change it – totally. I'm not sure if he's going away because he wants to let me get on with it, or because he can't bear to be around and see it change.'

'Maybe he's going away to avoid the fall-out, although Dad says he's going away because he thinks he's in love ... Oh! I'm sorry. I shouldn't have said that.'

Robert smirked. 'Don't worry. It's not a problem. Let's go to my office and do some brainstorming. I'd be keen to hear any ideas you may have. I'm assuming your mother is a golf widow too. Oh, I should ask though. Are you comfortable working with me, knowing how your father feels and that you will, effectively, be working with the enemy? I don't want to cause difficulties between you and your father.'

Jenna grinned. 'I don't really think it'll turn into a full-scale war, although, if it does, I may have to reconsider my allegiances. I can't honestly see Dad going that far though. He loves the club and like most of the current members, he's a bit stuck in his ways but he's a reasonable man. I think he'll try to talk you into keeping things the way they are but if he sees your plans make sense, he'll go along with them ... in the end.'

They strolled along the hall in silence for a few seconds and Jenna could feel his eyes on her.

'Are you sure about that?'

'Pretty much. But if he doesn't, Mum will make him,' Jenna said. She started giggling. She was feeling flustered again and she wished Robert wouldn't keep staring at her.

He chuckled softly and said, 'I asked for a pot of coffee to be sent up in an hour. We'll probably need it by then. ... What did you think of her, out of interest?'

'Who? Sherree or Beth?' Jenna asked tentatively, assuming he meant Sherree but as he'd just mentioned coffee, he might have meant Beth.

'Ah yes,' he said, almost singing the words, 'I'd almost forgotten the delightful Beth. Green Miles Golf Club seems to be a haven for beautiful young women, doesn't it? Have you noticed that most of the staff here are beautiful women, all under the age of twenty-five?'

'Er ... I ...'

'Sorry, that was tactless. You're now one of them.'

Had Robert just said she was beautiful? His comment made her stop in her tracks.

He must have noticed she wasn't beside him because he stopped and turned, giving her a curious look.

'Is something wrong? Oh, wait. Don't tell me. There's some sort of legislation about men calling their staff young and beautiful – or even women, perhaps. I suppose it's sexual harassment or something. I apologise.' He bowed his head in an old-fashioned gesture then turned and continued walking.

Jenna pulled herself together and caught up with him.

'Well, as I'm neither young nor beautiful, I won't make a claim against you.'

She noticed his head turn towards her but she avoided his eyes and looked straight ahead.

'You're wrong you know,' he said, 'but anyway, I meant Sherree. What did you think of Sherree?'

She stole a sideways glance but his face gave nothing away. He *was* saying she was beautiful ... wasn't he? Did he mean it or was he just flirting? Then she thought of his father and the twenty-one year-old Sherree and the compliment didn't feel like such a compliment any more. Perhaps Robert was as much of a womaniser as his father was.

'Don't feel embarrassed,' Robert was saying. 'I'm just interested to know from a female perspective, that's all. Please be honest. There's nothing I hate more than insincerity and flannel – and I promise, I won't tell my dad.'

He grinned at her and she wished her heart would stay still and stop doing silly back flips every time the man smiled.

'Well ... I think she's very pretty and I can see why men would find her attractive ...'

They had reached what was to be her office but Robert walked on and opened the door to his. He ushered her in.

'Take a seat,' he said, indicating the chair he'd occupied earlier, as he walked around the desk and sat in his father's chair.

He seemed to be savouring the moment. He leant his head back and stroked the arms of the chair with his fingers. He slowly spun it around, glanced out of the window for a second towards the fairways and the woods beyond, then spun back.

Jenna fidgeted in her seat. The sun had moved around and was now shining directly in her face. She had to lean to one side to keep it out of her eyes.

'Is the sun bothering you?'

She nodded and he stood up and pulled the blind half closed.

'Thank you,' she said. 'May I take off my jacket? It's rather warm in here.'

'Of course.'

She stood up and removed it and as she did so, her floral patterned blouse worked loose from the waistband of her knee length, figure hugging, navy blue skirt. She could feel Robert's eyes on her as she tucked it back in with the tips of her fingers and when she sat down, he was still staring at her.

'Thank you,' she said. After several seconds of silence, she dragged her eyes away from his.

'Don't mention it,' he replied. 'You were saying that you can see why men would find Sherree attractive.' He leant forward, rested his elbows on the desk and linked his fingers under his chin. His eyes were focused on Jenna's face and a hint of a smile showed at the corners of his mouth. 'Why is that, exactly?'

Jenna could feel herself blushing. He *was* just like his father, she thought. Well, he wasn't going to flirt with her and get away with it. She crossed her legs, rested one elbow on her knee, lifted her arm up and rested her chin on her loosely clenched fist. She leant forward to meet his eyes with hers, and in as sexier a voice as she could muster she said, 'Because men, in general, don't have very much imagination, and with women like Sherree, they don't have to use any. Long legs, large breasts, short skirts and low cut tops somehow translate into the word 'sex' in a man's mind, and all men are very keen on sex. Hence the attraction.'

She wondered if she'd gone too far. She kept forgetting this man was now her boss and he could fire her in a split second. To her surprise, he burst out laughing.

'Well, well, Miss Baker, you come with hidden claws and teeth at the ready, I see. I apologise. I had no right to toy with you. Tell me. Does that mean that women such as you, don't like the Sherrees of this world? It's a serious question. In the States, the women I know would refer to Sherree as 'a hoe' which means –'

'I know what it means. Some people here would refer to her as a tart or a slapper or something equally unpleasant, but is that really fair? Perhaps she's just a young, insecure, woman who foolishly believes that the only way to attract a man is to flaunt herself.'

'A man, or a rich, elderly man?'

Jenna shrugged. She didn't like where this conversation was heading. 'Perhaps she has a 'father complex', perhaps she just wants someone to look after her, perhaps she's had bad experiences with men her own age. Who knows? I don't think people should be judged by the way they look or dress. They should be judged by the way they act and treat other people.'

Robert raised his eyebrows.

'Sorry,' Jenna said. 'I'll get off my high horse.'

'Don't apologise. You didn't instantly despise Sherree, then? A lot of women would have.'

'I don't think I despise anyone,' Jenna said, 'and I suspect, if they were honest, many women would be envious of her.'

'Envious of Sherree! You surprise me. Why?'

Jenna blushed and hung her head.

'Please tell me. I'm really interested.'

She sucked in a deep breath and met his eyes. 'Because she does have an incredible body and I think I can honestly say, there are very few women alive who wouldn't kill for longer legs and bigger breasts – and to know that the eyes of every man in the room are focused on her, and her alone, even if it's purely sexual – in fact, especially if it's purely sexual.'

Robert's eyes seemed to search her face and then travelled the length of her body and back again.

'Well,' he said 'I don't think you need to be envious of Sherree on that score.'

Jenna wasn't quite sure what he meant by that but as his eyes seemed to burn into her, she had a vision of him leaping across the desk, pulling her into his arms and ripping off the blouse she'd carefully tucked into her skirt. She knew it was ridiculous but she felt excited, hot and very nervous and when she felt nervous, she giggled.

Robert seemed surprised by her laughter. He smiled and slowly stood up, taking off his jacket and hanging it on the back of his chair.

Jenna could see from the way the white cotton shirt stretched across his body as he moved that the athletic frame had only improved with age and she couldn't stop herself from appreciating the full length of it. When her eyes finally returned their focus to his face, she saw something in his which made her giggle all the more.

Suddenly, the phone in her office rang. She jumped up and dashed to the next room to answer it.

'Do you know,' he said, as she ran to her desk, 'you've got the sexiest laugh I've ever heard.'

Jenna was almost breathless when she answered the phone. 'Green Miles Golf Club,' she gasped.

'Jenna? Is that you? Why are you gasping for breath? What's going on there?'

'Mum! Er ... nothing. I had to run to get the phone. I'm clearly more unfit than I thought. What's the matter? Has something happened?'

'Why should anything have happened? I'm just calling to see how it's going – and to check that Roddy and his son are behaving themselves.'

Jenna wondered what her mother would have thought if she could have read Jenna's mind a few minutes ago.

'Mum! Honestly! Everything's fine. Dad and Roddy are playing golf and Robert and I are ... getting to grips with club stuff. I can't talk now but Dad's picking me up later so I'll pop in for a quick drink and tell you all about my first day.' Well, not all of it, she thought.

'Okay dear. See you later. Have fun – and don't take any nonsense. If Roddy, or his son try anything, you just kick them where it hurts and tell them to shove their job where the sun doesn't shine. Okay?'

'Mum! Okay. I'll do that. Bye.' Her mother still surprised her at times.

Jenna sat at her desk and realised that she'd rather like it if Robert did try something. She wondered whether she'd imagined the entire morning so far. Had she and her new boss really spent it flirting with one another? Whatever way you looked at it, that's what they had been doing.

She wondered what to do next. Should she stay where she was and wait and see what he did or should she go back in and ... and what? Their conversation could have led to very dangerous ground. She needed this job and, as gorgeous as Robert still was – and she had to face it, he was gorgeous – he had broken her heart once before. Could she risk it happening again, now that she was an adult and he was her boss?

She heard Robert's mobile ring and although she couldn't hear what he said, he didn't sound happy. Five minutes later, he came into her office.

'I've got to go,' he said. 'I'm really sorry to leave you in the lurch like this but my mum has had an accident. I can't get hold of Dad. No mobiles allowed on the course. Will you tell him, please? And I'll be back as soon as I can. Probably not today, though. Sorry.'

'Yes of course. I hope she's okay. Shall I get you a flight?' She picked up the phone to dial but he was heading towards the door.

'Flight?' he said, glancing back at her. 'I don't need ... oh. Mum's not in the States, she's visiting friends in London. I'm going to London. See you soon. Oh. Give me your mobile number. I'll let you know when I'll be back.'

'Yes. I hope it's not serious.'

She gave him the number and he keyed it into his phone.

'No, it's not. It's just her friend panicking, but I'd rather see her for myself, to make sure. She stepped off the curb and some stupid cyclist almost knocked her flying. She stepped back and tripped. Just bruises I think but she's at the hospital, so I'm heading there. I don't suppose Dad will understand but to me, Mum is far more important than Green Miles bloody Golf Club. See you.'

'Bye. See you soon,' she said. 'Oh, should I have your number in case...' but he was already half way along the hall and he didn't hear her.

Jenna spent the day exploring the club and searching the internet. She found a golf ball that laughed when it was in motion and thought how great that would be for teaching children to play golf. They'd really be keen to hit a ball that laughed. She studied the club brochure and noticed that there was an area of unused grassland near the driving ranges that would be perfect for a children's putting green or maybe, mini golf. Both Roddy and her father would have an apoplexy at the very suggestion of that, she thought.

She found a list of members and realised that either she or her mum knew nearly all of their wives. She started drawing up ideas for events they might find interesting or entertaining – hopefully, both.

She considered social networking options. What about a Facebook page called The Green Miles Golf Widows' Club, and a Twitter account? She could organise a newsletter, arrange coffee mornings, breakfasts, lunches and dinners where all the wives could meet up or perhaps just join their husbands, maybe sometimes even bring along their children.

Another option would be to have wine tastings, cookery lessons, even a book club. Her mind raced with ideas and when her father and Roddy turned up in her office, she was astonished to see that it was already one o'clock.

'Thought we might all have a spot of lunch,' Roddy said. 'Where's Robert? He's not in his office.'

'Ah … he had to leave. His mother has had an accident and –'

'Amelia! Is she hurt? What's happened? Where is she? When?'

Jenna was astonished to see him so upset. 'She's fine. It's not serious. She tripped and fell but it's only bruising, I think. Robert's gone to the hospital, just to be sure.'

'Hospital! I thought you said it wasn't serious! Why is she in hospital? Where?'

'They're just checking nothing's broken, I assume. I ... I'm not sure which hospital. Robert didn't say, only that it's in London.'

'London! Amelia's in London?'

Jenna's head was spinning. 'Yes. Robert said she's staying with friends. He didn't say whom.'

Roddy picked up the phone on Jenna's desk and dialled a number. 'Voicemail! Bloody hell! Robert, it's your father. I've just heard about your mother. Where are you? Is she all right? Call me as soon as you get this.' He hung up. 'I'm going to get my mobile, in case Robert calls that. Let me know if you hear anything. I think I need a stiff drink. Edward, join me?' He marched off along the hall.

'I'd better go with him, pumpkin. He's pretty shaken up. Can't remember the last time I saw him like this. ... Oh! Yes, I can ... Good God! So that's the lay of the land is it?' Edward said, dashing off after Roddy without another word.

CHAPTER FIVE

'So, how was your first day, darling?' Fiona asked.

She was curled up on one of the two sofas, a glass of wine in one hand and a book in the other when Jenna walked into her parents' sitting room that evening.

'Pretty good, all things considered. Dad's had a few too many whiskies, I'm afraid. Bit of a drama with Roddy. I had to drive home. He's gone upstairs to get changed and you may need to check on him.'

Fiona raised her eyebrows and tutted. 'He'll be fine, I'm sure. Grab a glass and pour yourself some wine. You can get a taxi home. I'll pay. So what was the drama with Roddy then? No doubt, it involved a woman. And what's the son like? I've been dying to hear.'

Jenna kicked off her shoes, grabbed a glass from the cabinet and poured herself a large glass of wine. She curled up on the other sofa opposite her mother and took two large mouthfuls of wine.

'I needed that. Well, where do I begin? Robert, needless to say, is even better-looking, now that he's a man. He's got some radical ideas about Green Miles and, quite frankly, I think there may be trouble. You may have to have a word with Dad at some stage.' She took another gulp of wine.

'Really? What sort of ideas? That sounds rather interesting.'

'I think it will be. He wants to make the place family friendly. Wants to involve the wives and kids and have other things going on, apart from golf.'

'Good God! No wonder there was a drama. I'm surprised the man's still alive.'

'That wasn't the drama! Robert says Roddy knows he's changing things and he's, sort of, okay with it. I'm not totally convinced Roddy realises just how much it's going to change but that remains to be seen. Dad has no idea yet either. I did try to mention it on the way home but I don't think he really heard me.'

'So what was the drama then?'

'Well. That's the oddest thing. It was actually about Amelia.'

'Amelia?'

Jenna nodded. 'Yep. She's come over to stay with friends in London and she had an accident today – nothing serious, although I haven't heard from Robert but Roddy got a call, Dad told me, and she's fine, just bruised and shocked. Anyway, Robert dashed off to London and when Roddy came to take us for lunch and I told him, he sort of lost it. It was as if Amelia was the woman he's in love with, not the lovely Sherree. Ooh! I met her too –Roddy's girlfriend, but I'll tell you about her in a minute. It was really weird. He started rambling – you know, like you do when you're worried sick about someone. Then he said he needed a stiff drink and marched off. Dad said something strange and dashed off to join him and they spent most of the afternoon in the bar.'

'Good heavens. That is strange. I'll have to ask your father all about it later. I'll let you know if I have any news. So, what's this Sherree like then? I bet I was right about her being young, wasn't I?'

Jenna topped up her wine glass and passed the bottle to her mother.

'Yes, she's very young. I think I heard Robert say she's twenty-one – which is pretty gross bearing in mind Roddy's sixty. I'm not sure about her, to be honest. She's very pretty, although she wears far too much make-up ... and jewellery. She actually jingles every time she moves, like one of those reindeers they have at the Christmas grotto. And, her clothes, or should I say, lack of them, leave a lot to be desired. I don't think she's very bright

45

either. She thinks Casablanca is in the Mediterranean. Probably thinks it's on the coast of Spain. Oh God! I sound like a real bitch!'

'She sounds delightful!'

'Actually, I think she's probably a nice person. She's certainly very friendly. I just feel sorry for her, dating a man like Roddy. Perhaps she just wants a father figure, although she did seem genuinely fond of him. I suppose it's possible.'

'Anything is possible where affairs of the heart are concerned, darling. I just wonder whether she'd find Roddy so appealing if his bank balance weren't quite so large. Tell me more about Robert. What does he think of Sherree? Did he give you any idea? It must be very odd, his father dating a woman younger than him.'

'He didn't really say, now I come to think of it. He asked me what I thought of her but he never said what he thought. He did say that most of the women he knew would have called her a hoe.'

'Oh dear. That doesn't sound too promising then, does it?'

Jenna shook her head. 'I'm not sure. Oh, I think Dad's coming down.'

'We're in the sitting room, darling,' Fiona called out.

Edward came in and flopped onto an armchair.

'I hear Roddy was upset about Amelia, darling. Is she all right?'

He seemed to be trying to keep his head up but it kept flopping onto his chest and he was clearly having trouble focusing.

'Shall I make you some coffee, Dad?' Jenna asked.

'Coffee would be good,' he slurred. 'Few too many snifters with Roddy. Poor chap's in a bit of a state. Had a couple of nasty shocks today.'

Jenna got up and headed towards the kitchen. 'I was just telling Mum about Amelia, Dad. She is okay though, isn't she? You said Robert called his father and said it was just bruising.'

'Er ... Amelia? Yes, yes. She's fine. Think Roddy may feel more for her than he lets on. Very strange. Not like him at all. Think Sherree may just be a distra ... distra ... you know what I mean.'

'A distraction, Edward?' Fiona said.

'Yes!' Edward said, throwing his hands in the air. 'That's the one. A distra ... oh never mind.'

'Are you suggesting that Roddy's still in love with Amelia? After all this time ... and everything that's happened. Surely not.'

'And surely, if that was really true, he wouldn't be going away for two months with Sherree – just the two of them,' Jenna added. 'It's very odd.'

'No idea. Just know the last time he was this upset was when he heard she'd got married, and the time before that, when he heard she was going to America and before that, when she was leaving him. In fact, every time I've ever seen Roddy upset, it was something to do with that blasted woman.'

Jenna went into the kitchen and made coffee, returning to the sitting room a few minutes later.

'Have I missed anything?' she said.

'Only your father's snoring, darling.'

Jenna grinned as Edward made several different sounds, all of which would have been more suited to a farmyard.

'Do you think it's true, Mum?'

'About Roddy still being in love with Amelia, you mean? I suppose it's possible. He was certainly besotted with her when they were together and I can remember your father spending an inordinate amount of time with him, drinking, when she left him, when they divorced, when she moved to the States and finally, when she remarried, I believe. According to Edward, Roddy has been visiting the States more often over the last few years, to see Robert. Perhaps he also saw Amelia and some spark has reignited between them – or maybe, just on his part.'

'But ... why would he go out with all these young women, then? And ... if he was so besotted with her, why did he cheat on her in the first place? You said that's why they split up – because of his infidelity.'

Fiona nodded. 'That's what I heard. Of course, I didn't really know Amelia and, as you know, I had as little to do with Roddy as possible, so I have no idea of the truth of the matter. I just heard gossip from the other wives, and your father, of course. He told me they were separating because of an affair but even he didn't know the full details – or if he did, he chose not to tell me. He's always been so protective of Roddy, as you know. It's all part of the 'brothers in arms' and all that RAF camaraderie. All for one and one for all and all that nonsense. Oh. That's the Musketeers, isn't it? Anyway, you know what I mean.'

Jenna watched her father's chest rise and fall in time with his breathing, the snoring having subsided, for the moment.

'Dad will miss him when he goes away, won't he?'

Fiona nodded. 'Yes. But it may actually do them both some good. Your father may remember that there are other things in life besides that silly club, and Roddy, after spending several weeks with a young woman in a relatively confined space, may also finally realise he's not a young man any more.'

'Either that, or he'll die of a heart attack! Well, you didn't see the ample charms of the lovely Sherree! Even Robert and Dad found it difficult to take their eyes off them, I mean … her. Sorry, I shouldn't have said that about Dad. Do you ... do you really mind Dad spending so much time at Green Miles? You know you'd only have to say the word and he wouldn't go so often, don't you?'

Fiona sighed. 'I know dear. Most of the time, I don't

mind. In fact, to be honest, I think it's helped our marriage survive. It's good for couples to have different interests and not live in one another's pockets all the time. He has his golf. I have my painting. Sometimes it irritates me that we don't do more together and, of course, it does annoy me when he won't hear a bad word about Roddy but on the whole, I'm happy. I know some women aren't though – like Amelia, I suppose.'

'Do you ... and Aunt Jennifer despise Amelia? I mean, for what happened. Is that why you never had anything to do with her?'

Fiona swirled the wine around in her glass and looked thoughtful.

'Jennifer did ... for a long time, but I think she's finally over that now. I ... well, I didn't despise her exactly but I did think she behaved appallingly. It *was* my wedding day, after all, well, mine and your father's of course. Jennifer was my bridesmaid and Roddy was Edward's best man, and Jennifer and Roddy were engaged. Well … there's a time and a place for everything and being found in the bridal suite screwing the best man when you should be serving champagne, as you were employed to do, is not a good way to make a first impression. I don't think I'll *ever* be able to get that image out of my head, completely, and I'll *never* forgive Roddy. Not for breaking my sister's heart or for ruining my wedding day ... or for having sex in the bridal suite before I did!'

Jenna giggled. 'Mum! You ... you went to their wedding though, didn't you?'

'Yes. That nearly caused a family rift too – between Jennifer and me, especially when she turned up at the church. She was furious but what could I do? Edward was Roddy's best man, so I had to go, to support my husband. It was all such a rush. One minute, Roddy's engaged to Jennifer, the next, he's walking up the aisle with a pregnant woman whom he'd met at my wedding just four months before! I've told you all this though.'

'You've never told me the details, just that you and Dad found Roddy in your bridal suite, having sex with one of the catering staff, whom he later married, and that he'd been engaged to Aunt Jennifer at the time.'

'Oh. Well, Jennifer said he'd only broken off the engagement due to nerves and then that he was infatuated with Amelia and he'd soon snap out of it, and then that he'd only married Amelia because of the baby. I must admit, I thought that too, but if you'd seen the way he looked at her when she walked down the aisle towards him.' Fiona let out a long, loud sigh. 'Well, all I can say is that I don't think your father has ever looked at me quite like that – and I know he loves me. The man looked as if he'd just seen the centre of the universe, won the jackpot and all his ships had come in at once. It was the strangest thing but there was a sort of aura around him. He almost ... glowed!'

'Wow!' Jenna exclaimed.

'With bows on. Believe me dear, it was amazing.'

'And then he starts having affairs. I'm not sure I'll ever understand men.'

'Only men understand other men, darling. I'm afraid that's just a fact of life.'

'Exactly what I said.' Edward sat bolt upright and rubbed his eyes. 'It's a fact of life, these days. Nothing we can do about it. Not Roddy's fault. Not the boy's fault either, although I suspect the mother's got a lot to answer for.'

'What are you babbling about, darling?' Fiona said.

'There's a pot of coffee on the table beside your chair, Dad. I thought you'd need more than one cup.'

'Oh. Good thinking, pumpkin. Bit of a head coming on. May have an early night.'

Jenna poured a cup of coffee and handed it to him.

'Well, Edward, what were you talking about?' Fiona

persisted.

Edward sipped the coffee and glanced at his wife over the rim. 'What? When?'

'Just now! You said it's a fact of life and it's not Roddy or Robert's fault.'

'Oh! Er ... shouldn't have said anything. Forget it.'

'Not a chance, especially now you've said that. What is it?'

'Shush, Fi.' He inclined his head in Jenna's direction. 'Not now.'

Jenna saw him. 'Oh, for heaven's sake, Dad! I'm thirty years old. Nothing you could say would ever shock me.'

Edward cleared his throat. 'This might. Besides, it mustn't go any further. I promised Roddy.'

'Well Roddy will be gone in less than a week and are you saying that you don't trust your own wife and daughter to keep a secret? Is that it? Well, thank you very much. It's so nice to know that after thirty-five years of marriage your own husband doesn't trust you.'

'I do trust you, darling!'

'But not enough to tell me one of Roddy's silly little secrets.'

'It's not a silly little secret! It's important and he's embarrassed. I'm surprised he told me, to be honest but he's so upset about the boy being gay that it just slipped out and ... oh!'

Jenna and Fiona stared at Edward in stunned silence.

'W ... which boy?' Jenna muttered after several seconds.

'You mustn't repeat this. Do you hear me, Jenna?'

When her father called her Jenna, she knew he was being serious but right now, she was struggling to make sense of what he was saying. There was only one 'boy' in Roddy's life and that boy was Robert. Was her father seriously saying that Robert was gay?

'You ... you mean Robert?' Her voice sounded

51

strangled, even to her own ears. 'Are you telling me that Roddy thinks Robert is gay?'

Edward shook his head. 'He doesn't think it, pumpkin. He knows he is. The boy told him this morning before they met us for breakfast. I don't think Roddy would have told me but the shock of Amelia's accident and several whiskies and ... well, it just tumbled out. Robert said he doesn't want children and when Roddy asked why not, he told him he was gay. It's a tragedy. No more sons. This could mean the end of Green Miles Golf Club.'

CHAPTER SIX

'Daisy, are you busy? I really need to talk.'

Jenna had intended to go home and have an early night but as soon as she left her parents' house, she knew she wouldn't get a wink of sleep until she'd discussed this with her best friend. She'd promised her father that she wouldn't tell anyone about Robert being gay, but Daisy wasn't anyone; she'd known her all her life and they were like sisters and Jenna knew she could trust Daisy not to breathe a word.

'Sure. Adam's meeting a friend he was at university with, so you can come here, if you like, or I can get him to drop me at yours.'

'I've just left Mum and Dad's and I'm in a cab, so I'll divert to you. See you in about ten minutes.'

The cab got to Daisy's in six minutes just as Adam, Daisy's husband, was walking towards his car.

'I think that man once drove for Ferrari,' Jenna said as she left the cab and staggered, comically, towards Adam. 'You off out?'

Adam kissed Jenna on the cheek and gave her a hug. They'd been at junior school together and Jenna had known him almost as long as she'd known Daisy.

'Bet that made you happy. You've always liked fast cars,' Adam said.

'And you've always liked fast women,' Jenna replied, seeing Daisy standing at the door. 'Speaking of which ...'

'Hey you! Watch it!' Daisy said, grinning. 'Adam, bring us back some chips will you, if you're not too late, with ketchup ... and lots of vinegar ... ooh, and a pickled onion.'

'Bring me back a man!' Jenna declared.

Adam chuckled. 'With ketchup, vinegar and a pickled onion, Jenna?'

'As long as that's the only thing pickled. And I don't want Joe, the guy who works there. I want a tall, dark and handsome man ... oh, and check he's not gay.'

'Sure thing. See you girls later and don't drink too much.'

'We're just having a chat!' Daisy said.

'Yeah. I know your chats and they usually include at least one bottle of wine, possibly two.'

'What happened to the diet?' Jenna asked as they waved Adam goodbye.

'It's Monday. I never diet on a Monday. Too depressing. I've just seen an advert on TV for chips and I've got a real craving for them.'

'Craving! Anything you want to tell me?'

'Yeah, right. You have to give up alcohol when you're pregnant and there's no way I'll last nine months without a glass of wine. I've told Adam if he wants kids, we're adopting.'

'I think I might have to do the same,' Jenna said.

'Oh God! Is something wrong? You went for your smear the other day didn't you?'

'What? No. Sorry. I was being a drama queen. Oh, that's also appropriate. Open some wine and I'll tell you.'

Jenna followed Daisy into her kitchen and grabbed two wine glasses whilst Daisy opened the bottle. They strolled into Daisy's sitting room and Jenna flopped onto the sofa.

'Okay. You know I told you last night on the phone about my new job and that it was working for Robert Miles and you know how I always dreamed I'd marry him one day.' She took a gulp of wine.

'Yes, get on with it. Ooh! Don't tell me. He's come back for you. He's spent the last ... however many years it's been since that kiss at his sixteenth birthday party, thinking about you and he's realised it was true love after all and –'

'He's gay.'

Daisy almost dropped her glass of wine. 'He's what?'

'You mustn't tell anyone, Daisy. I promised Dad and he'd kill me if it ever got back to Roddy – or Robert, by way of gossip. Promise me.'

'I promise ... but I'll have to tell Adam. You know I will. I've never been able to keep anything from him for longer than ten minutes and besides, I talk in my sleep, apparently, so he could find out that way. It's better if I tell him. He won't breathe a word.'

'Okay. You can tell Adam. I thought you would anyway, but no one else.'

'I promise. So ... how do you know this? Did he come right out and tell you? Don't tell me. You tried to have your wicked way with him and he said he wasn't that kind of guy.'

'It's not funny, Daisy. And he didn't tell me. Dad did. Roddy, Mr Miles, that is –'

'I know who Roddy is, Jenna.'

'Of course you do. I think I'm still in shock. Well, he and Dad were drinking all afternoon because Amelia had had an accident –'

'Who's Amelia?'

'Robert's mother. Will you stop interrupting.'

'Will you get on with it then.'

'Roddy told Dad that Robert told him this morning that he is gay and that's why he doesn't want children.'

'Who doesn't want children? Roddy or Robert? It doesn't matter. I don't care. Wow! So the man of your dreams also dreams about men. That's a bit of a bummer. Oh God! I didn't mean to say that. Honestly, Jenna, I didn't!'

Jenna grinned. 'You're forgiven. I'm really depressed though. And ...what's really weird is – until he dashed off to check on his mum – I'm absolutely positive, he'd been flirting with me. Well, we'd been flirting with one another, I suppose but he kept giving me these really deep, intense looks. He's still got the most gorgeous eyes I've ever seen by the way ... and his smile. Wow! ... you know – the type that makes you melt.'

'Like Daniel Day-Lewis, as Hawkeye in 'The Last of The Mohicans', you mean?'

'Exactly like Daniel Day-Lewis, although I still think those looks the guy who played Uncas kept giving whatshername, were pretty hot. Anyway, I know it's stupid and I know he would never have married me anyway, even if he wasn't gay, but I've had this silly crush on him for so long and when I saw him this morning ...' Jenna let out a long sorrowful sigh.

'That bad, huh?'

'It felt like my heart leapt from my chest and danced all over his body then did back flips on all the tables, just for good measure ... and yet, when he shook hands with me, I felt nothing ... Absolutely nothing! Nada. Niente. Zilch.'

'Niet. Oh, that means no. How do you say 'nothing' in Russian?' Daisy asked.

'The same way you do in other languages – you keep your mouth shut.'

'Very funny. That's a skill you've yet to learn. Ooh! Isn't it something like nee-chee-vo or nichy-evo or nichy-ego or ... Nick-had-to-go?'

'Non! Although wasn't that what they said when they got rid of their last Tsar: "Sorry, folks, but Nick had to go." I think it is something like nichyego, actually ... but I don't really care. I've got a broken heart. Learning Russian won't help.'

'Drinking Russian might. I've got a bottle of vodka in the fridge.'

'I think it's a good thing,' Daisy said an hour or so, and several glasses of vodka, later. 'Now you can finally forget the gorgeous Robert Miles and fall in love with a real man. Not that Robert's not real, of course, or a man,

56

but, well, I think part of you has actually been waiting for him.'

'You might be right, although I don't think I have,' Jenna said. 'I thought when he moved to the States that I'd never see him again. That's what is even more stupid about the whole thing, though. I knew when he kissed me, all those years ago, that it meant nothing to him but it was really nice and ... well, no one I've kissed since has had the same effect on me. I'm sure I heard music and fireworks and –'

'It was a birthday party. They had music and fireworks. Of course you heard them.'

'No, I meant proper music, you know, classical stuff. It was definitely Tchaikovsky's 1812 overture. Definitely. That's why I've got it as my ring tone on my iphone – to remind me.'

'You're such a drama queen. He was deaf, you know – Tchaikovsky.'

'So would you be, after all those bells and trumpets and cannons. The point is, no one has ever matched up to Robert Miles.'

'I hate to point this out, Jenna but you were twelve. I'm not saying you can't be in love when you're twelve. God, in the old days, girls were having kids at twelve ... actually, girls still are having kids at twelve. Anyway, he kissed you, then he left and you never saw him again. That was eighteen years ago. You've been out with about eight men since then and you always find fault with them, the minute they start to get serious. It's as if you push them away, as if you're saving yourself for someone. Well, not saving yourself, exactly, that ship sailed when you were sixteen, but you know what I mean.'

'I don't think I have been. I think I just never met the right man. It was different for you. You and Adam started dating when you were four! Okay, not actually dating but everyone always knew you two would get married, even when he left and went to uni in Bristol. Why did he go to Bristol, by the way? No, it doesn't matter. The thing is, you were destined for one another.'

Daisy nodded. 'That's true. When he went to Bristol – and even I can't remember why he chose Bristol – perhaps it was because of the bridge. He really liked that bridge –'

'People commit suicide off there you know. I might do that, if it's true about Robert.'

'Yeah, right. Don't interrupt. When Adam –'

'Not if it's raining though. Someone jumped off there, years and years ago holding an umbrella. I suppose because it was raining and they didn't want to get wet – and the umbrella saved their lives. It acted as a parachutey sort of thingy.'

'Stop interrupting! When ... wait a minute. If you were committing suicide, why would you care if you got wet, especially as the bridge is over a river – so you'd get very wet if you landed in that and not just smashed yourself to bits on the concrete round the side.'

'No idea. Perhaps they had hair like yours that goes all frizzy in the rain and they wanted to look their best before they died. I don't know. Why did Adam want to jump off the bridge, Daisy?'

'Adam didn't want to jump off the bridge. He just liked it. That was why he went to uni in Bristol. Anyway, as I was saying, when he went there I thought it was over. He said we were just 'on a break' while he studied but we all know what 'on a break' really means so I went out with someone else. Then he did, but the day he came home we met in the street by chance and we've been together ever since.'

'That is *so* romantic,' Jenna cooed, wiping an imaginary tear from her eye, 'even though I've heard it about a million times. Perhaps that's why he wanted to jump off the bridge then. Because he thought it was over too.'

'Will you shut up about people wanting to jump off the bridge. No one wants to jump off the bridge.'

'I do,' Jenna said, studying the bottom of her empty glass.

'Honey, I'm home!' Adam called from the hall. 'And I come bearing gifts. Chips, with ketchup, vinegar and a pickled onion for you, my love,' he said. He strolled into the sitting room and handed Daisy a paper wrapped bundle. 'And the same for you, Jenna. Oh ... and this is my friend from uni, Tom Piper. That is what you wanted isn't it?' He handed Jenna the bundle of chips and winked. 'I'll get plates. Tom, you know Daisy of course, but I don't know if you met Jenna at our wedding or not. This is Daisy's best friend, Jenna Baker.'

Tom stepped forward from the dimly lit hall and smiled at Daisy, then at Jenna.

'Pleased to meet you,' he said. 'I don't think we did meet at the wedding. I'm sure I would have remembered that. Adam tells me you started a new job today. Was it a bad first day?'

Jenna smiled back at Tom. He was tall, dark and handsome, just as she'd jokingly ordered but he wasn't quite as tall, or as dark, or as handsome as the man who was plaguing her thoughts.

'Pleased to meet you too,' she said, 'and no, I don't remember meeting you at the wedding but there were lots of guests, so I might have done and forgotten or I might not have done, and remembered but it was a long time ago now.'

Adam returned with the plates. 'I've put the kettle on. I'll make you a coffee in a minute, Tom and by the looks of that vodka bottle, I'd better make some for you two.'

'We were learning Russian,' Daisy said, stuffing the pickled onion into her mouth, whole. She grinned at Adam with a pickle for teeth.

'Gorgeous as always,' he quipped. 'Tom's going to be

moving here for a while. He works for 'Viewmore Homes' and he's overseeing a proposed new homes development, over on Claremont Cliffs. Aren't you Tom?'

Tom smiled. 'Yep. I'm really looking forward to it. It's been a while since the company started a new project but people need homes and the Claremont Cliffs' site has been crying out for development.'

'Really? I thought there was some problem with it?' Jenna remarked. 'I can vaguely remember Dad saying that someone wanted to build there once but they couldn't because someone stopped them but I can't remember why.'

Tom shook his head. 'I don't know about that. Possibly, in the past permission was refused but times moves on and local authorities change. What was once a 'no-go' suddenly becomes a prime development opportunity. I've just rented an apartment in a block built by one of our competitors. It's a couple of miles along the coast and on the sea road but the views are spectacular. Just imagine what they'll be like from the top of Claremont Cliffs. You could probably see the coast of France.'

'That'll come in handy,' Daisy said. 'Next time we go on a 'booze cruise', you can wave at us.'

'I think you're on a bit of a booze cruise now, sweetheart,' Adam said. 'Don't mind her, Tom. She's clearly had too much to drink. I'll go and make that coffee.'

Tom smiled. 'It's not a problem, Adam. I tend to go on a bit when I get excited about work.'

'What do you do, Jenna? You didn't say when I asked you earlier, whether your day was bad.'

'Didn't I? Sorry. Er ... I used to be an estate agent but now I'm a personal assistant to the new Chairman and President of Green Miles Golf Club.'

'I've heard about Green Miles. It actually borders the

Claremont Cliffs' site on two sides. Some of the properties we're planning to build would back onto the edge of the golf course. It's a really prestigious club. Incredibly difficult to get membership apparently and unbelievably expensive to join. Maybe you could put in a good word for me.'

'Maybe. But things are changing so you may not need it. Robert has big plans for Green Miles,' Jenna said as a tear ran down her cheek.

Tom spotted it and handed her his handkerchief but she wiped the tear away with the back of her hand.

'I think it's time I went home,' she said. 'I'm getting a bit emotional. Must be overtired.'

'You're not driving, are you?' Tom asked.

Jenna shook her head. 'My car's in for repairs. I'll get a taxi.'

'I'll take you home, Jenna,' Adam said.

'I can take her, Adam. I've got to head home soon anyway and there's no point in you going out again ... if that's okay with you, Jenna,' Tom said.

Jenna nodded. 'Yep. That's good. Do you know where I live?'

'No, but Adam can give me the address and I'll put it in the Sat Nav.'

'Okey-dokey.' She stood up and put on her shoes. 'I'm ready.'

'Okay,' Tom said, grinning. 'Forget the coffee, Adam. I'll have one at home. What's Jenna's address?'

Adam told him and he put it in his phone whilst Jenna and Daisy hugged one another and stumbled into the hall.

'Are you sure you don't mind, Tom? Adam said. 'You may need to help her to her door.'

'It'll be my pleasure.'

Adam was right; Tom did have to help Jenna to her door. He had to help her find her key, too and put it in the lock and turn the handle.

'Thank you,' she said. 'Would you like to come in for a coffee?'

Tom studied her face. She wasn't his usual type; not leggy or buxom enough for his liking but she wasn't bad looking. In fact, she looked very pretty leaning against the door frame with the yellow lamp from the street light shining on her face, giving her a warm and rather cosy, glow.

'Coffee would be good,' he said, helping her inside. And anything else that may be on offer, he thought.

He'd just finished with his latest squeeze and he was going to be in Claremont for a few months if things went well with the development plans, so he'd need to have someone around. He never had trouble finding women but this project would demand a lot of his time and attention, so he wouldn't have much spare time to trawl the bars – not that it looked as if Claremont had many bars to trawl, at least, not the sort of bars he'd want to be seen in.

Jenna seemed pleasant enough. She wouldn't be an embarrassment on his arm and in the right clothes, she would possibly be quite stunning. The fact that she was also the best friend of Adam's wife was a bonus. He needed to get Adam on his side if the Claremont Cliffs' project was to succeed. Adam worked in the planning department of Claremont Council and, more importantly, his father was a local councillor and Chairman of the Planning Committee.

'Er ... I think you may need to make the coffee,' Jenna said. 'I think I need to sit down.'

Tom grinned to himself. Things were going very well. He'd only arrived in Claremont this morning and already he'd rented a luxury apartment at far less than its true rental figure; he'd got his foot in the planning department door and he'd found himself a girlfriend without even trying.

He ambled into the kitchen of Jenna's tiny two-bedroom cottage and glanced around. It was smaller than his bathroom. He switched on the kettle. May as well pretend to make coffee, he thought. One thing was for sure though, after tonight, they would be going to his place for sex.

'Jenna, can you show me where you keep the coffee, please,' he called.

She struggled to her feet and he hovered in the doorway. He knew she would have to brush up against him to get into the kitchen.

'Excuse me,' she said.

He slid his arm around her waist as she stepped in front of him and he pulled her close. He could see she was trying to focus.

'I know we've only just met,' he said 'but there's just something about you, Jenna. I've wanted to kiss you since the moment I laid eyes on you.'

Her eyes met his and she smiled at him.

It worked every time, he thought. He leant his head forward, brushed her lips with his and kissed her. It was a soft, lingering kiss and he could feel her body moulding to his as he pulled her closer. He gently pushed her back against the wall and leant into her, one hand slowly making its way towards her breasts and one leg easing itself between hers. He wondered for a split second why she hadn't wrapped her arms around him yet. That's what they usually did but he didn't really care.

He slid his hand up and cupped her left breast. Not great, he thought but enough to be interesting. Then he started caressing her as his mouth moved down her neck.

'Robert,' she whispered.

Tom's head shot up and he stared at her face. She had her eyes closed and he wondered whether she'd actually fallen asleep. Oh well, he could just carry her upstairs, have a quick one and get home in time for the football on

63

Sky.

He bent down to lift her into his arms just as her phone rang. It was the 1812 overture ring tone. She immediately opened her eyes at the sound, gave him an odd look, as if she had no idea who he was or what he was doing there, and dashed to her bag to answer her phone. Unable to keep his balance, Tom's head hit the kitchen door frame with a resounding thud.

Jenna peered over her shoulder then answered her phone.

'Hello,' she said, suddenly sober.

'Hi Jenna, I'm so sorry to call you so late. I tried a couple of times but you were engaged. Then things got a bit manic here. Oh, sorry, it's Robert, Robert Miles.'

'I know,' Jenna said, glancing back at Tom. 'What time is it?'

'Sorry. Were you in bed? It's eleven-ish, I think. I wouldn't normally call this late but I did say I'd call you and I hate it when people say that to me and don't.'

Jenna sighed. Definitely gay, she thought. A heterosexual male would never even consider that; it was a girl thing.

'Me too,' she said, 'and don't worry about the time. I was just ... making a cup of coffee. I've spent the evening with a friend and I've only just got home.'

'Oh! That's good. I just wanted you to know that Mum's fine. A few bruises but nothing serious and after a couple of gin and tonics, she's feeling a lot more like her usual self.'

He laughed and Jenna thought it sounded like one of those CDs of soothing mood music her aunt Jennifer was always listening to – not that they seemed to soothe Jennifer's moods.

'That sounded as if my mum is an alcoholic and is only herself after a drink,' he added. 'She's not, I assure you.

64

Two glasses are her usual limit.'

Jenna thought about the three large glasses of wine she'd drunk tonight followed by more than a few glasses of vodka and wondered what Robert would have to say about that. Not that it mattered. Robert was out of bounds. Any hopes of a romance with him had to be firmly dismissed.

'Sorry,' he said, 'I'm waffling. How was your day? I hope it wasn't too boring.'

'No! It wasn't boring at all. I did quite a bit of research online and I've got a few ideas I'd like to discuss with you.'

'That's great. I'll look forward to it. See you tomorrow then. I'll be driving down in the morning so why don't we meet for breakfast at the club at nine.'

'That sounds like a … good idea.' She was going to say 'perfect' but of course, it wasn't.

'Good night then ... Jenna.'

He said her name as if he were whispering it in her ear and she felt her heart flip.

'Good night ... Robert,' she whispered back.

She could hear him breathing rhythmically on the other end of the connection as if he didn't want to hang up. Then Tom called her name from the kitchen and seconds later, the phone went dead.

'Sorry, I didn't realise you were still on the phone,' Tom said. 'I was looking for the coffee.'

'I hope you don't mind, Tom but it's late. I'm more than a little tipsy and it's been a really long day. Can we take a rain check on the coffee? I really need my bed.'

He sidled up to her. 'Sure,' he said, 'want some company?'

Jenna realised they'd been kissing. She couldn't really remember how or why it had happened but she was pretty certain it had and from the way he'd been leaning against her when the phone rang and the fact that her blouse was hanging out of her skirt, she wondered whether that was all. She could vaguely remember feeling his hand on her breast – but she may have imagined that. Excessive alcohol did that to her. More than once she'd woken up, unsure whether something had actually happened or if she dreamt it but as she hadn't been to bed, she was sure that this hadn't been a dream.

'Tom ... I ... not tonight.'

Tom didn't seem pleased but he smiled at her. 'No problem. I'd like to see you again. How about dinner tomorrow?'

'Er ... not tomorrow. Daisy and I go swimming on Tuesdays.'

'Wednesday then? Please. I'm new here and I'd really like the company.'

He did seem nice, Jenna thought and she hadn't been on a date for about five months now. And Robert, the love of her life, was gay.

'Okay,' she said. 'Wednesday it is.'

He made his way to the door after giving her a quick kiss on the lips.

'Night,' he said, closing the door behind him.

'Good night,' she said, bolting it firmly.

If only Robert hadn't been gay, she thought and made her way upstairs to bed.

CHAPTER SEVEN

So Jenna had a boyfriend, Robert thought. That was definitely a man's voice he'd heard in the background and she'd said she'd spent the evening with a friend. She hadn't said boyfriend though, so maybe he was just that – a friend.

He poured himself more coffee, flopped onto the sofa and flicked the TV on with the remote. Of course, she had a boyfriend. She was young, free and single and she was pretty – very pretty. He should have realised she'd have a man in tow. Why was it that he either seemed to pick the wrong woman, or the wrong time? No wonder his love life was such a disaster.

His phone rang and he glanced at it, sighed loudly and pressed the button to send the call to voicemail. He hated doing it but it was for the best. That's what the therapist had said anyway. Robert wasn't so sure. He thought being ignored by someone would only make you angrier, not help you get over a broken relationship but talking to her never seemed to have any effect either, and he'd been doing that for months.

'She's still calling you, then?'

Robert's head shot round to see his mother, Amelia, limping towards him. He jumped up and rushed to her side, linking her arm through his and leading her to the sofa he'd just vacated.

'I thought you'd gone to bed. You need to sleep and you shouldn't be hobbling around on that foot, you know. The doctor said you should rest it.'

Amelia lowered herself slowly onto the sofa and smiled.

'Doctors! What do they know? First they think it's broken, then it's sprained. Then they say it's just bruised. I thought medicine was a science, not guesswork. I'm fine, just a bit battered and bruised. You know it'll take more than a mad cyclist to do away with me – and I've been sleeping all afternoon. I want to hear about your first day. Well, I suppose that should be, first few hours. You needn't have left to come and see me, you know. I expect your father was furious.'

'I thought he would be but he wasn't – at least, not when I spoke to him on the phone. He was playing golf when I left so I didn't get a chance to tell him but when he called, all he was concerned about was whether you were okay. He didn't even mention the club or the fact that I'd run off and left everything on my first day.'

'Well, that's a turn up for the books. He must be mellowing in his old age. Either that, or he's losing his mind.'

'It's odd, you know, Mum. The last few times I've met up with him, I started to think that maybe, he's changed and that the club isn't the be all and end all of his life any more, especially since he's now taken up sailing but yesterday, when we were there, he was back to his old self. It's as if the place has some sort of influence over him.'

'What? You mean like he's possessed or something? Well, they used to say the place was haunted, so maybe ...' She trailed off and laughed.

Robert grinned. 'Yes. That's obviously the reason. Perhaps I should run 'Ghost Walks' as part of the new initiative to change the club. Who is it supposed to be haunted by? Wait, don't tell me. The broken-hearted Eleanor.'

'Actually, they say it's Theodore. He walks the corridors looking for his lost love.'

'Of course he does.' Robert shook his head. 'I'll put it in the brochure.'

'That'll please your father no end. The Green Miles

Golf Club Ghost.'

'I'll ask him to lead the walks. Seriously though, the strange thing is, when I told Dad that I intended to change things at the club because I wanted to make it more family friendly, he really didn't seem that bothered. Every time I said anything, he just said that the club would be mine and I could do with it as I saw fit and he was certain that, whatever I did, would be in the best interests of the club and the Miles' family.'

'Poor Roddy. He's clearly deluded himself into thinking that once you settle in, the club will suddenly become as important to you as it has been to all the Miles' men before you. He's in for a nasty shock, isn't he?'

Robert smirked. 'I think he's already had one today ... well, two, with your accident – he was clearly shocked by that, oddly enough.'

'Yes, that surprised me. What was the other shock?'

'Oh. We were having a conversation about me passing the club on to my son and, to cut a long story short, he now thinks I'm gay.'

'What?' Amelia's laughter echoed around the room and she clasped her hand to her side. 'Oh, I clearly shouldn't laugh like that, it hurts. What on earth gave him that idea?'

'I did. Somehow. You know what he's like. He never really listens and what he thinks he hears is rarely what was actually said. He jumped to conclusions and the look on his face was priceless. I was going to explain but I thought it might do him good to think that I'm so far removed from the Miles' mould, there's no hope of getting me to tow the family line.'

'I almost feel sorry for him. When are you going to tell him you're not? Gay I mean.'

'In a day or two. No harm can come of it, after all. It's not as if he's likely to broadcast it to all and sundry, is it? I might leave it until the dinner dance announcement and when I do my little 'Thank You, Dad' speech, I'll say that

I hope to find the right woman so that I can pass the club on to my son.'

'Ah. How sweet.'

'Isn't it? Of course, it would have been even better if I could have produced a potential candidate – but I think she's got a boyfriend.'

Amelia's grin faded and she sat bolt upright in spite of the pain. 'Oh! Are you telling me you've met someone ... at the club?'

'What? Oh. I hadn't meant to say that. Yes. She's my new personal assistant. I don't know much about her but ... we just sort of clicked. It was really odd. The minute I shook hands with her, it felt, I don't know, sort of warm and reassuring.'

'Magic, you mean?'

Robert pulled a face. 'Yes Mum. You've been watching too many old romantic movies. No. It just felt ... nice, somehow. She's really easy to talk to and, well, we were sort of flirting with one another for the short time I was there.'

'Does the future Mrs Miles have a name?'

'Oh! Her name's Jenna. Jenna Baker – and she won't be the future Mrs Miles. I told you, I think she's got a boyfriend.'

'Jenna ... Baker. Her father isn't ... Edward Baker is he?'

'Yes. Oh, of course. You must know Jenna's parents from the old days. What were they like? It's odd but I don't really remember meeting the mother. I met Edward at the club and on the few occasions he came to our house, but you and Dad never socialised with them as a couple, did you? Why was that? Edward and Dad have been friends ... forever, as far as I remember.'

Amelia sighed and leant back against the cushions. 'Would you pour me a gin and tonic please and I'll tell you something I should have told you a long, long time ago.'

'That sounds ominous! Either that or it's another line from the movies.'

'Sometimes I feel as if my life is one long movie, darling. One of those comedy dramas that turns into a tragedy, even though you were expecting a happy ending.'

Robert knew she wasn't being serious. 'You're still only fifty-three, Mum. There's plenty of time for a happy ending. Just because your first two marriages didn't work out, doesn't mean the third ... or fourth one won't.'

Amelia laughed. 'Or the fifth, sixth or seventh. I mean, you only have to look at people like Elizabeth Taylor to know that, or some of the movie stars of your generation.'

Robert poured his mother's drink and a whisky for himself. Then he gently lifted Amelia's legs onto the sofa so that she could lie back in comfort. He grabbed a throw from the back of an adjacent chair and covered her legs with it. He then, sat opposite her and waited.

'Well. I've told you that your father and I met at a friend's wedding but ... that's not strictly true. I didn't tell you the complete truth of it because ... I didn't behave very well and I suppose, I didn't want you to think badly of me.'

'I could never think badly of you, Mum. You know that.'

Amelia nodded and smiled lovingly at him. 'I know ... and I probably should have told you this before but ... it had never really seemed important and it didn't affect you. At least, I didn't think it did. Perhaps I was wrong.' She sipped her drink.

Robert leant forward and took her free hand in his. 'Mum. Just tell me.'

'Okay. I was eighteen, still at college, my dad had left Mum and me, and we'd moved back here to England. I was waitressing for a wedding catering company at the weekends – that part you know. One of the weddings was

71

Fiona and Edward Baker's. Roddy was Edward's best man. It really was like something you see in the movies, Robert. I was serving, glasses of champagne on a tray, and someone knocked into me by accident. Roddy saved both me and the tray of glasses from falling to the ground and when I looked up into his eyes ... well, it was love at first sight ... for both of us.'

Robert smiled sardonically as his mother stopped to take a sip of her drink. As romantic as her story was, the irony wasn't lost on him. His father was still falling in love with waitresses. To his knowledge, every one of his father's *amours* had been with a waitress.

'We couldn't keep our eyes off one another ... or our hands and ... we ended the day by making love ... in the bridal suite.'

Robert's head shot up.

Amelia nodded. 'Needless to say, Fiona and Edward came in and caught us. All hell broke loose as you can imagine but the worst of it was ... your father was actually engaged at the time to Fiona's bridesmaid, who also happened to be ... Fiona's sister.'

'What? And he didn't tell you? God! He's even worse than I thought!'

'No! I mean, yes. Don't think badly of him, Robert. It was me. It was my fault. Roddy told me he was engaged before he even kissed me. He said that he'd have to break off his engagement and that he wanted to be with me. We should have waited but ... these things happen. The moment we kissed, we knew that was it.'

'Wow! What happened then? He obviously did break off the engagement – or did she break it off? Wait. I've just realised. You said she was Fiona's sister. That means, she's Jenna's aunt.'

Amelia nodded. 'Yes. Her name is Jennifer. She was ready to forgive him but he ended it and she took it very badly. Understandably, I suppose, although personally, I

72

think it's better to know that your fiancé doesn't love you as much as he should *before* the wedding. Fiona was furious, as I said, partly because we'd broken her sister's heart but also because we'd ruined her own wedding day. Roddy and Edward tried to control the situation and keep it from the other guests but Jennifer threw a fit and promptly made an announcement at the wedding reception that Roddy had been 'shagging some tart' in the bridal suite. I'm sure you can picture the scene.'

'Vividly. So ... Fiona has hated you ever since. Edward didn't though. I can remember him being friendly to you on the few occasions you were at the club and always when he came to our house.'

'Fiona didn't either, oddly enough. She didn't want to be friends, obviously, but she was never rude to me when we met. She never really forgave Roddy though and Jennifer wouldn't let it rest. She ... caused trouble at every opportunity. She was very bitter.'

'Caused trouble? How?'

Amelia let out a long, deep sigh. It was clearly painful to relive this, Robert realised.

'Your father and I were inseparable – in those days. From the day we met, we were together. Shortly after, I discovered I was pregnant with you and Roddy was over the moon. We got married very quickly. Edward was his best man so Fiona came to our wedding, but so did Jennifer. You know the part when they ask if anyone knows of any reason why the bride and groom should not be wed. Well, Jennifer thought of several. All ludicrous of course but she was very ... vociferous. She had to be ... assisted home. One of the things she said was ... that you weren't Roddy's child and she persisted with that story for many years. It was all very unpleasant.'

'Did ... did Dad ... believe her?'

'Thankfully no, and as you grew up, your resemblance to Roddy and the rest of the Miles men made her claims

73

farcical. That's one of the things I loved your father for. He never doubted our love – in those days.'

Robert fiddled with his glass, swirling the contents round and round.

'I've never asked you for details because I knew you were so upset but, what happened at my sixteenth birthday party? I can remember the row but ... I got drunk and I can't remember what happened after that. The next thing I remember was us leaving Dad the next day and going to stay with one of your friends. I assumed it was because of Dad's ... affairs and the fact that he was always at the club.'

'I'm not really sure how it all got so out of hand, to be honest. Jennifer persisted with the story about you but she also said that Roddy was having affairs. Then she said that I was. Roddy and I ignored them because we knew they weren't true but ... I think that sort of thing eats away at you. We were fine for the first few years and it wasn't until his father signed the club over to him that things started going seriously wrong. His father didn't leave him to run it. He watched over him and constantly criticised. Roddy started spending more and more time there, trying to please his father and I spent more time on my own. The rest of the club wives were either friends with Fiona, so they didn't want to know me, or were absolute bitches and loved spreading the rumours Jennifer was feeding them. Roddy and I just slowly drifted apart, I suppose.'

'But you didn't drift apart, Mum. You had that row.'

'Yes. I ... I met someone at the sailing club I'd joined, and we became friends. One day he kissed me and ... Roddy saw it. I pushed the man away – his name was David – but Roddy had gone. I waited for him to come home but he didn't. He got drunk and ... slept with one of the waitresses at the club. I suppose, in some way, he felt he was getting his own back or something. He told me the next day and I explained about David. We patched things

74

up but the damage was done. We didn't trust one another any more so we drifted further apart, had rows, the usual stuff that causes marriages to fail. Then, that day of your party, I found Roddy in his office with ... a red-headed young woman. That is all I can tell you about her because she had her head in your father's lap and I'm sure I don't need to explain. That was it. He said nothing was going on. I said it was obvious something was. He made up some ridiculous story. I didn't believe him. We had that dreadful row and you and I left.'

'Shit! Dad tried to get you back though, didn't he?'

'Get *us* back Robert. He wanted you in his life as much as he wanted me but I told him that he would have to give up the club – and that he wouldn't do, not for anyone. I shouldn't have given him that ultimatum but I was hurt and angry and we all do foolish things. So I filed for divorce on the grounds of adultery. He didn't contest it and when I said I wanted to go to the States and take you, he didn't fight me on that either. Not because he didn't care about us but because he wanted us to be happy. I've told you that before. Roddy did everything he could to make us happy – other than give up the club.'

'And women,' Robert said. 'That's why I want to change it so much.'

'I know, but don't let your desire to change it become as big an obsession as the club itself was to Roddy. I'm sure I don't need to say this to you, but I'll say it anyway. Don't let it take over your life. Now, tell me more about Jenna Baker. She's got a boyfriend you said. Is it serious? One thing you should learn from how your father and I met is that until a person is married, there's still a chance they could choose you – and come to think of it, it doesn't seem to matter even if they are married.'

CHAPTER EIGHT

'Morning, Daisy,' Jenna said, answering her phone and grabbing her raincoat from the coat rack in her shoebox sized hall, then taking a final look at herself in the mirror. 'Please note, I didn't say *good* morning. My head feels as if a bunch of Russian Cossacks are dancing on my brain. I swear here and now that I'll never look at another bottle of vodka for as long as I live.'

'Yeah, yeah. Heard it all before. I feel fine. It must be you. You need to drink more.'

'Very funny. Are we still on for swimming tonight?'

'That's what I'm calling to ask you? I hear you and Tom got rather friendly last night and he asked you out.'

'What? How did you hear that?' Jenna asked.

'He called Adam bright and early to – now let me get this right – thank him for introducing him to such a wonderful young lady. I thought he must be referring to someone he met at the pub but apparently, he means you!'

'You really are *so* amusing. Did he really say that?'

'Yep. You didn't waste any time did you? No sooner do you discover that Robert is more likely to be interested in Adam than he is in you, than you're off bewitching the next available man. So, what happened? Did you do the dirty deed?'

'No! Mind you, I think if Robert hadn't called me when he did, we may well have done. Not that I would have remembered because I was pretty out of it.'

'Robert called you?'

'Yep. Just as Tom was starting to examine the merchandise – at least I think he was. His hand was halfway up my blouse, from what little I do remember, when my phone rang. I asked Tom for a rain check. Not on sex – on coffee. We were supposed to be having

76

coffee.'

'Call it whatever you like, honey,' Daisy said. 'I think the man's in love. Anyway, if you'd rather see Tom tonight instead of going swimming that's okay with me and let's face it, you could do with the sex. I was beginning to wonder if you'd taken vows of celibacy. How long's it been?'

'No idea. So long that I can't remember. Anyway, no, I don't want to see Tom tonight. I'm seeing him tomorrow. That's soon enough.'

'Oh.' Daisy sounded disappointed. 'You don't seem that keen. I thought he was rather tasty. I wouldn't mind a nibble myself, if I didn't have Adam, of course.'

'Okay, we'll swap. You can have Tom, and I'll have Adam.'

'No chance! Isn't it time you were going to work?'

'I'm out the door as we speak. Robert and I are having breakfast to go over my ideas for the club. It feels weird though. Now that I know he's gay, I mean. This time yesterday, I was drooling all over him, flirting my little cotton socks off, and imagining him throwing me onto his desk and ripping my clothes off. Today, whenever I look at him, I'll be imagining him doing that to some man – and now that you've mentioned Adam, it'll probably be him I see. Oh God. I wish I hadn't sworn myself off the vodka. I'll need a drink by lunchtime at this rate.'

'Just treat him as we do Gray. Actually, there's an idea. Gray's single. We could fix him up with Robert. Is he seeing anyone?'

'How should I know?'

'Then make that your first priority. Find out if Robert's free and we'll devise a cunning plan to get him and Gray together.'

Jenna hesitated. 'I don't know, Daisy. I'm not sure it would feel right. I know this sounds really silly but I don't think I'm ready to see Robert with another man. Not

77

because he's gay, simply because I'd still be wishing it was me.'

'I know. You've got to accept it, though. Robert Miles is not the man for you. But maybe, Tom Piper is.'

Jenna arrived at Green Miles at eight forty-five and was surprised to see Robert already seated at the same table they'd sat at yesterday.

'Morning,' she said, telling herself that she could handle this. She just had to forget he was gorgeous and remember he was gay and he was her boss. 'I'm not late am I? Mum picked me up because Dad's got a bit of a hangover and didn't think he should be driving. We've been debating the pros and cons of alcohol and, despite it all, we've decided in alcohol's favour.'

She was waffling and she tried to suppress the inevitable nervous giggles but she failed. If only he wouldn't look at me like that, she thought.

'Good morning,' Robert said. 'You're not late, I'm early. Did you ... sleep well?'

She wondered why he'd used that sarcastic tone and then she remembered that he must have heard Tom last night. It almost sounded as if he was jealous but of course, that was ridiculous.

'Very well, thanks. I went to my friend, Daisy's for the evening and another friend gave me a lift home and popped in for coffee but I was so tired that I went to bed instead ... alone ... he went home ... I mean. Sorry, I'll shut up.'

She saw his raised eyebrows and suddenly felt ten years old again.

'No, please. I'd love to hear about your social life.'

Bastard, she thought. Okay, he was definitely gay. That was bitchy.

'I apologise, Robert. Would you like to see the results of my research yesterday?' She pulled out her iPad as she spoke. 'You said you'd like to get the wives and children involved. Well, I found a golf ball that laughs when it's moving and that got me thinking that it would be fun to have a mini version of the course, for the younger children. There's a large area near the driving ranges that would be ideal. As you know, the course here is 6269 yards long, and includes copses, ponds and fairway bunkers. I thought the children's course could include sandpits and paddling pools and a few wooden obstacles for them to scramble over – just to keep them entertained. Obviously, it would only have a few holes but it would give them a taste of the real thing and –'

'Morning Miss Baker, morning Mr Miles. What can I get you?' Beth stood grinning down at them.

'Jenna?' Robert said.

'Oh. I'll just have toast please and coffee, and please call me Jenna,' she said to Beth.

She avoided Robert's eyes. She'd felt them studying her the entire time she'd been talking although she'd kept her eyes focused firmly on her iPad.

'Same for me please,' he said, still looking at Jenna.

Jenna noticed he didn't tell Beth to call him Robert.

'Er ... I suppose you also know that this course is actually famous for having an ancient oak tree surrounded by a gigantic holly bush slap bang in the middle of the seventh fairway, directly in line with the cup? I've discovered that's what the hole is actually called – a cup. Anyway, players aim for the tree because of that, but if they're unlucky enough to lose their ball in the holly they don't try to recover it. We could have something in the children's course to replicate the holly bush. Not something prickly or dangerous obviously, but something that takes the ball away so that it's lost to them, so that they learn there are certain areas other than bunkers and ponds to avoid. Although, as they'll be sandpits and paddling pools on the children's course, they might not try to avoid them. I may need to rethink that part.'

'Jen –' Robert began.

'My mother and I know many of the members' wives and I thought we could consider social networking options like having a Facebook page called The Green Miles Golf Widows' Club or some such thing and a Twitter account. I could do a monthly newsletter and we could have coffee mornings, breakfasts, lunches and dinners. We could have Murder Mystery evenings with the proceeds going to charity. Who killed the Club President? might be an idea for one. Or –'

'Jenna!' Robert said so loudly that it made Jenna jump. 'Look at me. Please will you look at me.'

She raised her head slowly and her eyes met his – those piercing midnight blue eyes.

'I wasn't being sarcastic,' he said. 'I'm sorry if you thought I was but I truly wasn't. I would be interested to hear about your social life even though it's strictly none of my business. I ... I don't have any friends here yet and it would be nice to hear about yours. Perhaps I might even meet a few of them one day. I'd like us to be friends, Jenna ... if that's at all possible.'

'Oh,' was all she could think of saying.

'Is it ... possible? Us being friends? I thought we ... hit it off yesterday.'

'Er ... I ... I can't see any reason why not, although ... it could make things awkward ... if ... if you ever want to get rid of me, I mean.'

She saw an odd look flash across his eyes and a strange smile curve the corners of his mouth and the ten-year-old girl was back with a vengeance. If he wasn't gay, she would have sworn that was a look of desire she'd seen and that mouth – well if that wasn't a prelude to a kiss, she didn't know anything about men. A sudden thought struck her. Perhaps Robert wasn't just gay, perhaps he was ... bisexual, and somehow, that just made things worse.

'I don't think I'll ever want to get rid of you, Jenna,' he declared.

Jenna suddenly wished she hadn't taken the job after all. How could she tell her boss that she just wasn't ... that sort of girl?

'Here you go,' Beth said, putting their plates of toast and pot of coffee on the table. 'Anything else?'

'No thanks, Beth,' Robert said. 'I think we've got everything we need.' He spread butter on his toast and poured both of them some coffee. 'I think your ideas are fantastic. I love the one about the children's course – and a laughing golf ball! That I've got to see – and hear. I also love the social networking suggestions and calling it Green Miles Golf Widows' Club is brilliant. The coffee mornings etc. are excellent ideas. In fact, I love them all. Well, all except murdering the Club President.' He smiled broadly. 'I hope you don't want to do that.'

At this precise moment, actually I do, she thought but she smiled back at him instead and bit into her toast, pretending it was his throat.

'There you are, my boy.' Roddy marched into the restaurant and joined them at their table. 'Beth,' he yelled, 'I'll have the usual. Don't mind if I join you two, do you? Morning, Jenna.' He poured himself a cup of coffee from the pot.

Robert's demeanour changed instantly, Jenna noticed. She smiled at Roddy and wondered why he didn't have a hangover like her dad.

'Of course not,' Robert said. 'We were just discussing plans for the changes we're making to the club. Did you know there are golf balls that actually laugh? We're going to be using them on the children's course we're having beside the driving ranges.'

Roddy spat out the coffee he'd just drunk and his head shot round so that he could look Robert full in the face.

'A children's course? Laughing golf balls? Are you

mad?'

Robert didn't seem at all surprised by his father's outburst.

'Not as far as I'm aware. We're also having women's breakfasts and lunches. Oh, and there's going to be a Facebook page called the Green Miles Golf Widows' Club and I'm turning the old Library into a family room. I believe it was a suggestion Mum made many years ago. And, of course, women will be allowed to join and I'm having certain days when the club will be open to everyone and –'

'Over my dead body!' Roddy boomed.

Robert sipped his coffee. 'I do hope not, Dad but that reminds me, we're having Murder Mystery dinners too. Who Killed the Club President? I believe is to be the first one.'

Roddy banged his fist on the table. 'No! This is your mother's doing. I would never have believed her capable of such revenge but this is because she thinks I chose the club over her, isn't it? When you said you were going to make changes, I thought you meant modernisation and allowing women in the bar in the evenings, and ... and possibly to play golf on one day a week or something, not this ... this treachery. Well, I won't allow it.'

'Actually Dad, you can't do anything about it. You've already signed the club over to me, remember? Please don't get so upset. You go off and have fun with Sherree and when you come back, you may be pleasantly surprised.'

'Never. I'll cancel my trip and I'll fight you all the way. You will not make a mockery of me, Robert, let me tell you. God, it's bad enough that you're a homo –'

'Dad! I think that's quite enough,' Robert said, getting to his feet. 'We can continue this in my office.'

'Your office! You planned this all along, didn't you? I thought that maybe we could build some bridges and that if I left you to run the club, you'd understand how important it is. My father never trusted me to run it and watched over me for years. I was determined not to do the same to you. I trusted you! How could you do this to me? How could *she* do this to me?' He turned on his heels and stormed out.

Robert watched him go and then resumed his seat. 'Well,' he said, his face almost as white as the chalk face of Claremont Cliffs, 'that went well.'

'Are ... are you okay?' Jenna asked, reaching out her left hand to him without thinking.

He took it in his right hand and stroked her knuckles absent-mindedly with his thumb. She felt an odd tingling sensation run up her arm and across her chest and wondered if she were having a heart attack, although, from Roddy's outburst, he was a more likely candidate for cardiac arrest than she was.

'I'm fine,' he said, staring at her hand in his. 'I must admit though, I knew Dad would hate what I wanted to do but I didn't expect an outburst like that. Do you know, I really thought that, once he'd got used to it, he might come to like it. I ... I don't think, until this very morning, that even I understood what this place means to him.'

'He'll come round, I'm sure.'

'Really? You heard him. I'd be surprised if he ever speaks to me again. I'd joked about it but I didn't think he'd be quite this irate. It's too late for him to do anything, of course and even if he tried to oppose it, the Chairman and President have the final say – and that's me.'

'Well, you could perhaps not make so many changes or you –'

'No! All my life, I've resented this place. I don't want other kids to feel like I did. The stupid thing is, it could have all been so different if he'd just listened to Mum and made a few small changes all those years ago.' He shook his head.

83

'Robert. Please don't take this the wrong way and please don't think I agree with your dad – because I don't – but, well, do you think that perhaps, you're as much obsessed with changing this place as your dad is with keeping it the same? I'm just saying this because ... my dad spends a lot of time here but Mum and I don't resent it anywhere near as much as you seem to.'

Robert looked up into her eyes. 'That's funny,' he said. 'My mum said almost the exact same thing to me last night. It's possible that I am, I suppose but don't forget, things are different between you, your mum and your dad, and me, my mum and mine. I don't expect your dad ever had affairs, for example, or told you to stay at home because you'd only get in the way at the club. Your dad never let your mum take you thousands of miles away without so much as asking if you'd perhaps like to stay with him or at the very least, come back for the holidays. Your dad ... Sorry, I didn't mean to go on about it.'

'That's okay,' Jenna said but she was a little surprised by his words.

His phone rang and he glanced at the screen. He sighed loudly and answered it, still holding Jenna's hand in his.

'Lou,' he said. His voice sounded cool and detached, 'please stop calling me. I'm sorry but it's over. How many times do I have to say it? You cheated on me and I told you at the start that was something I'd never tolerate in a relationship. It was your choice and you made it. I spent weeks trying to help you come to terms with it but I've had it. No. Don't start crying. It won't work. I've been ignoring your calls because that's what the therapist said was best for you. That clearly hasn't worked so I'm telling you for the last time. I will never take you back. Please don't call me again. You need to move on, Lou. You need to find someone to make you happy. I'm going to hang up now. Goodbye.' He pressed the end call button, then dialled a number. 'Hi Greg. I've just spoken to Lou ... yes, the calls are still coming. I wondered if you'd keep an eye on things for me. I don't think there'll be any major dramas but you never know. Okay, thanks. Call me if there's a problem. Bye.'

He smiled sadly at Jenna and squeezed her hand tightly. 'Why is life such a complicated, fucking mess?'

Jenna didn't think he wanted her to answer so she stayed silent.

'I'm going for a walk around the course to clear my head,' he said, abruptly releasing her hand. 'I'm really sorry you had to be dragged into that scene with my dad and ... I'll understand if you decide you'd rather not work here after all, especially now that we both know how he really feels about the changes. Think about it and let me know. I also apologise for you having to hear about my love life. I was in a relationship which, as you heard, ended badly several months ago but, no matter how many times I say it, she still keeps calling. I thought by moving here, she'd finally get the message. It appears not.'

He turned and walked away.

Jenna didn't know what to do. The morning hadn't gone at all the way she'd imagined it would. The scene with Roddy had been more than a little upsetting. She hadn't expected him to take it well but she certainly hadn't expected such an outburst and nor had Robert. She was now beginning to wonder how her own father would react. When she'd told Robert yesterday that her father may lead the battle to stop the changes, she was half joking. Now, she wasn't quite so sure. She would have to speak to her mum about it, pretty quickly.

Then there was the conversation she overheard with Robert's ex. She couldn't help but notice that he'd called Lou 'she'. Was this just how he referred to his ... partners or was Lou actually female? she wondered. He'd also said he wouldn't tolerate cheating. That, at least put her mind to rest on one point. If he was bisexual, at least he was

85

only with one sex at a time. Not that that made any difference. She couldn't date a man unless he was totally heterosexual; that's just the way she was.

Jenna looked around her and realised that, since Roddy's outburst, she was the only person in the restaurant and that even the staff were keeping clear. She gathered her things together and made her way to her office. The only thing to do was to keep busy, she told herself, so she went on to the internet and started researching wine tastings, cookery lessons and book clubs.

CHAPTER NINE

'It was unbelievable, Daisy. He just went mad and stormed off,' Jenna said.

They were swimming leisurely, side by side, doing lengths of the pool at the Claremont Leisure Centre. The Centre sat a mile out of town and consisted of a small indoor pool, a few pieces of gym equipment and two rooms used for occasional yoga or fitness classes.

Next door to the Leisure Centre was a pub, the Claremont Arms and Jenna had asked Daisy to ask Adam to meet them there later, for a drink. She had, rather foolishly, she now thought, suggested Robert might like to meet up for a drink later, to take his minds off things, and she didn't want to meet him alone.

'So you felt sorry for Robert and asked him out for a drink,' Daisy said.

'Well ... yes. He'd already told me he didn't know anyone around here and he was so quiet all day that I just thought it might do him good to go out and meet some people.'

'And the phone call from his ex? That sounds a bit off, doesn't it?'

Jenna had told Daisy all about the phone call before she'd told her about Roddy's outburst.

'I don't know what to make of it,' Jenna said. 'He definitely said 'she', so either it was a woman or he refers to his partners as 'she'. I've never heard Gray call his partners that, though.'

'He doesn't. So now you think Robert swings both ways. You couldn't deal with that. You'd just never be sure, would you?'

'No. I've got to stop thinking that there could be a chance that I could have something with Robert. That's one of the reasons I suggested the drink tonight. Adam's going to ask Gray to join us, isn't he?'

'Yes, but I thought you said you weren't ready to see Robert with someone else.'

'I'm not, but it might do me good. It might actually help to get him out of my head.'

'It's not your head you need to get him out of. It's your heart – and you can make a start tonight. Adam's asked Tom to join us too. You can take him home with you and get him to give you a good seeing to.'

'You're just an old romantic, aren't you, Daisy?'

Daisy laughed. 'To the core. Speaking of which, why aren't you tugging at the reins to get Tom's kit off? You wanted to have your way with Robert the minute you saw him again.'

'I know. I think that's the problem though, in spite of everything, deep down, I'd still rather have sex with Robert.'

'Well you can't, so forget it. Now let's get out of here before I turn into a prune.'

Robert was feeling unsure of himself and he hadn't felt like that in a very long time. Since the row with his father, he'd been doing a lot of thinking. Perhaps his mum and Jenna were right. Perhaps he was as obsessed with changing Green Miles as Roddy was with keeping it the same. He wondered whether there might be some sort of compromise but he doubted it. Roderick Miles didn't compromise and, he realised, neither did he.

That was only part of what was troubling him though. The other part involved Jenna. He had returned to England to take over the club for two reasons. One was to change the club and get some sort of closure on his childhood; the other was because he thought Lou might finally realise he meant what he said.

When he'd discovered, through a friend, that she'd

cheated on him and she'd admitted it, he'd ended the relationship immediately. One thing his parents' marriage had taught him was that infidelity always causes havoc. She hadn't taken it well and was still calling him several months later. He hoped that distance would help her come to terms with it. It would at least stop her turning up on his doorstep at all hours of the day and night.

What he hadn't expected was to meet Jenna just a few days after he arrived. He hadn't fallen in love at first sight, like his mum and dad had – at least, he didn't think he had but there was definitely a very strong attraction and he was sure that Jenna felt something for him; he'd seen it in her eyes.

In the normal course of events, this would have made everyone happy, but this wasn't normal. Her dad would take his father's side regarding the club and that would mean very bad feelings between himself and Edward. Jenna would be caught in the middle of that. Then there was the fact that his dad had dumped Jenna's aunt for his mum. That might put a bit of a spanner in the works at future family gatherings.

He picked up his car keys and headed towards the door, feeling even more dejected than he had earlier. No matter how he turned it over in his head – and he'd been doing little else all day – there could be no future together for him and Jenna. It wasn't just the present situation that would prevent it, even if that could be overcome, it was also the past. They could be friends and nothing more.

He now had another reason to resent his father and as he got into his car and drove to the pub, he decided there would definitely be no compromise. When he'd finished, Green Miles Golf Club, would be unrecognisable and his father would know how it felt to lose someone or something he loved.

By the time he pulled into the pub car park and strode towards the door of the pub, he was in a very bad mood.

He hoped that seeing Jenna and meeting some of her friends would cheer him up but the minute he set eyes on her, it had quite the opposite effect.

He was the last of the group to arrive and he immediately spotted Jenna squashed into the corner of a booth with a man in his early thirties, sitting next to her and leaning, somewhat possessively, Robert thought, towards her. Next to him sat another man, also in his thirties, and Robert had enough gay friends in New York to realise where his sexual preferences lay. Seated opposite Jenna were a very pretty, young woman and a guy, both also around thirty and clearly a couple. Something in the pit of his stomach made him feel that he should turn around, go home and call her to say he couldn't make it. He was seriously considering doing just that, when Jenna caught his eye and waved at him.

He took a deep breath, pushed his shoulders back and marched forward as if he were a gladiator heading into the arena to fight a coalition of lions.

'Hi,' Jenna said, smiling up at him. 'These are my best friends, Daisy, her husband Adam, and Gray. We've known each other for ever, well, since junior school, and this is Tom, Adam's friend from uni. Everyone, this is Robert.'

Robert noticed that she hadn't introduced Tom as her boyfriend, even though, one look at Tom made it clear that he considered Jenna his 'property'.

'Hi,' Robert said. 'It's good to meet you all. What are you all having to drink? I'll get a round in.'

'Hi Robert,' Daisy and Adam said simultaneously.

Tom just smiled, nodded and seemed to move a little closer to Jenna, if that was possible. Gray tipped his head to one side, pursed his lips and held out one, long dainty hand. Robert took hold of it and gave him a firm handshake. He saw Gray's eyes dart towards Adam, then back to him. Then Gray smiled up at him, a little sadly,

Robert thought.

'I'll come to the bar with you,' Gray said. 'I know what everyone wants, apart from you, Tom. Same again is it?'

Tom just nodded.

Robert could feel Gray watching him as they strolled towards the bar.

'You've been friends with Jenna for most of her life then?' Robert asked.

'Uh-huh. Jenna, Daisy, Adam and I have been friends from our first days at school. We're very close and we tell each other *everything*.'

Robert wondered if there was a hidden meaning in that comment because Gray gave him a very pointed look but maybe Gray was just stating a fact – and he was becoming paranoid.

'That must be nice. I've lost touch with the majority of guys I was at school with and most of my friends now, are in the States. There are a few over here whom I must look up when I get a chance. It was very kind of Jenna to invite me here tonight to meet all of you.'

'Jenna's a very kind girl. We all love her to bits.'

'And Tom? He's Jenna's ... boyfriend ... I take it. Have you known him long?'

'Have I known him long or has Jenna known him long? Gray replied.

He looked directly into Robert's eyes and Robert felt a little uncomfortable, as if Gray could read his mind.

'Okay. Has Jenna known him long?'

'No.'

Robert smiled at him. 'You don't give much away, do you?'

'You'd be surprised! But I like to know who I'm dealing with and I don't like people who play games, well ... I like some games, if you know what I mean ... but I don't like people pretending to be something they're *clearly not, darling,* especially if it involves my friends.'

'Are ... are you saying that you think I'm pretending to be something I'm not?'

'You tell me.'

'There's nothing to tell, Gray. What you see is what you get. You might not like it but there's not much I can do about that.'

He met Gray's eyes and they stared at one another for a few seconds. Gray grinned at him and slipped his arm through Robert's. Gray put the drinks on a tray and slid the tray towards Robert.

'Come along then, darling,' he said.

They walked back to the booth with Robert carrying the tray and Gray's arm still linked through his.

'Well, it looks as if you two are getting along nicely,' Daisy said, grinning broadly.

Jenna felt as if she wanted to cry. Seeing Robert and Gray together like that and watching them chatting and swapping jokes and sarcastic comments with Adam and Daisy all evening, made her feel as if her heart were being slowly shredded.

She knew she should be happy for them but she wasn't. The only way she could deal with it was to force herself to pretend that she couldn't care less about Robert Miles and that Tom, who had been cloyingly attentive all evening, was the love of her life. So instead of moving her hand out of reach every time he tried to touch it, she finally let him take it in his.

She thought she saw Robert's eyes narrow when Tom rubbed the middle finger of his other hand suggestively back and forth across her knuckles, and again when Tom whispered in her ear what he'd really like to be doing with it, making the colour rush to her cheeks, but she was sure she must have been mistaken.

The problem was, she realised, the more she pretended, the keener Tom got and the keener Tom got, the more she wanted to stand on the table and tell the world that it was Robert she wanted and she didn't care if he was gay, bisexual or anything else, for that matter, just as long as she could be his.

'Well, I don't know about the rest of you but I've got work tomorrow,' Adam said. 'Me and the missus are going to head off. Jenna, we'll drop you on the way.'

'That's okay, Adam,' Tom said. 'I can take Jenna home.'

Jenna kicked Daisy's foot and gave her a pleading look.

'Don't worry, Tom. I need to pick up some clothes from Jenna's place and you know us girls, we'll be yapping for ages. You go home and we'll take Jenna,' Daisy said.

'You didn't tell me ...' Adam began but Daisy must have kicked him and he clearly got the message. 'Oh, yes. I'd completely forgotten. Do you want to come with us, Gray or –'

'I'll come with you,' Gray said.

Tom gave Jenna a questioning look but she smiled at him and hoped he wouldn't suggest he'd come along anyway.

They made their way towards the door. Reaching the car park, Robert turned to Jenna and smiled.

'Thanks for inviting me tonight,' he said. Then to the others, 'It was great to meet you all.'

'We'll be here again on Friday, *darling*,' Gray said. 'We'd love you to join us if you're free. We start earlier than tonight, around seven, and usually finish up in the Claremont Ghurka, if you like Himalayan food.'

Robert's eyes darted to Jenna's face as if he were seeking her confirmation.

'Yes, please do,' she added.

'Thanks. I'd love to. See you all on Friday then.'

Robert got into his Audi TT, waved and drove off. Tom drove off in his BMW convertible, after giving Jenna a quick peck on the lips and confirming their dinner date for the next day.

'Well, what an interesting evening,' Gray announced, sliding into the back seat of Adam's Fiat Punto, next to Jenna. 'I'm assuming, as you clearly didn't want the lovely Tom to take you home, darling, you still have the hots for the delicious Robert.'

Jenna forced a smile. 'Not at all, honey. He's all yours. I'm just tired and I'm seeing Tom tomorrow anyway. He can wait until then.'

'Barely, darling. The man was pawing you like a Black Bear on an ant hill. Even I felt embarrassed and poor, dear Robert, well, … I thought he would beat the man to a pulp any second.'

Jenna and Daisy's heads both shot round to look Gray full in the face, Daisy from the front passenger seat. Even Adam looked at him through the rear view mirror.

'You don't mean that you think Robert fancied Tom, do you?' Jenna exclaimed.

Gray looked stunned. 'Good heavens no, darling! He fancies you, Jenna and it's as clear as my baby soft complexion.'

'But he's gay!' Adam said.

'Believe me, Adam, if that man's gay then I'll become a eunuch and you all know how much chance there is of *that* happening! And, as for Tom, well, dear Robert may be lying about his sexuality for reasons best known to himself, but there's something about the lovely Tom that just isn't right. I can't put my finger on it yet and the man clearly would rather I didn't exist but I'm determined to get to the bottom of it ... ooh! You know what I mean.'

'N ... not gay? What do you mean he's not gay? He told his own father he was and whilst I know he's bearing a rather large grudge against him, I can't see that he'd lie to his own father about something like that,' Jenna said.

'Don't shoot the messenger, darling. I call it as I see it.'

'But tonight – in the pub. You linked arms with him and laughed and joked with him. You even put your arm around him at one stage and he didn't move away,' Daisy said. 'He must be gay.'

'Why? I link arms with Adam and put my arm around him. That doesn't mean he's gay, or that he fancies me or that I fancy him.' He tapped Adam on the shoulder. 'No offence, darling, you know I love you.'

'None taken,' Adam said, grinning.

'Yes but Adam knows you and he knows what you're like,' Jenna said. 'Robert only met you tonight and, no disrespect, Gray, but you don't exactly hide the fact you're gay, not that you should.'

'That's the point. Apart from the fact that I can tell if someone's gay or not from ten yards, when I did that, if he were gay, he would have given me some indication. He didn't. Tom would have pulled away, because he's the type who is clearly uncomfortable around gay men but Robert just saw it as the friendly gesture it was. He's obviously got gay friends in New York and he's perfectly at ease with them, and because I'm your friend, he's at ease with me.'

'Perhaps ... perhaps he is gay but ... well ... he just didn't fancy you,' Jenna said.

Gray twisted in his seat to look her full in the face. He had a startled expression on his face.

'Not fancy me! Are you mad, woman? I assure you, if he were that way inclined he would one hundred percent, without any shadow of a doubt, fancy me! I'm horrified that you could even think such a thing!'

'I'm sorry, honey but ... well, I just don't understand it then. His dad wouldn't have told my dad if there was the slightest doubt about it, and my dad wouldn't have told me – well, he didn't intend to tell me, it slipped out – don't makes any jokes about that. The point is Roddy definitely believes it and he actually said that Robert told him, to his face.'

'Well, the only thing Robert seemed interested in tonight,' Gray said, 'was how long you and Tom have been an item. Not that I told him, of course. I can be so cruel sometimes.'

CHAPTER TEN

'I don't know how I got through today, Daisy, to be honest,' Jenna said when she called her on the phone after work the following day. 'I just couldn't get to sleep last night and when I did drift off, I dreamt that I was chasing Robert who was chasing Gray who was chasing Tom who was chasing me! They say your subconscious tries to solve your problems whilst you sleep. Well, I think mine's just telling me my life's going round in circles.'

'Did Robert say anything to you?' Daisy asked.

'I didn't see him all day. When I got in there was a note on my desk saying that he wouldn't be around much and could I make some calls to get quotes for the work to design the children's course. He left me a list of people to call and said I should just tell them my ideas and ask them to come up with some rough costings. The note also said I should start work on the newsletter and get quotes for the Murder Mystery dinners. Basically, he just told me to get on with it.'

'So you haven't spoken to him either?'

'Nope. Not a word. I wonder if he's annoyed about last night.'

'Why? Unless he thinks we were trying to fix him up with Gray and even then, I don't see why he'd be annoyed. He shouldn't tell people he's gay if he isn't,' Daisy said. 'Are you still seeing Tom tonight?'

'Yeah, but I'm not sure I want to, really. He seems nice but ...' Jenna trailed off and sighed.

'I know ... he's not Robert. Well, I think you should go. You might have fun. Call me if there are any developments.'

Jenna hung up but her phone rang again a few seconds later.

'Jenna, this is your father. Roddy's told me about that boy's plans to destroy Green Miles and your mother was right. That golf club is no place for you to be working, especially as someone's assistant. I think you should call the young upstart right now and tell him that you no longer want to work there. Then come round here, I need to hear everything you know about this.'

'Dad! Firstly, Mum didn't say any such thing. She said I shouldn't work for Roddy, and I'm not. Secondly, Robert is not an upstart. Roddy knew he had plans and if he was so concerned that Green Miles should stay the same stuffy, pompous, place it's always been, he should have made that clear before he signed it over. Perhaps if he'd actually listened to his son he would have known what Robert intended. No. Don't interrupt, I haven't finished. Thirdly, I can decide for myself who I will and won't work for. I know I didn't want the job but now I'm there, I plan to stay. I hope it won't cause friction between us because you're my dad and I love you but I like Robert's plans and I think most of the wives and children will too.'

Jenna could feel herself shaking. She and her father rarely argued and she hoped that this wouldn't blow up into something both of them may regret. She'd told her mother about Roddy's outburst and Fiona had said that it was best to stay out of it and see what happened. Jenna now wondered if that had been the right decision.

'Dad?' she said tentatively. 'I'm sorry but I really do think Robert will improve Green Miles, if you and Roddy and the other members would just give him a chance.'

'I'm disappointed, Jenna. Very, very disappointed,' Edward said, then he hung up.

Jenna was stunned. Her father had never hung up on her before. He was clearly more upset than she'd realised. She couldn't leave things like that; she had to go and talk to him even though she was supposed to be having dinner with Tom. She had collected her prized but rather dated,

Toyota Celica from the garage on the way home; she could drive to her parents and leave her car there.

She dialled Daisy's number because she didn't have Tom's, explained briefly what had happened, then dialled the number Daisy gave her and told Tom that she'd meet him at the restaurant. She showered, slipped a v-neck, geometric patterned dress on over her underwear and pulled on a metallic knit shrug. After a quick flick of mascara and swipe of lipstick, she grabbed her raincoat, jumped into her car and headed to her parents. When she let herself in with her key, she could hear them arguing.

'Sometimes, Edward, I think you're as bad as Roddy. It's a golf club for heaven's sake, not the Ark of the Covenant. Things change. Just look around you. Nearly every golf club in this county, in this country even, allows women members except Green Miles. They all have open bars and restaurants, except Green Miles. Many of them have other functions and events except –'

'That's the whole point, Fiona! Green Miles is one of the last few remaining clubs of its kind. We don't want the hoi-polloi coming and going with their wives and hordes of children. We don't want weddings and parties and riff-raff churning up our greens racing around on carts, shouting and swearing. We –'

'You want to live in the early nineteenth century when men like Theodore Miles were in command and women and children did as they were told and were seen occasionally but never heard. When servants bowed and scraped to you and you could shut yourself away in your silly club and all pretend you are so much better than everyone else. Well darling, I've got news for you. This is the twenty-first century and you and Roddy are certainly *not* better than everyone else.'

'You're being ridiculous! There is no point in having this discussion.'

'We're not having a discussion! A discussion is when

two people have a conversation and actually listen to one another. You never want to hear anyone's opinion any more unless it's the same as yours. Well that's it, Edward. I should have said this a long time ago. It's that bloody, stupid club or it's me. You choose. Frankly, at this precise moment in time, I couldn't care either way but if you think Roddy is so wonderful then perhaps you should move in with him. I'm going to the pub!'

Fiona stormed into the hall almost knocking Jenna over.

'Mum! Oh God! What's going on?'

'Ask your father. I need a drink and I'm having it with the hoi polloi. You're more than welcome to join me.'

Edward marched out of the sitting room into the hall. 'Fiona!' He saw Jenna and scowled. 'You have a lot to answer for, Jenna.'

'Don't you dare blame Jenna! You were the one who wanted her to take the job. Well, Edward, you reap what you sow, dear. Come on, Jenna.'

'Dad! I ...'

Her father turned his back on her and marched back into the sitting room, slamming the door behind him and her mother grabbed her arm and dragged her out onto the driveway, slamming the front door behind them.

'Shit!' Jenna said in shocked disbelief. 'How did things get so crazy, so quickly?'

'Don't use bad language, darling.' Fiona dialled a number and booked a cab. 'Your father will come around, don't worry. He spent the day with Roddy and that always spells disaster. That man needs someone to put him in his place, and pretty damn sharpish too. Roddy, I mean, not Edward, although, this evening, I could have cheerfully hit him with the whisky decanter and felt a greater loss for the spilt whisky.'

'Mum!'

Jenna was horrified and shaken. In all her thirty years,

she'd only heard her parents row a few times and never anything like this. She was still shaking when she got into the cab Fiona had called and by the time they reached the pub, she realised she needed a drink more than her mother did.

'What will you do, Mum?'

'I'll have a few drinks and then I'll go home.'

'No. I ... I mean. You told Dad to choose. What if he ...' She couldn't bring herself to say it.

Fiona laughed although not happily. 'He won't darling. Edward may be silly at times but he's not a fool. Roddy is his friend and he cares about him deeply but I'm his wife and I know he loves me. He'll apologise and then we'll reach a compromise ... because that's what people who care about each other, do. He'll sulk for a day or two but he'll come round, so don't you worry. I think we'll have champagne and your father's paying,' she declared, waving a joint credit card in her hand.

'Bloody hell!' Jenna said, glancing at the clock over the bar, nearly an hour later. 'I'm supposed to be meeting someone for dinner tonight and I'm fifteen minutes late already. I'll call and cancel.'

'Is it a young man?' Fiona asked.

'Yes. I met him at Daisy's the other night. He's a friend of Adam's.'

'Don't cancel, darling. You go. You deserve to have some fun.'

'I can't leave you like this, Mum.'

'I'll be fine, don't worry about me. It may surprise you but I have been in a pub on my own before. Now go and enjoy yourself and don't worry about your father either. Things will work out and when he sees sense, he'll apologise to you and me both. Now go.'

Jenna wasn't sure her mother was right but she finally left and raced down the road to Carluccio's, the Italian restaurant where Tom was waiting. She called Daisy on the way to tell her what had happened and said she'd let her know as soon as she heard anything.

Tom didn't look very pleased when Jenna pushed open the door.

'I'm so, so sorry, Tom,' she said, having reached the table, gasping for breath. 'There's been a bit of a drama at home, as I mentioned earlier, and I couldn't get away.'

Tom glared at her. Then a smile formed on his lips. 'No problem, Jenna. It's nothing serious I hope.'

'I'm not sure,' she said. 'I ... I think it may be.'

'Sit down and have some wine.'

She took off her raincoat and a waiter dashed over to take it from her.

'Thanks,' she said and sat down. She took the glass of wine from Tom and blinked several times in an attempt to hold back the tears pushing at the corners of her eyes.

'Do you want to talk about it?' Tom asked.

She shook her head. For some reason, she didn't, at least, not to him. 'No. I'd rather talk about something else, if you don't mind. How are things progressing with the development plans for Claremont Cliffs?'

She didn't really want to hear about them, not tonight anyway. Plans to change Claremont Cliffs or any plans involving any sort of change to anything, anywhere, were the last things she wanted to talk about but she wasn't sure what else to say, so she sat and listened and ate and drank while Tom told her how wonderful it was all going to be. All the time he was talking, she had images of herself, her parents, Robert, Roddy and Amelia all standing on the edge of the cliffs which were crumbling beneath them, and one by one, they all fell over the edge and into the raging sea below.

When her phone rang she was astonished to realise that she'd eaten her meal and a dessert and that Tom was paying the bill and getting ready for them to leave. He glowered at her as her phone played its usual 1812 overture and she tried to give him an apologetic smile but felt she failed.

'Hello darling, it's Mum.'

'Mum! Are you all right? Where are you?'

'I'm fine, darling. I'm at home. I just wanted to check that you were okay.'

'I ... I think so. Is ... Dad with you?'

'Don't worry about your father, darling. He'll come home when he's cooled off. He's left a note saying he's staying at Roddy's tonight and he'll be back tomorrow – which of course means, he'll drink himself into oblivion and come home with a hangover.'

'Oh God, Mum!'

'Don't worry, darling. I keep telling you, everything will be fine. Trust me. I've known your father for more than thirty-seven years. It'll all work out, I assure you. I'm going to bed now and I just wanted to say that I'll call you tomorrow when there's any news. I don't expect your father to surface before the afternoon and then he'll sulk for a few hours and then, he'll come home, so it'll probably be late evening. Please don't worry though. I wouldn't have given him the ultimatum if I'd thought there was the slightest chance of him choosing the club over us. He just needs a little time to realise he's wrong – like most men do.'

'Tom, I'm really, really sorry but ... I can't. Not tonight.' Jenna said, gently pushing him away from her. 'I'm still upset about things at home and ... I just wouldn't be able to ... well, you know what I mean.'

They'd driven to her cottage in virtual silence and all the way, she'd been trying to think of something to say. She knew that he expected her to ask him in and she also knew that it wouldn't just be for coffee, so when he pulled up outside and walked her to the door, then put his arms around her and started kissing her, she had to stop him before he began to think he would be spending the night.

She met his eyes and she thought he was going to explode because his face was so red. The muscles tightened around his mouth and the look in his eyes was a mixture of surprise and anger but he quickly recovered and reached out for her again, forcing his lips into what she could tell was a false smile.

'It'll take your mind off things,' he said. 'I'm very, very good at making women forget about anything else except the multiple orgasms I'm giving them. You won't have to do a thing.' He ran his finger down the side of her face and across her lips. 'Just lie back and let me take you to heaven.'

She wished she hadn't laughed. She hadn't meant to but she just couldn't help it. It wasn't her usual nervous giggle either; it was a full blown, laugh out loud, burst of laughter, and Tom clearly wasn't pleased. But come on, she thought, did he really expect her to take that twaddle seriously? Did men think stuff like that actually worked on women?

'What's so funny about that?' he said. 'Believe me, babe, you don't know what you're missing. I can guarantee you've never had a man like me before.'

She thought he was probably right, although not in the way he obviously meant it.

'I'm sure it'll be my loss,' she said, suppressing her chuckles, 'but even so, I must still say no. I'm just too tired to have ... multiple orgasms tonight. I really feel I'd like to be wide awake to ... fully appreciate that experience.'

She could tell that he wasn't sure whether she was being serious or making fun of him, but she didn't care. She just wanted him to leave.

He seemed to decide she was being sincere.

'Okay,' he said, leaning forward and giving her a quick

104

kiss on the lips. 'I'll take another rain check but next time, I'm going to show you exactly what you've been missing and that's a promise.' He winked at her and smiled provocatively. 'What are you doing tomorrow?'

'Oh! Er ... I'll probably be at my parents' house tomorrow ... and Friday, we're all in the pub.'

He stiffened visibly then grinned. 'Okay. I'll tell you what. I'll meet you at the pub on Friday and I'll cook you dinner at my place on Saturday night. You'll be hungry by then, because we'll have spent all Friday night and all day Saturday, in bed and believe me, being under the covers with me is like being between the covers of the Kama Sutra.'

Jenna nearly laughed again but the mention of Saturday made her remember the dinner dance and that made her remember how awful the past two days had been.

'Saturday is the annual dinner dance at the club, which I don't usually go to but because I'm working there I ... oh ... but I don't know what's happening now ... and ...' Tears rolled silently down her cheeks.

Tom tried to brush them away but Jenna shook her head and stepped away from him.

'I'm sorry, Tom but I really want to be alone now,' she said. 'I'll see you on Friday. Good night – and thank you for dinner. I really am sorry.'

She opened her front door and stepped inside, closing it before he had a chance to say anything else. She heard his footsteps on the path and his car door slam. The engine revved and with a screech of tyres, he drove off.

Tom was less than happy. On Monday, everything seemed to be going so well. Now, just two days later, it was beginning to feel as if he may have lost his touch. His initial enquiries about the possibility of buying, and getting planning consent for the Claremont Cliffs' project had been met with far less enthusiasm than he'd been led to believe he could expect and, in spite of what he'd been telling Jenna, things were not looking promising.

The council confirmed they wanted someone to buy the site from them, and yes they were happy to consider some sort of development project but it seemed they were envisaging something very low density and environmentally friendly. Two hundred executive homes and two blocks of luxury apartments definitely wasn't what they had in mind, they now said. But the *pièce de résistance* was that there now seemed to be some question as to who owned the land and whether any building developments would be permitted in any event. Why the hell Adam couldn't have mentioned that before Tom had come here, he had no idea.

Then there was Jenna. He was beginning to think that she was leading him a merry little dance. He usually managed to get women into bed with him on the first night but this was the third night he'd seen her and so far, all he'd got was a quick grope of her breast. It wasn't as if she was even his type, so why the hell was he wasting his time on her with nothing to show for his efforts? The problem was, she was Daisy's best friend so, if he wanted to keep Adam happy, he knew he'd have to keep Jenna happy too, for the time being, at least.

Let's not forget that shit, Robert Miles, Tom thought. He had already put a spanner in the works. One of the unique selling points of the proposed two hundred executive homes and luxury apartments was going to be their proximity to – and if he could wangle it – membership of, the prestigious Green Miles Golf Club. Who would want to be a member of the downmarket, open to all, club that Robert was planning to turn it into?

He needed a drink – and that was another problem with Claremont – it was nothing short of a dump. He drew up outside the one wine bar – the only wine bar he'd seen, which looked half decent and stomped up to the bar. He spotted a couple of young women out of the corner of his eye and thought one of them looked exactly his cup of tea, so he bought a bottle of champagne, grabbed three glasses and strolled over to their table.

'Hi, lovely ladies. I'm celebrating a rather profitable deal,' he lied, 'and I've got the champagne but what I need are two gorgeous women like you to share it with. I'm Tom and you are ...?'

'I'm Beth and this is Sherree,' the plainer of the two said.

'That's S-H-E-R-R-E-E,' Sherree said, her jewellery jingling as she stretched out her hand.

'I'm very pleased to meet you both,' Tom said, suddenly feeling that he might get lucky tonight after all.

Jenna had mixed feelings about telling Tom to go. She kept trying to convince herself that she liked him but when he said ridiculous things like he had just now, all she wanted to do was tell him to get lost. Every time he touched her, she couldn't stop herself wishing that it was Robert and tonight, if it had been Robert, she would have dragged him up to bed without a second thought. Tonight of all nights, she didn't want to be alone and yet, she'd rather be alone than end up in bed with Tom.

Perhaps she wasn't giving Tom a fair chance, she thought, trying to think of anything other than Saturday night and the dinner dance and by extension – the row with her dad. The tears came again and this time, she didn't brush them away. She flopped onto the sofa and sobbed so loud that the 1812 overture on her phone was almost drowned out by the din.

She finally heard it but by the time she got to it, the caller had rung off. When she saw that it had been Robert, she cried even louder.

'I need a drink,' she said to herself when the tears eventually stopped. She got up and poured herself a very large gin and tonic – having sworn herself off vodka – and when that was gone, she poured herself another, then another.

She wasn't sure if the bells she could hear were in her head or on the TV but when she realised the TV wasn't on, she struggled to her feet to see where they were coming from. Finally, she decided they weren't in her head. After a couple of minutes, she recognised them as her doorbell.

She staggered to the door and even though it was late, without thinking, she yanked it open.

'I don't want to have sex with you!' she slurred. 'Please go away.'

'Jenna?' Robert exclaimed.

Jenna's mouth fell open and she would have fallen flat on her back if Robert hadn't reached out and grabbed her arm.

'Are you okay?' he asked in a concerned manner. 'I've just heard what happened between your mum and dad. I tried calling you but there was no answer.'

Jenna tried to focus but all she could think of was what she'd just said to him.

'I didn't mean I don't want sex with you, Robert,' she said, trying not to slur her words. 'I meant I don't want sex with Tom. I thought you were Tom but you're you.'

Robert grinned at her. 'Yes, I'm me and I think you need to sit down.'

He helped her to the sofa and lowered her down onto the seat.

'No!' she said, leaping to her feet but she felt herself sway and grabbed his jacket to steady her. 'I *need* a drink.'

'I think you've had several,' he said, coaxing her back down. 'I'll go and make us some coffee.'

'I don't want coffee. I want to go to bed ... but first, I want a drink. Ooh! I didn't mean I *do* want sex with you either at the door, no, I mean not sex at the door but sex anywhere, even though I do, but I don't – because I couldn't deal with it.'

Robert made no reply but when she was able to focus, she could see he was looking at her with a confused expression on his face.

'I think I'd better shut up,' she said, leaning back against the sofa cushions and closing her eyes.

She could hear noises from the kitchen but everything seemed to be coming from a long way off and she was sure she could feel herself falling.

'Robert!' she screamed as she slid off the sofa.

He dashed into the sitting room and caught her before she landed on the floor.

'You saved me!' she said. 'I ... I was falling. Oh. I ... I thought I was falling over Claremont Cliffs.' Then she burst into tears.

He gently lifted her onto the sofa and sat down beside her, holding her in his arms. He rocked her slowly back and forth and stroked her hair.

'Shush,' he whispered. 'It's okay.'

'It's not!' she sobbed into his shirt, nuzzling beneath his jacket. 'Everything's gone wrong. Dad and Mum have rowed and Dad's gone to live with Roddy, and Roddy is really angry, and Dad hates me, and Roddy hates you ... and me, and Roddy doesn't really love Sherree. He loves your mum – at least, we think he did, but now he hates her and I don't want to go to bed with Tom even though he says I can have lots of orgasms if I do, and be in the Kama Sutra ... and he wants to build on the cliffs but we're all falling over the edge so he can't ... and you don't like Gray but maybe you like Tom instead, or even Adam ... but you don't like me even though I've loved you all my life – well, not all my life but lots of it, and ... um, I forget now but everything's gone wrong.'

'Jenna. D... did you just say you loved me?'

She raised her tearful eyes to his and she thought she

saw something deep and tender in his dark eyes but she was having trouble focusing so she wasn't completely sure. She lifted her arm and ran her hand through his hair and the feel of it against her skin sent a thrill of anticipation through her. She'd been right all those years ago – his hair was as soft as a kitten's fur.

'Oh Robert,' she said shifting her position so that she could wrap her other arm around his neck.

She felt her lips brush his and although it wasn't the 1812 overture, she heard bells chiming – twelve of them, she was certain.

'Jenna, please,' she heard him say and his voice was a caress.

'Nothing matters, Robert,' she said.

'You're drunk. You don't know what you're saying or doing. It's midnight. I think perhaps you need to go to bed.'

'Yes please! Please take me to bed, Robert. I know exactly what I'm saying. I've wanted you since your sixteenth birthday party when you kissed me. I can't remember why you did kiss me but you did and I feel ...' She struggled to think of the right word but when it came to her, it wasn't the word she was expecting. 'I feel ... sick!'

She wasn't sure what happened next. She thought he lifted her up and then held her hair back whilst she threw up in the downstairs cloakroom. She was aware that he washed her face and hands and was sure he made her rinse her mouth with water and then with the minty mouthwash she kept on the shelf above the sink. She knew he lifted her into his arms and carried her upstairs. She felt him hold her in his arms as he slowly removed her metallic knit shrug and lifted her dress over her head.

She could remember him saying, 'These need washing.'

'Kiss me, Robert,' she pleaded, leaning against his firm

body and she felt goosebumps cover every inch of her as he gently eased her down onto the bed.

She felt him kiss her on her forehead and she closed her eyes waiting for his mouth to travel downwards to her lips. This night would be heaven, she thought.

CHAPTER ELEVEN

Jenna's head was thumping. She tried to open her eyes and it took her several attempts before she managed it. Her mouth felt as if she'd swallowed a bag of cotton wool and her chest ached. She glanced towards her clock and saw that it was five-thirty. That meant she didn't have to get up for at least another hour and a half. She could go back to sleep and ... she suddenly remembered last night and she reached out her hand for Robert.

He was gone. She forced herself up on her elbow and her eyes searched the darkened room. She flicked on the bedside lamp – and wished she hadn't. There was no sign of him. No shoes, no hastily removed clothes, nothing. She lifted the duvet a touch and realised that she still had her bra and pants on. Had he made love to her and then put her underwear back on her? Why would he do that? She looked for her dress and shrug but they weren't on the chair or discarded on the floor.

She flopped back onto the pillows utterly confused. Last night Robert had made love to her, she could remember it so well. It had been ... she couldn't remember, but they had made love, she was sure of it. He'd carried her upstairs. She'd kissed him and he'd smothered her body with kisses from head to foot – hadn't he?

She tried to remember exactly what had happened but she couldn't and yet she was sure she'd felt his lips on hers, his hands caressing her breasts and sliding down between her legs. She could remember the longing she felt, the yearning for him to take her and yet ... she still had her underwear on. She racked her brain. Had he regretted it? Had he put her bra and pants back on to make her think that nothing had happened? Surely he wouldn't have done that?

Hadn't he told her he loved her? No, she'd told him but ... oh my God! 'You told him you loved him!' she screamed. She tossed and turned and pulled the duvet over her head, making little squealing sounds.

What had she done? What had they done? Had they done anything? Had she dreamt the whole thing? Had Robert even come round at all? Why couldn't she remember?

She threw off the duvet and crawled out of bed, staggering to the shower. She saw her dress and shrug hanging over the edge of the bath and when she touched them, they were still damp. Had she rinsed them? Why?

Then she remembered. She'd been sick. Robert had held her hair for her. Oh God, she groaned. That part she could remember. Was that before or after she told him she loved him? Had she told him or had she just imagined that?

Her head felt as if the wall was banging against it, not the other way around so she grabbed two headache tablets and decided she'd have to go back to bed. When she woke up again, she might remember. She stumbled back to her bedroom and stopped. One final thought occurred to her and she called out his name. He could have dressed and now be downstairs making coffee. The only sound she heard was from the clock her grandmother had given her, and it chimed six times telling her it was now six o'clock.

Daisy couldn't stop laughing when Jenna phoned her to tell her.

'It's really *not* funny,' Jenna insisted. 'What am I going to do?'

'Sorry, Jenna but you'd be laughing too if I'd just told you that I thought I'd had sex with my gay boss and I thought I'd told him that I loved him but I couldn't really remember and the only thing I could remember is

113

throwing up all over him.'

'I didn't throw up all over him – at least, I don't think I did. Oh God. Maybe I did. How can I face him? What can I say?'

'You could always call in sick so you don't have to face him. Either that or you just go up to him and ask.'

'Yeah, right! What do you suggest I say? "Robert, did we have sex last night or did I imagine the whole thing?" That would go down well, wouldn't it? The sex was so great I can't even remember!'

'I think you've answered your own question. However drunk you were, even you would remember having sex. Besides, do you honestly think he would then put your underwear back on you? I think you can safely assume there was no sex and that it was just a dream you had. Personally, I wouldn't kiss someone who's just thrown up, anyway – no matter how much mouthwash I've forced down their throat. I think the kissing was all on your part. As for the telling him you loved him, there is a very strong possibility that that bit, you did.'

'Oh God! My life is falling apart. I've made my father hate me. Because of me, my parents might be getting divorced. I'm sexually harassing my boss, telling him I love him and trying to get him into bed even though I know he's gay. The one guy who wants to sleep with me, I'm not interested in. I'm verging on becoming an alcoholic. I'm throwing up over people. Have I left anything out?'

'No, I believe that about covers it – and just think, Jenna – it's only Thursday. Heaven knows what else you'll have done by the weekend!'

There was nothing else to it. Whether she wanted to or not, Jenna knew she'd have to go to work and face Robert. For a split second, she wondered whether he might decide that he did actually want to get rid of her, even though he'd said he never would, and that made her feel even more depressed. She could then add losing her new job to her list of this week's achievements.

She was more than a little relieved when on arriving at her office, once again, there was no sign of Robert, but he'd left her a sealed envelope on her desk. Her stomach churned whilst she opened it, and she didn't know whether to laugh or cry when she read the contents.

Good morning, Jenna,

I'll be out of the office again for most of the day but I've left you my mobile number in case you need me. If you're feeling up to it, would you continue contacting the Murder Mystery people etc. I've read the draft newsletter you left on my desk yesterday and I think it's perfect. Perhaps you could start sending those off to the wives/partners of all the members.

I hope to see you later, if not, then definitely tomorrow.

I also hope you're feeling okay. Here are some emergency supplies in case you need them. I'm sure things will sort themselves out and that your mum and dad will be fine but if you need to talk, please call me and if you need to go home, then don't worry about the club – just go.

Have a good day.

Robert

She could feel something in the envelope and she tipped it out. It was a packet of 12 headache tablets and it claimed to combat headache and sickness – *fast*.

She picked up the phone, dialled Daisy's number and told her about the note and its contents.

'Well, it's not quite a bouquet of roses but I suppose it shows the man cares about you. Of course, it also means that you didn't imagine all of last night. Part of it did happen. Unfortunately, it does seem to be the part where you threw up, but at least it means you're not completely losing your mind. I'm glad you called actually. Did you know that Robert's meeting Adam for lunch?'

'No. Oh God, you don't mean ...' Jenna let her voice trail off for dramatic effect.

'What? Oh very funny. No. Well ... at least, I don't think so.' Daisy giggled. 'It's apparently something to do with the Claremont Cliffs' site but don't ask me anything else because I have no idea. Adam wouldn't tell me. He's being very secretive about it and ... wait a minute, perhaps you're right!'

They both giggled knowing full well that Adam was as straight as a die, in more ways than one.

'How odd though,' Jenna remarked. 'Robert didn't mention anything to me about Claremont Cliffs – not that there's any reason why he would, of course, but he didn't say anything in the pub the other night, did he?'

'No, but he did seem very interested in what Tom was saying about the development backing onto Green Miles Golf Club land, so maybe Robert is concerned whether it'll have an impact on the club.'

'Or maybe he's not just thinking about changing the club, perhaps he's thinking about expanding it. It would make sense in a way. Some of the bigger clubs have both, eighteen hole and nine hole, courses and imagine how fantastic it would be to play along the cliffs. That would be a real challenge on a windy day.'

'Sorry, what were you saying?' Daisy said. 'I fell asleep when you started talking about golf. Only teasing – although if you start going on about it at the next dinner party we have, I'm signing you up for a lobotomy. Anyway, you could be right. The club would then have the entire sweep of land to the east of Claremont and to the north. Surely that would please Roddy? The Miles' men have always wanted to take over the town, especially Theodore – seeing that it was named after the family he blamed for ruining his life.'

'Ooh! I didn't know you knew anything about the

Miles' men.'

'I don't. I only remember Mum telling me some tale about Theodore Miles buying Claremont Manor to get revenge but I can't really remember it. Next time you tell Robert you love him, ask him to tell you the story.'

'You're *so* amusing,' Jenna replied with a hint of sarcasm. 'I think I'll look it up on the internet. Now go away, I've got important golf related thingies to get on with. Call me if you find out why they're meeting for lunch though. I need to know exactly what Robert is doing – not that I'm stalking him or anything.'

'Right. And you call me if he comes back and tells you what he *didn't* do to you last night.'

Jenna hung up and was just about to Google 'Theodore Miles' when she heard a woman's voice outside Robert's office.

'Hello-o?'

'In here,' Jenna called out, getting up from her desk and walking to the door. 'May I help you?'

'Ah. You must be Jenna Baker. Wow. You look almost identical to your mother when she was your age. You must be around thirty, right?'

'Er ... yes. Sorry ... do I know you?' She studied the tall, slim, elegantly dressed woman and thought she'd seen her somewhere before. Her hair was dark brown, almost black and her eyes were a deep, dark blue.

'Not exactly,' the woman said and smiled, 'but you do know my son, Robert. I'm Amelia Stone, formerly Amelia Miles. Is he around?'

'Amelia! ... I mean, Mrs Miles. I mean ... Mrs Stone. Sorry. I'm so pleased to meet you.'

'You can call me Amelia,' she said, grinning. 'May I call you Jenna?'

'Yes. Yes of course. Er ... Robert's out of the office, I'm afraid. I'm not sure when he'll be back.'

'Oh well, never mind. He did tell me he would be out

for most of the day. He also tells me you've got some wonderful ideas for the club. Do you have some time to tell me about them? Could we possibly have a spot of breakfast, unless you're too busy, or you've already eaten? In which case, just join me for coffee, please. I'm sure Robert won't mind, and it's my treat.'

'Er ... no, I haven't eaten. That would be great. Thanks,' Jenna said, wondering if she could really face food.

'Good. You'll have to bear with me, I'm afraid. I'm still limping a bit on this silly foot.'

Jenna noticed she was using a stick to help her.

'Is it very painful?'

'Only when I put pressure on it but I can't sit at home all day resting. The friends I'm staying with very kindly offered to drop me here today so that I could see Robert ... and have a chat with my ex-husband.'

'Ah. Er ... I don't think Mr Miles will be in today.'

'He'll be here at eleven this morning,' Amelia replied. 'I called him and told him to be.'

'Oh!' Jenna said. She couldn't think of anything else to say.

'So, Jenna, how do you like working for my son?' Amelia asked as they ambled towards the restaurant.

'I ... I like it very much.'

'Okay, that's the safe version. Now why don't you tell me the truth? Robert's told me everything that's been happening.'

'Oh,' Jenna said again, praying that he hadn't told his mother *everything*. Then she realised that if someone threw up over her then said they loved her and tried to get her into bed, she probably wouldn't tell her mum. She'd tell Daisy and Adam and Gray though.

'He told me about Roddy's little scene and he also mentioned that Roddy had dragged your father into this and that Edward and Fiona had rowed. That must have been very upsetting for you. Roddy can be an absolute idiot at times.'

Jenna could feel the relief sweeping over her. It appeared Robert may not have told her everything. 'It was,' she replied. 'Very. And I still don't know what's going to happen with Mum and Dad. I can't bear the thought of them splitting up over a stupid golf club. Oh! I mean. Er ... I didn't mean –'

Amelia lifted her hand in a halting gesture and smiled. 'Don't worry, Jenna. I totally agree. It *is* a stupid golf club but both my ex-husband and my son love it so I have to pretend it's not. And, in case you thought I'd take offence because Roddy and I split up over the stupid club – and his affairs, as you've no doubt heard – don't worry about that either. I don't take offence at the truth, although other factors were also involved.'

Jenna smiled back. 'I ... I didn't think Robert loved the club. I thought he ... resented it.'

'He both loves it and resents it. He loves it because, as ridiculous as this may sound, he's a Miles and this place eats into the hearts of Miles' men. Even I sometimes wonder whether Eleanor cursed the male line and that's why Theodore stalks the halls. Not that I believe in all that hokum. Robert resents it because he blames it for keeping his father from him and because he sees it as the reason Roddy and I divorced, which as I said, is partly true. However, Roddy and I had other problems and I think, if we weren't both so stubborn, things might have been different. Let's sit by the window.'

Apart from two other men in the restaurant, the place was empty. Jenna followed Amelia to the table and Beth came to take their orders.

'Just some toast and coffee for me, please,' Amelia said.

'I'll have the same, please,' Jenna said.

'I haven't seen your parents for years but your father

was always a sensible, rational man and he loved your mother very much,' Amelia said. 'Unless those things have changed over the years, I don't think you'll have too much to worry about. Edward would never let this club come between him and his family, I'm certain of that.'

Jenna smiled. Then a thought occurred to her. 'You said that Robert told you about my parents' row and he knew about it when he ... when I spoke to him yesterday but he didn't say how he knew about it.'

'I believe Miss Starr told him about it. Miss Sherree Starr. She is Roddy's latest ... girlfriend. You've met her, I think Robert said.'

Jenna was surprised. 'Yes, I have but ... how did she know and why did she tell Robert? Sorry, I shouldn't be asking you this but I just don't understand.'

'Well, I don't know the precise details and he only told me briefly when I called him this morning but I believe he bumped into her in a wine bar last night. Your father turned up at Roddy's in a bit of a state, so Roddy told Sherree to spend the evening with a friend. Something like that anyway.'

'I see,' Jenna said, even though she didn't. 'Did ... did Robert say anything else ... about last night, I mean?'

Amelia looked thoughtful. 'No. Oh, apart from the fact that he was concerned how this whole thing was affecting you, of course, and that you'd discussed it briefly last night but that he needed to talk to you properly about it as soon as he got a chance. I expect your young man has been a great comfort to you.'

'My young man? Sorry I ... what young man? Oh! You don't mean Tom?'

'Don't I? I thought you had a boyfriend.'

Beth brought over their toast and coffee. 'Sorry it took so long,' she said to Jenna, clearly not realising that Amelia was her boss's mother. 'There's a bit of a drama in the kitchen, I'm afraid.'

120

'Nothing serious, I hope,' Amelia said, pouring her coffee.

'Beth, this is Mrs Miles ... Stone! This is Mrs Stone, Robert's mother.'

The colour drained from Beth's face. 'Roddy's wife!' She was obviously surprised.

'Ex-wife, actually,' Amelia said, spreading butter on her toast. 'You were telling us about the drama.'

'No! I mean. It's nothing serious. Just ... just an ex-employee who's ... got a bit of a problem and ... well ... it's not important. She was just leaving anyway. Let me know if you need anything else,' Beth said and dashed off towards the kitchen.

'Nothing changes, I see,' Amelia said. 'You were telling me about your boyfriend.'

'Oh, er. I don't have a boyfriend. At least ... no. Tom's not my boyfriend. He's the friend of a friend and he's taken me out once ... or twice, but he's definitely *not* my boyfriend.'

'That *is* good news,' Amelia remarked.

Jenna thought that was a very odd thing to say but then again, the entire week had been odd so far, so she shouldn't be surprised by anything.

'What did you mean about Eleanor cursing the male line and Theodore stalking the halls?' Jenna asked. 'I know you weren't being serious, but is there supposed to be a curse and a ghost? I've never heard about it. Perhaps we could have ghost walks and decorate the rooms they occupied, or something.'

Amelia chuckled. 'That's almost exactly what Robert said – although not the part about the rooms, and he was joking. I can see though, that you and he are definitely on the same wavelength. No wonder he likes you so much.'

Jenna couldn't believe her ears. Had Amelia just said that Robert liked her – a lot?

'Well, let me tell you the story then. It's rather long but

121

I'll try to keep it as short as possible. You know, of course, that it was Theodore Miles who bought Claremont Manor and the entire estate in 1813 and turned the house and part of the grounds into Green Miles Golf Club?'

Jenna nodded. 'Yes, and that prior to that, he'd been a dashing and heroic, young Royal Navy captain. Well, it's doesn't say 'dashing' in the brochure, I made that bit up, but from looking at his picture, that's the impression I got.'

'And you were right, he was. He was also very handsome, like all the Miles' men. Unfortunately, prior to his exploits in the Napoleonic Wars, he was also very poor. His uncle bought his commission in the Royal Navy. Anyway, his mother lived in Claremont and, so the story goes, he came home on leave one day and found the lovely Eleanor Claremont tending to his sick mother. Eleanor had brought her a basket.'

'That sounds so funny,' Jenna said. 'Taking someone a basket, I mean. I know it's what the gentlewomen of the time used to do – take provisions to the poor in a basket, but why didn't they just say they took provisions. After all, what would the poor want with a basket and, of course, the gentlewomen always took the basket back with them. Sorry, I tend to waffle.'

'No. I agree entirely. It just sounds more genteel, I suppose. Well, needless to say, Theodore fell in love at first sight, which is hardly surprising. The poor man had been at sea for over a year, and had seen very few young ladies, let alone one as pretty as the lovely Eleanor. This was sometime around 1805 or 1806, I can't recall exactly and Theodore wasn't even a captain then, just a lowly lieutenant. Clearly, Eleanor felt the same because they met regularly at his mother's house. No gentlewoman would have taken that many baskets unless there was an ulterior motive – other than helping the poor, of course. Why are you smiling? It's a very sad story, I'm sorry to say.'

Amelia grinned.

'Sorry,' Jenna replied. 'I was just thinking that I can see where Robert gets his sense of humour from.'

'Roddy also had a wonderful sense of humour once – but that was a long time ago. The man takes himself far too seriously these days. I'm so glad Robert doesn't do that. Anyway, Theodore asks Sir Henry Claremont for Eleanor's hand in marriage but Henry won't hear of it. She's his only child and a naval lieutenant is far beneath his daughter in both wealth and social position. He shows poor Theodore the door and forbids his daughter to see him again. Well, like so many others in the early 1800s, Theodore makes his fortune during the Napoleonic Wars and on his return, he finds the Claremonts facing ruin due to Sir Henry's excessive gambling. He also finds Eleanor engaged, despite having told him secretly that she would wait for him. The fiancé's rich and he'll restore the Claremont finances.'

'But Theodore's rich now. He could do the same and Eleanor still loves him, doesn't she?'

'Yes, but in those days, people rarely broke off engagements. It just so happens though, that the fiancé falls off his horse and breaks his neck, just weeks before the wedding. There were rumours , apparently, that Theodore had a hand in that, but who knows.'

'You mean Theodore may have murdered his love rival? He doesn't look the type – although, there is something steely in those dark eyes of his. What happened then? I assume he stepped in and saved the day. Married Eleanor and saved Sir Henry from ruin. Oh ... but then he wouldn't have bought Claremont and Eleanor wouldn't have cursed the Miles' men. Clearly, I'm wrong.'

'Not entirely. Theodore does marry Eleanor, and a fairly large sum of money changes hands on the wedding day. He tells Sir Henry that his further financial assistance comes by way of him purchasing the Claremont estate, and Sir Henry and his wife moving to another, shall we say, far less grand establishment, a few miles away. Sir Henry has no choice and he has no heirs so, rather than face total ruin, he finally agrees. Eleanor's caught in the middle but despite it all, she loves Theodore. Unfortunately for her, Theodore sees her engagement as a betrayal and he never forgives her. He turns part of the estate into a golf club, and what had been Eleanor's bedroom, into his office. He has a new and rather grand house built at the other end of the estate and calls it Torrent Hall, named after his ship, HMS Torrent. That's where Roddy lives now – not on the ship – in the new house. It doesn't form part of the club. Theodore then takes several lovers and keeps poor, heartbroken Eleanor virtually housebound.'

'That's awful! Surely he could see she had no choice? If he really loved her he would never have treated her in such a dreadful way.'

'He was a very proud and stubborn man. He would rather have found her living in penury than to have found that she'd given herself to another man for money. I think he was bitter and blinded by revenge. But it gets worse. Theodore clearly exercised his conjugal rights because dear Eleanor gives birth to a daughter less than a year later. Ten months – yes ten months after that, she dies, shortly after giving birth to their son and that's where the story has different endings. Some say that on hearing that Eleanor's very sick, Theodore rides through a ferocious storm to reach her and beg her forgiveness. God knows where he's been – probably with one of his women. Anyway, Eleanor forgives him and he stays by her bedside for three days and nights until she dies. Others say she died alone, cursing the Miles' men with her dying breath.'

'Oh God! I'm not sure whether I prefer the first or second version. The romantic in me wants to think of them exchanging declarations of love and forgiveness on her

124

deathbed but part of me wants to slap Theodore round the face and curse him for being such an utter bastard!'

'Well, I think the ghost comes with either. Theodore is supposedly walking the halls looking for his lost love, and whichever one you choose, he loses her. The curse, of course, only comes with the second. Personally, I lean towards that one. I'm not sure I could forgive a man who had treated me so appallingly. But one never knows – unless one's in a similar position. That's put a bit of a dampener on the morning, hasn't it?'

Jenna grinned. 'I almost wish I hadn't asked. It's a great story though. Perhaps we could have an Eleanor and Theodore dinner theme, starting with a tour of the room that was once hers and is now the office and have someone reciting their story during a dinner. We could serve food similar to what they would have eaten. It's a shame Robert couldn't turn part of the clubhouse into a hotel. We could have themed weekends where guests could dress in nineteenth-century costumes and ... Oh! Sorry, I'm waffling again.'

'No! I think you might be on to something. He told you then, that he's actually in the hotel business. Of course, the dinners would have to be candlelit. I would mention it to him. I think he'll be impressed.'

Jenna wasn't sure whether Amelia was being serious or vaguely mocking but she came down on the side of serious.

'Actually, I didn't know he was in the hotel business. Robert hasn't mentioned what he did in New York.'

'Oh! Well then, as I said earlier, you and he are *clearly* on the same wavelength. Well, well, well.'

CHAPTER TWELVE

Amelia asked Jenna if she could use Robert's office for her chat with Roddy. She also asked her not to mention it to Robert if he phoned because she wanted to tell him about it herself, depending on how things went.

Naturally, Jenna agreed to both so when her phone rang at ten-thirty and she saw that it was Robert, she didn't tell him that his mother was sitting opposite her.

'How are you feeling this morning?' he asked.

'Er ... I'm fine, thank you, Robert.' She said his name so that Amelia would know it was him.

'Good. Do you fancy a spot of fresh air?'

'Sorry? I'm not sure I follow you. Do you want me to go outside?'

He laughed. 'Yes. There's something I want you to see. I'd come and get you but I've got an appointment later so it would be quicker if you met me here. I don't suppose you drove to work did you? If not, just get a cab and take the money out of petty cash.'

'Okay,' she said hesitantly. 'Where are you?'

'Oh. I'm at the top of Claremont Cliff Road, near the old restaurant. Meet me there. See you in about fifteen minutes. Bye.'

'Er. That was Robert, obviously. He ... he wants me to meet him at Claremont Cliffs now, so ... I'll see you later if that's okay. I'm not sure when.'

'Good,' Amelia said. 'He's gone to look at it then. Now remember. Don't tell him that I'm here. He knows I'm going to be here sometime today but he mustn't know about Roddy, so if he says he'll come back with you, make sure it's not until after twelve. We probably won't be anywhere near that long but I'd rather be on the safe side. I know he's got a lunch appointment at twelve-thirty so we should be okay. Have fun.'

Jenna called a cab and she was on her way to meet Robert just a few minutes later. On the way, she called her mother to see if there was any news her end and to tell her about Amelia and Roddy, which came as something of a surprise. Fiona said that she had nothing to report but that she was sure Edward would be home that evening. Jenna sat back, closed her eyes and wondered why she was meeting her boss at the top of a cliff and whether she should apologise for trying to get him into bed with her.

A vision of him pushing her over the edge made her open her eyes and sit bolt upright. She decided not to mention last night and wait and see whether he would. Less than a minute later, she found out.

'Hi,' he said, grinning broadly. 'You look much better than I expected you to.' Then he adopted a serious, concerned expression. 'Do you remember anything about last night?'

'Er, thanks. I think, and … no, I don't. It's all a complete blur of gin soaked inebriation.' She decided lying was her best course of action. 'I don't get like that very often, honestly, but it had been a really rough night what with Mum and Dad and ... everything. Unfortunately, when I do, my memory totally fails me. I could wake up in a harem and I'd have no idea how I got there.'

'Well, if you do, and you find out, let me know. I'd quite like to wake up in a harem. Seriously though, you don't remember ... anything?'

Jenna shook her head. 'Nope! Nothing, Nada, Zilch. Oh!' She remembered her conversation with Daisy and suddenly realised, she'd got drunk on Monday and Tuesday nights too. She was definitely becoming a lush. She needed to get herself under control.

'What's wrong? Memory returning?' he said, sounding rather anxious.

'No. You don't happen to know how to say 'nothing' in

Russian, do you? And don't say, by keeping your mouth shut. I know that.'

Robert gave her a quizzical look. 'No idea. Why?'

'No reason. Just a conversation Daisy and I were having the other day.'

'Daisy's lovely. Adam's great too – and Gray. In fact, all your friends are nice,' Robert said. 'Let's walk a little, over here.'

Jenna couldn't help but notice he hadn't mentioned Tom but then, Tom wasn't really her friend. She stole a sideways glance at him as they strolled along the cliff path. He was smiling and when he suddenly turned to face her, she saw something in his eyes that made her heart start its usual gymnastics.

'So you really don't remember *anything* about last night?'

She coughed lightly to try to clear a sudden lump in her throat and when she spoke, she sounded like a mouse. 'Not a single thing.'

He took a step closer to her. 'Jenna, there's something I need to tell you and I hope you won't get upset. You ... you really don't remember a thing? Not a single thing?'

She hesitated, panic seizing her, and started to giggle almost uncontrollably.

Robert just watched her with half a smile on his face and questions in his eyes.

'Okay,' she said when she was able to speak. 'I ... I can vaguely remember you arriving but not what we said and I ... I think I can remember being ... unwell but that really is all.'

She took a few steps to the side, pretending to be looking at something on the ground but as there was only grass, she started walking again.

'You were ... unwell,' he said, 'and you were very drunk. The only reason I asked was because ... I undressed you and put you to bed and I didn't want you to think that anything happened or that I took advantage of you because I didn't and I wouldn't and I left your underwear on you, so don't panic.'

'Oh,' was all Jenna could say.

'You don't seem very shocked,' he said, clearly relieved. 'In fact, you sound almost disappointed.'

Her eyes shot up to meet his. She could feel herself blushing and again she started giggling.

He creased his brows. 'I think you do remember,' he said.

She shook her head. 'I don't. Really, I don't.'

His eyes searched her face and then, grabbing her hand, he led her towards the cliff edge.

'Oh God,' she said, only half-joking. 'You're not going to push me over, are you?'

He turned to face her and his eyes narrowed.

She remembered she'd told him about falling off the cliff, so she quickly said, 'It seems to be a recurring nightmare of mine, recently.'

'Well, I have no intention of pushing you over,' he said. In fact, we shouldn't get too close. Apparently, these cliffs are prone to collapse. The sea washes away the footings and all the overhanging chalk eventually cracks under the strain. A bit like an avalanche, really. But don't worry, I won't let go.'

He squeezed her hand and Jenna glanced down at her hand in his. She looked around her at the wild grasses and gorse bushes bordering the cliff edges, at the clumps of dying daffodils and meadow flowers scattered here and there, at the birds flying overhead and at the bright, cornflower blue sky with not a speck of white cloud. The May sun had yet to reach its peak in the morning sky, and cast a carpet of glistening diamonds of light on the water of the glass-like English Channel. Jenna smiled. This was bliss, she thought, something she had not experienced for some time.

'So ... you really don't remember anything else then?' Robert asked again.

'What? Sorry. I was just thinking how incredibly beautiful this is. How absolutely ... perfect.'

Robert swung her round to face him. He slid his arms around her waist and looked her directly in the eye.

'That's a coincidence,' he said. 'I was just thinking the same thing about you.'

'Robert!' she started to say but his mouth came down on hers in a kiss as unexpected as it was tender.

Her mind raced and she put the palms of her hands up and pushed against his shirt but all she felt was the hardness of his chest and the warmth of his skin beneath and it sent a thrill through her body like nothing she'd ever felt before. The kiss deepened and instead of even attempting to push him away, she wrapped her arms around him and edged herself closer.

Bizarrely, she heard Tom's voice in her head saying he could give her multiple orgasms, except she realised it wasn't Tom's voice in her head, it was her own, talking about Robert, and she believed it. She was already having them – well, almost.

Then she heard it. The 1812 overture, just like the first time he'd kissed her, eighteen years ago, except this time, it sounded tinnier and kept repeating the same chords over and over again. She felt Robert ease himself away and when their eyes met, the passion was evident in his. He was breathing heavily and she wondered what he would say. She also wondered why she could still hear the 1812 overture.

'Jenna,' he said, 'I think that's your phone.'

His words didn't register in her romance-addled brain at first but then she realised what he'd said.

'Oh! Yes. Sorry.'

In a trance-like state, she fumbled in her bag for her phone. Robert turned and walked a few steps away from her obviously to give her some privacy.

'This had better be an emergency, Daisy or that's where you'll be when I get my hands on you,' she whispered.

'What? I can't hear you. It must be a bad connection. Can you hear me?'

'Yes. I can hear you, Daisy,' she said as Robert glanced in her direction and smiled lovingly. She smiled back.

'I'm calling to tell you where Robert is. Adam's on his way to meet him now. They're meeting there first and then going to lunch.'

'Really. Thank you. I'll speak to you later.'

'Wait! Don't you want to know where they're meeting? You said you did!'

'Let me guess. Is it Claremont Cliffs, near the old restaurant?'

'That's exactly it. And you were right. He is thinking about extending the golf course and having a nine hole course too. Has he called you and told you?'

'Actually, Daisy, he's standing right in front of me,' she said, lowering her voice. 'And he was standing a lot, lot closer before you called. I'll talk to you later. Bye.'

She hung up before Daisy had a chance to say anything else.

Robert grinned at her. 'Everything okay?'

She nodded, now unable to speak at the thought that he might – hopefully – kiss her again, possibly even more than just kiss her. Claremont Cliffs was usually deserted on a weekday.

'Good,' he said, taking two large strides towards her and reaching out to grab her arm. He pulled her close. 'Now, where were we?'

He kissed her again and she revelled in the feel of his lips on hers, his arms wrapped so tightly around her that her body seemed moulded to his. A vision of Edvard Munch's 'The Kiss' popped into her head. No, she thought, Gustav's Klimt's 'The Kiss' was more apt. It was

131

bright and golden and ... all rational thought escaped her as she lost herself completely in the overwhelming sensations racing through her.

When they finally came up for air, all she could say was 'Wow!'

Robert smiled. 'Wow indeed,' he repeated, still holding her hand. 'Jenna, I need to ask you about Tom.'

'Tom!' she exclaimed. She'd totally forgotten about him. 'Oh er. He's just a friend of Adam's. He asked me out and we went for a drink but he's not my type and ...' Not only had she forgotten about Tom, she realised but she'd also forgotten Robert was gay – or bi-sexual or whatever.

'So ... you wouldn't be upset if he ... didn't get this site for his development, then?'

'Not in the least. Speaking of types, I ... I didn't think I was yours.'

Robert's brows knit together. 'Actually, I don't think I have a 'type'. I like all women. Oh, that came out wrong. I meant, I'm happy with any woman. No. So did that. God! Kissing you has made me tongue-tied. What I meant was I don't prefer blondes, or brunettes, long legs or short, large ... well, you get the general idea. With me, it's a feeling. I see someone I like and that's it – although sometimes I get it very wrong, like I did with Lou. What made you think that, anyway?'

'Er. I'd like you to be honest with me, Robert. I ... I'd rather know the truth. I ... I'd hate to think this is ... some sort of game.'

Now he looked really confused, she thought, but she couldn't come right out and ask him. She'd promised her father that it wouldn't get back to Robert or Roddy that anyone else knew.

'I really don't know what you mean. Why would you think this is a game? Are you saying that you don't feel that there's something between us? Something special?'

132

'No. I ... I think there is, for me at least but ... well, do ... do you just like women or ... do you ...?' She couldn't say it.

'I don't ... wait a minute. Are you asking me if I also like men? Are you suggesting that you think I might be bisexual?'

Jenna avoided his eyes, bit her lower lip and hung her head.

'Shit!' he said. 'What made you think I might be ... oh God! You think I'm gay, don't you? Dad told your dad didn't he and your dad told you?'

Jenna just nodded.

'So ... that's what you meant last night about me not liking you and liking Gray, only not, or whatever it was you said. I don't suppose you remember that either but ... wait a minute. Oh my God! Is that why you invited me for a drink on Tuesday? To see if you could fix me up with Gray. You were there with Tom. Adam was with Daisy and that left me and Gray. No wonder he said what he said. So that means they all think I'm gay too – all your friends.'

Jenna nodded again but looked up when Robert didn't say anything further. She met his eyes and she could see a heap of questions in them. The first one took her by surprise.

'So, why did you let me kiss you then and why did you kiss me back – if you thought I was gay? And why did you kiss me last night?'

She shook her head. 'We thought you might be bisexual and whilst I didn't think I could deal with that and I'm still not sure, if I'm totally honest, I've loved you for so long that ... I didn't really care.'

'You said that last night, too,' he said. 'What do you mean, "we thought"? Have you and your friends been discussing my sexual preferences for the last few days?'

His voice had grown cold and his midnight blue eyes

133

had turned as black as thunder. She could see there was a storm brewing but she had to know.

'Are ... are you saying you're *not* gay then?'

'Yes. I'm not gay. I'm not bi-sexual either. I'm a heterosexual, red blooded male who, until a few minutes ago was seriously considering making love to you right here, right now, despite the fact that Adam will be here any minute. Oh God. I hope he doesn't think I've lured him here to try to have my wicked way with him!'

'Of course he doesn't! ... Why have you lured ... I mean, asked him, to meet you here? Why did you ask me here?'

Robert's eyes scanned her face. 'Because I'm thinking of buying this land and building a nine hole golf course here, amongst other things. I wanted to ask Adam's opinion before I submitted plans and made an offer.'

'That's what I told Daisy you might be thinking,' Jenna said, feeling pleased with herself.

'Jesus Christ! So you're not content with discussing my sexuality amongst your friends, you are also discussing my business. I suppose they all know about my row with Dad too.'

'Why are you getting so angry?' Jenna pleaded, feeling the tears welling in her eyes. 'I'm sorry. I suppose we shouldn't have been talking about you but ... I tell my friends everything and they tell me and –'

'That's how rumours get started and that's how people end up getting hurt,' he said in a raised tone. 'I'm not angry, I'm ... disappointed.'

Jenna's eyes shot to his face. She remembered vividly the last person who had said that, only yesterday and how that had turned out. She couldn't prevent the tears from flowing.

'Then you shouldn't have told your father you were gay! It was your fault the rumour started in the first place, so don't start shouting at me just because I told my friends!'

She spun round and stormed towards the road.

He was in front of her in an instant and pulled her back into his arms. 'I'm sorry, Jenna,' he said. 'You're right. It was my fault. I shouldn't have let my father think I was gay. It was stupid but he jumped to conclusions and ... well, I thought it would do him good to think it for a few days. I suppose, I did it to ... hurt him in some small way. I suppose it was a sort of ... revenge. I didn't think for one minute he'd actually tell anyone. I'm not sure whether I should somehow, be pleased. Perhaps he's not such a stuffed shirt.'

'I ... I think he was ... drunk,' Jenna said, sniffing, but feeling much better now that she was back in his arms.

'Oh,' Robert said.

'Is everything all right?' Adam called from the car park.

Jenna and Robert's heads shot round to see Adam walking towards them. Robert released her from his arms but his fingers still held hers.

'Everything's fine, Adam,' Robert said. 'Oh, by the way, I'm not gay – or bisexual. I just thought I would mention that.'

Adam grinned. 'To be honest, Robert, I never really thought that you were and Gray knew you weren't the second you shook his hand.'

'That's good to know. Not that I think there's anything wrong with being gay. Some of my best friends have male partners and I think it's a shame we feel we have to label people but there it is. Tell me, should I put a notice in the local paper or will word of mouth suffice?'

Adam grinned. 'Word of mouth reaches more people than the local rag ever will. That, my friend, you can count on. So, you're considering expanding the golf club to this site then? I have to admit that's much more likely to be accepted by the committee than Tom's plans are, but I don't have any influence either way.'

Robert grinned. 'I wouldn't ask you to use it if you did,' he replied. 'I don't believe in underhandedness. I just really wanted some advice about the land because you've lived here all your life and you know the planning history. Shall we take a little stroll around and then head off for lunch?'

'Lunch!' Jenna said. 'Oh heavens! I must get back in case your mum ... I mean, my mum, calls. Sorry, I must dash. Bye.' She ran to the car park, dialling the cab firm's number as she went.

CHAPTER THIRTEEN

Amelia watched Roddy march towards her at exactly eleven o'clock and was struck by how attractive he still was. For a sixty-year-old man, he looked remarkably fit. His ink black hair was greying at the sides of his temples but he clearly made no attempt to disguise it and his undeniably handsome face was deeply tanned from spending so much time out of doors. He still held himself well too, possibly from his years in the RAF but mainly from an innate air of confidence. She found herself smiling fondly at him.

'Well, I see you've made yourself at home, Amelia. Is this what you wanted all along? For you and the boy to take over the club and ruin it, out of revenge,' Roddy said, glowering at her.

Amelia's smile disappeared, along with the fond memories that had surfaced to the front of her mind.

'You can be such a bloody fool at times, Roddy and you're being utterly ridiculous, as usual.'

'I'm being ridiculous! You're the one who's being ridiculous. You've been harbouring a grudge for all these years because of something you thought you saw and because you think I chose the club over you. And this is your revenge. I suppose you've called me here to rub my face in it. Well, I won't listen. I'm not in the least bit interested in anything you have to say to me.'

Amelia took several deep breaths. She did not want this to turn into a row; the last time they had one of those, it changed their lives completely.

'Then why did you agree to come here when I told you I wanted to talk to you?'

Roddy just glared at her.

'Oh, sit down Roddy, for heaven's sake.'

To her surprise and relief, he did.

'Well. Say what you want to and let's get this over with,' he said.

'I want to talk to you about Robert. No! Please let me speak without interrupting, Roddy. You can have your say when I've finished.'

He had opened his mouth to interrupt but again to her surprise, he closed it and waited.

'I know you think Robert bears a grudge against you and this club and –'

'I *know* he does. Sorry, continue,' Roddy butt in.

'Thank you. Well, that's true, he does, but he also loves you and you may be surprised to hear this but he also loves this club. Not quite as much as you do and definitely *not* in the same way, but he does love it. He wants to change it to improve it. No, Roddy! Please let me finish. Robert's not doing this to *hurt* you, Roddy, he's doing it to make sure no other kid has to go through what he did. He's doing it because he *loves* you! He always has. He worshipped the ground you walked on when he was a boy – as much as I did, in those days. But you kept pushing him aside and at the same time, you kept telling him how important this club was.'

'I didn't push him aside! I tried to involve him. I wanted him to know how much the club meant and that one day, it would all be his. Sorry, but I had to say that. You've got it all wrong, as usual.'

'I have *not*!' Amelia banged her fist down on the desk. 'One of your main problems, Roddy, is you never listen. You only hear what you think people are saying, not what they actually say and if you don't agree, you don't give them time to explain. How many times did you tell Robert he couldn't come here because he would be in the way?'

'He got hit by Edward's golf ball! Surely you remember that? He *was* in the way. I didn't want him to get hurt again.'

'Of course I remember that! He suffered from concussion for almost two days, not that that seemed to matter to you. You just went back to your game. I had to rush him to hospital.'

'He told me he was all right! You know that. He stood in front of me and told me not to worry, that he didn't want me to stop my game and that he'd just go and lie down for a while. I remember it to this day! How was I to know he'd collapse when he got home? Someone came and told me on the course that you'd telephoned, and I came to the hospital straight away.'

'Of course he told you to play on. He knew how important the bloody stupid game was to you and don't give me any of that "but it was a competition" nonsense. I didn't care then and I care even less now! Can't you see? He was being brave for you! He didn't want to let you down. He loved you so much that, even though he was in pain, he hid it from you, made his own way home, then collapsed in a heap at my feet. Can you imagine how that felt?'

Roddy's eyes held Amelia's for several seconds. 'It must have been terrifying,' he said. 'I'm sorry. I should have taken him to the hospital right away. That was a mistake on my part.'

'Finally, after all these years!'

Roddy shook his head. 'It isn't after all these years, I knew at the time, it was my fault I just ... I don't know. I think it suddenly hit me, seeing him lying there, how I could have lost him, so, when he regained consciousness, I vowed not to let him wander around the course again. He always did that ... wandered, I mean. He always seemed far more interested in the trees and the birds and the views than he was in golf. Huh! I suppose I should have seen then that he wasn't like the rest of the Miles' men – that he was different. That should have been a clue.'

Amelia had softened towards Roddy as he spoke but at

the mention of Robert being different, she was furious.

'And that's another thing. All this "Miles' men" nonsense and let's not forget all the "you need to go into the forces, son, that'll make a real man of you". Talk about giving someone an inferiority complex! And he wasn't even sixteen! It's a wonder he has become the strong, confident, successful man he has after sixteen years of that! It's a good thing we left when we did, otherwise he may have turned out like ...'

'Like me you mean? Go on, say it! That's what this is really all about isn't it? Me and my "constant affairs" as I remember you called them. And you talk about me never listening and only hearing what I wanted. That's rich coming from you. How many times did I tell you that what you thought you saw that day, wasn't what was actually going on? But would you listen? No! You just stormed off to your own lover and then you have the audacity to divorce me for adultery!'

'What lover? I didn't have a lover. You know damn well I didn't but you did! First the little waitress from the restaurant, then the redhead and don't try to deny it again, Roddy. The woman had her head in your lap!'

Roddy jumped up from his seat. 'She did not! I told you. You wouldn't listen to me then but you'll listen to me now by God!'

He strode around the desk, pushed Amelia's chair away from it, and spun the chair around so that Amelia faced him. He leant forward, placing his hands on the arms either side of her chair with his face just inches from hers. He was evidently livid.

'Roddy! Stop it! Go and sit down! Let's talk about this like sensible adults.'

'We've rarely talked about anything like sensible adults,' Roddy said. He had calmed down slightly but he remained in his position towering over her. 'Now listen to me. I swear on my life and my son's that this is the truth.

The woman was from Claremont Jewels and she was showing me a bracelet I'd had made – for you. I was going to give it to you that –'

'I've heard this before, Roddy. You produced the bracelet three days later. Three days, Roddy! Are you still saying you expect me to believe that story? You had it made *afterwards,* to back you up!'

'I did not!' he hissed. 'I spotted a slight fault in the spelling of your name – there was an 'e' instead of an 'a' at the end, and when she bent down to look at it, one of her contact lenses fell out. My chair had casters, like this one has, and she asked me to stay where I was in case a caster ran over it or I trod on it, getting up. She got down on her hands and knees looking for it and saw it under my chair. She asked if she could lean forward to get it. I said yes but when she leant on the arm, the chair moved and she fell forward. You came in at that exact moment, took one quick look and stormed out.'

Amelia stared into his eyes. She'd heard that ridiculous story before and she hadn't believed it then, even when he produced the bracelet which was beautiful and had their names engraved on it with the words 'one look, love forever', so why on earth did he expect her to believe it now? Then it dawned on her suddenly, after all these years – it *was* the truth.

However ludicrous it seemed, it was true and when she cast her mind back to the awful day, and saw herself standing in the open doorway of his office, she realised two things. The door had been wide open. He'd have closed it if he was planning on having sex with someone, and the shocked expression she'd seen on his face wasn't because he'd been caught out; it was because a woman's head had landed in his lap, taking him completely by surprise.

Roddy sighed deeply. 'What's the point?' he said. 'Even I realise now how unbelievably stupid that sounds.'

141

He removed his hands from the arms of the chair and was about to stand up straight when Amelia reached out to touch him. She hadn't intended to, it was just instinct and it was instinct for him to react to her touch, even after all these years. Before either of them knew what was happening, they were kissing deeply and passionately, and she was in his arms for the first time in more than eighteen years.

Jenna arrived back at the club in a rather dazed state. One minute she and Robert had been kissing, the next, arguing and then they were back in each other's arms again. She wasn't sure what that meant – on the relationship front but it didn't really matter. They could work that out. The only thing that mattered was that he wasn't gay and now there was a very real possibility that he could be hers, even if only for a short time.

She thought it was better if she kept away from her office for the time being as Amelia and Roddy would be in the middle of their chat so she decided to go into the kitchen. She remembered Beth saying something about a drama this morning with an ex-staff member and she wondered what it was.

She strolled into the kitchen and was surprised to find Sherree there, crying and being comforted by Beth.

'What's wrong?' Jenna said, not knowing whether she should stay or go.

They both looked round, clearly shocked.

'It's nothing,' Beth said a little too hastily. 'Just ... just a little drama. She's fine.'

Sherree tried to hide the fact that her face resembled a muddy zebra crossing, the fake tan almost gone to reveal pale white, silky smooth skin, streaked by heavy lines of thick, black mascara.

'Don't be ridiculous,' Jenna said, 'if you'd rather not tell me that's fine but please don't lie to me. Sherree is

142

clearly devastated. Is there anything I can do, or would you rather I leave you alone?'

They were hardly alone. The chef, the catering manager and three other members of the catering staff had all been huddled around Sherree when Jenna had walked in but they had quickly found other things to occupy their attention.

'There's nothing anyone can do,' Sherree shrieked between heart-wrenching sobs. 'Roddy will never forgive me. Never!'

'Shush!' Beth said, looking embarrassed. 'You mustn't keep telling people. I've already told you, he needn't find out. You're going away on Monday, so he'll never know and Robert won't tell him that you –'

'But I spent the night with him!' Sherree shrieked. 'All night! Of course, Roddy will find out. Of course, Bobbie will tell him. He'll do anything to get revenge on Roddy. Roddy told me that himself.'

Jenna heard the words but they didn't register until Beth gave her a sideways glance and screeched very loudly, 'Sherree, shut up for fuck's sake!' Then the meaning hit Jenna in the face like a laughing golf ball mocking her for her stupidity.

Robert had told her himself that he had simply undressed her and put her to bed. What he hadn't told her was that he'd then left her, gone to the wine bar, picked up Sherree and spent the night making love to her instead! The bastard!

But he'd already known about her parents' row and Amelia had said it was Sherree who had told him. That just made it worse. He must have left Sherree, gone to her place to possibly try it on with her, then gone back to Sherree to carry out his plan for revenge and spent the night with her.

Or he ... what the hell! Did it matter? Whichever way she looked at it, Jenna realised that Robert had dumped her and shagged Sherree. Suddenly, Jenna didn't care whether Sherree was all right or not; she had to get out of there before she started smashing things.

'I'm clearly in the way,' Jenna said. 'I'll leave you to it.'

She turned and ran out of the restaurant and she kept on running until she was gasping for breath. She stopped and was surprised to find herself in the woods that made up part of the eastern boundary of Green Miles Golf Club. She looked around, bewildered and spotted a large tree stump. She walked over to it and dropped down onto it, letting her head fall into her hands and crying so loudly that she startled a flock of sparrows that had perched on a nearby tree.

'I've never stopped loving you, you know,' Roddy said.

He and Amelia were lying on the sofa in what was now their son's office, wrapped in each other's arms. Roddy had lifted her up and carried her there when they were kissing, deadlocking the door on the way.

They both knew that making love at just gone eleven in the morning in Robert's office wasn't a particularly sensible thing to do, but they really didn't care. For both of them, it was as if they'd been transported back in time to the first day they looked into one another's eyes.

Amelia sighed contentedly and snuggled closer to him. 'I never stopped loving you either.'

'Then ... why did you leave me?' Roddy said, twisting around so that he could see her face. 'We could have worked it out. I ... I thought you left me for ... that man I saw kissing you, months earlier.'

'David, you mean? No. I told you, David kissed me and I pushed him away. There was never anything between me and David. I left because ... it was too painful to stay. I loved you so much but I also hated you at times. After the first time you slept with that waitress, then all those letters from Jennifer, and finally when I found you and the redhead, everything just blew up for me. All the years of ignoring those rumours and –'

'What letters from Jennifer?'

'Oh. I didn't show them to you. I didn't believe them at first so I just threw them away. When Jennifer realised the rumours weren't having any effect, she started sending me letters saying you'd been seen with other women and how much you seemed to like waitresses. Well, when you saw David kissing me that day and thought I was cheating on you and you came here, got drunk and *did* sleep with a waitress, I ... I started having doubts, I'm sorry to say.'

'I'll never forgive myself for that,' he said, 'but why didn't you tell me about the letters?'

'Because I knew you'd get angry and would probably threaten her with legal action, as you once did, and that would have caused tension between you and Edward and Fiona so I just ignored them. It was easier. I shouldn't even have read them but you know what it's like. Some part of you just has to. Then after your one-night stand with the waitress, well, things were getting worse between us. You were spending nearly all your free time here and we didn't seem to be having sex as much as we used to and I thought, well … I started to think there may be some truth in the letters after all. I loved you so much that it broke my heart and I could see Robert getting more and more withdrawn so when I saw you and the redhead, I ... I just had to leave.'

Roddy let out a long, sorrowful sigh. 'Jennifer sent me letters too, saying you were having an affair. I didn't show you mine because I knew they'd upset you but I kept them and I eventually told Edward to speak to her because if they didn't stop, I would take action. That was just a few weeks before you left. I think I've still got them, somewhere. I think that's why I started spending even more time here. I couldn't bear the thought of losing you

145

but I didn't know how to make you stay.'

'I know you let us go because you thought it would make me happy but I never really understood it, especially as you had tried to get me to come back.'

Roddy shrugged. 'I don't think I was thinking straight, to tell you the truth. Then I started drinking and when you said you were thinking of going to the States, I found comfort wherever I could get it.'

Amelia smirked. 'Jennifer was right about that. You do like waitresses.'

'Jennifer was wrong about that. I loved one waitress. You! All the others, including that first one-night one, were just my way of trying to find you again – and I know that sounds utterly ludicrous. You're right, I do say some ridiculous things sometimes.'

Amelia looked into his eyes. 'I think you say the loveliest things sometimes too,' she said. 'The only reason I married Joshua Stone, after moving to the States, was to convince myself that I was truly over you. How ridiculous is that? I'm not saying I didn't care about him – I did but I never loved him as I loved you. That's why it ended in divorce.'

Roddy tightened his arms around her. 'And the only reason I took up sailing, was in the hope that you might think I'd changed.'

'I didn't want you to change Roddy. I ... I just wanted you to spend more time with us.'

Roddy kissed her on her forehead. 'I wanted so much to impress my father, and when you gave me that ultimatum, well, I thought you were having a long-term affair anyway and ... I don't know, I think I thought the club was the only thing that was truly mine. I ... I couldn't let it go. It would have disappointed my father and I don't think he would have spoken to me again. I should have put you and Robert first but I honestly believed you'd leave me anyway.'

'Hmm,' Amelia murmured. 'On the subject of fathers not speaking to their sons, that's what this *chat* was about. I think you need to go and talk to Robert.'

Roddy's eyes scanned her face. 'I will,' he said, 'but first, there are one or two things I need to say to you. Well, not say exactly, more like ... do.'

Amelia knew precisely what he meant by the way he kissed her.

CHAPTER FOURTEEN

Jenna tried to pull herself together. She knew she should go back in case Amelia was looking for her but she couldn't. Not yet anyway. She wiped her eyes and took her phone out of her handbag, dialling Daisy's number.

'Daisy! Something awful's happened. I really need to talk to you. Will you meet me for lunch?'

'Of course I will. Tell me where and I'll be there in fifteen minutes. Is ... is it about Robert ... or your mum and dad?'

'It's about Robert. He didn't have sex with me last night but he did have sex with someone else.'

'What! I'll pick you up in ten minutes.'

'Wait,' Jenna said. 'I'm ... I'm not at the club. I'm in the woods.'

'What the hell are you doing in the woods?'

'I ... I ran here to get away.'

'From Robert?'

'From Sherree.'

There was a pause before Daisy answered. 'I'm leaving now. I'll be just inside the driveway by the main gates, in five minutes flat. Meet me there.'

Jenna stood up, brushed some moss from her skirt and marched towards the long drive and main gates where she found Daisy waiting at the entrance to the club. She got into her car and they headed for the Claremont Arms pub.

'Tell me then,' Daisy said as soon as they were moving.

'I'm not sure where to begin. With Robert kissing me this morning then lying, with Amelia and Roddy, or just –'

'Wait! Robert kissed you ... this morning! Is that what was happening when I called you?'

'Yep!'

'Wow! I want details ... hold on though … before that.'

148

What do you mean, Amelia and Roddy? What's happened between them?'

'Who cares? You're missing the point. This isn't about Amelia and Roddy, or even Robert kissing me this morning. Well, I suppose it is about that but it's really about who Robert spent last night with – the whole night – after he left me.'

'Yes. Of course it is. Sorry. Tell me.'

'Sherree! He spent the entire fucking night with Sherree! Or maybe that should be, he spent the entire night fu –'

'Yes! I get the picture. It won't help you to keep saying it. How do you know?'

'Because she told me! Well ... not me exactly but I was there. I should have gone into the kitchen earlier.'

'Sorry, but you're losing me. I think you'd better start at the beginning.'

Jenna let out a long, sorrowful sigh. 'Okay. Amelia turned up because she'd arranged to meet Roddy at eleven, for a chat. I think she wants to see if she can sort things out. Anyway, we had breakfast together which was nice except she said some strange things, although she did tell me the entire story about Eleanor and Theodore – and boy, was that depressing. The Miles' men are certainly big on revenge, the bastards. She also told me about Robert meeting Sherree. Oh God. If I'd just gone into the kitchen then, I would have known about them before that womanising rat kissed me.'

'Whoa! You're starting to sound like a parrot. Why do you keep going on about the kitchen? Did you see Robert and Sherree together in the kitchen?'

'No! Robert wasn't in the kitchen. He was with Adam on Claremont Cliffs.'

'Now you've really lost me. Skip the start. Get to the end. Oh ... but I still want to know about the kissing bit.'

'Okay. He calls and asks me to meet him at Claremont

149

Cliffs so I go. He asks if I remember anything from last night and finally he tells me that he just put me to bed. I thought it was sweet because he didn't want me to think he took advantage of me.'

'I thought it was you who tried to take advantage of him. Never mind. Go on.'

'Well, one thing leads to another. He says I'm gorgeous or some such line and then he kisses me. I hear the 1812 overture but it's you. We start kissing again and I tell him that I thought he was gay. He gets cross, and I start to cry. Then he hugs me. Then Adam arrives so I go back to the club.'

'Wow! Er ... why did you tell him you thought he was gay? I thought it was supposed to be a secret. Are you saying he definitely *isn't* then, or did he get cross because he is and it was a secret? Although, if he slept with Sherree ... God I'm confused.'

'What? I told him because he kissed me! I had to know. He says he isn't and I think he got cross because we've all been discussing it, not because he secretly is and doesn't want anyone to know. Anyway, this is the really important part.'

'I think him kissing you and not being gay is fairly important. Though why the hell you told him we were all discussing it, is beyond even me. You can be so dumb at times, you know. Oh. Sorry, no, I guess the important part is that he slept with Sherree. How do you know that? Remind me, I'm lost again.'

'I didn't tell him ... exactly. He guessed we had, and if you'll shut up and listen I'll tell you how I know.'

'Sorry, I'm all ears.'

'Okay, I go into the kitchen and there's Sherree balling her eyes out, an entire department store of make-up running down her face and Beth is trying to comfort her. And bear in mind, this is around eleven-thirty and she was in there crying when we had breakfast. Anyway, I ask

150

what's wrong and if I can be any help and she shrieks – and I do mean shrieks, "No one can help me. Roddy will never forgive me," or something like that. Then Beth says that Robert won't tell him. Then Sherree shrieks again, "But I spent the night with him, the whole night and Bobbie" – she calls him Bobbie – "and Bobbie will do anything to get revenge. Roddy told me so." Again maybe not those exact words. To be honest, I'm in such a state of shock I can't really remember, but then Beth looks at me with a horrified expression on her face and tells Sherree to "shut the fuck up" or something, which frankly, someone should have told her to do long before today. Then I run off into the woods, crying my eyes out.'

'Shit!' Daisy said, pulling into the car park of the Claremont Arms.

'My sentiments precisely.'

'So ... you think Robert left you, all nicely tucked up in bed dreaming that you were having sex with him, and went off to have sex with his father's girlfriend?'

'I don't think. I know! Even Amelia said as much. Well, she didn't say they'd had sex but she told me about them meeting in the wine bar and that Sherree had told Robert about my mum and dad's row.'

'Okay,' Daisy said, linking arms with Jenna as they walked towards the pub door, 'but that means he was with her *before* he came round to you, not *after*.'

'Yes, but don't you see? That's why he didn't want sex with me. He had already arranged to go back and spend the night with her! Aren't you listening? I heard Sherree say so, in the kitchen. Robert – Bobbie spent the whole night with her!'

'Oh. So it wasn't because he was gay that he didn't want sex with you ... or because you were blotto and had just thrown up over him? It was because he'd had another offer – and please note, I didn't say better.'

'Thanks. No. I don't know why he didn't want sex with

me. Maybe he didn't have the time. I only know why he *did* want sex with her. Don't you see? He did it to get revenge on his dad. And I told you, he's not gay. He was in the wine bar with Sherree. She told him about my mum and dad. He came round. That bit I don't get – why he bothered to come round to me unless he thought he could have a quick one with me then go back to her. Perhaps he's a womaniser too, like his dad. But he put me to bed instead because I was too drunk, even for him. Anyway, he went back and spent the night with her.'

'I see,' Daisy said. 'Well, to be honest, I don't but anyway. Why did he kiss you this morning then? And why does him sleeping with Sherree yesterday have any bearing on him kissing you today?'

'What? It means he lied. About everything! He pretends to be a nice guy, the type who would never take advantage of a drunken woman and then he screws someone to get revenge on his dad!'

'So ... it's not because he had sex with Sherree that you're so annoyed or that he spurned your advances so that he could go and have sex with her, it's because of the reason he had sex with her. Is that right?'

'Yes. No. I don't know. I need a drink.'

'I'll buy,' Daisy said, yanking open the door. 'And you're absolutely certain he *did* have sex with her?'

'I've told you several times ... Yes!'

'You're positive he didn't just see her with someone else and it's that person she had sex with and that Robert chatted to her and now she thinks he'll tell his dad that he saw her?'

'Oh. That hadn't even crossed my mind. I ... I suppose it's possible but ... no. Because just being seen with someone doesn't mean you've had sex with them, so she could deny it.'

'That's true. I mean look at you and Tom. Anyone seeing you in the pub the other night would think you

152

were doing it like rabbits and they'd be completely wrong. Of course, it's possible that Robert just took her home and put her to bed too and … like you, she just *thinks* he had sex with her. Maybe he just has a very caring nature. Don't give me that look! I'm trying to be helpful.'

'Fine. But I don't think she imagined it. You didn't see her this morning. She definitely had sex with someone last night.'

'Okay. It was either Robert or he actually saw her having sex with someone else. Yuk! That's weird. He could have seen her kissing someone and *assumed* they were going to be having sex.'

'It was Robert. It must have been. He even told me this morning how much he loves all women and will go out with anyone. God! He's even worse than his father! How can I be in love with a man like that?'

'So you are still in love with him then, in spite of Sherree? Of course you are. Don't answer that. Okay, I can see you'd be angry if he had had sex with you and then he'd gone off and had sex with Sherree, then come back and kissed you this morning, leading up to having sex with you again. But he didn't. He put you to bed. Went off and slayed his particular dragon and came back to you. Perhaps I'm missing something but I don't see the problem, especially now we know he's not gay. Now, he can be all yours, assuming you want to date someone you think is a bastard, and I suppose we can safely assume, you do – want to date him, I mean. We know you think he's a bastard.'

Jenna leant against the bar. 'I hadn't thought about it like that. But it's not right. You don't have sex with someone for revenge.'

'So if it wasn't for revenge but because he actually fancied her and wanted to screw her before he slept with you, that would be okay. Is that what you're saying?'

'Yes. No! I … I don't know any more.'

'I hate to say this honey, but I think your nose has just been put out of joint because he isn't quite the knight in shining armour you've believed him to be for the past, God knows how many years, and because he screwed Sherree and not you. Of course, that's nothing compared to how his dad's going to feel but that's not our problem. Large red wine and one orange juice, please,' Daisy said to the barman.

Jenna let out a long, deep sigh. 'I'm utterly confused now. I need to go to the ladies to splash some water on my face and tidy myself up a bit. I've just realised, I've been sitting on a tree trunk in the woods, crying for the last hour.'

'As one does,' Daisy said.

Jenna was feeling a little better by the time she arrived back at the club, an hour later. Daisy had made her see that Robert having sex with Sherree wasn't what really mattered, at least, not to them. Roddy would feel differently, of course.

What mattered was *why* Robert had sex with Sherree. After all, Daisy had reasoned, if Jenna had had sex with Tom on Wednesday night purely because she wanted sex, and then Robert had turned up and she'd had sex with him because she loved him, she wouldn't expect Robert to get all uppity about it. People make mistakes and you can't hold it against them, providing they don't repeat the mistake, of course.

No. The only thing that mattered was why he'd done it and whether Jenna could live with the answer. So they'd made a list.

Reasons for Robert having sex with Sherree – what to do now:

a) For revenge on his father – sensible women would avoid/possible to forgive and forget

b) He's a cold-hearted, deceitful, bastard – should be

154

avoided, if at all possible

c) He's a womaniser – see b) above

d) He fancied her – forgive and forget/everyone makes mistakes/mustn't happen again

e) Purely for the sex – see d) above

They had both agreed that, until they knew for sure one way or the other, Jenna should 'approach with caution'.

She went straight to her office and was surprised to find a note on her desk from Amelia. It simply read:

Gone Sailing.

Jenna couldn't help but feel that was a little odd, bearing in mind Amelia's bad foot but perhaps the meeting with Roddy hadn't gone well and Amelia needed the fresh air. Either that, or it had gone very well indeed and Roddy had taken her out on his yacht.

There was no sign of Robert and no note from him, so she assumed he hadn't yet returned from lunch with Adam. That was probably just as well; she wasn't quite sure how she would react when she saw him again. Come to that, she wasn't quite sure how he would. They'd parted on friendly enough terms but she somehow felt that he might have a little more to say about her discussing his sexual preferences with all and sundry.

What she needed was to keep herself busy so she sat at her desk and started sending out the newsletter to the wives and partners of the golf club members. It was headed 'Green Miles Golf Club' and it read:

Hello and welcome to the first newsletter from Green Miles Golf Club.

We're writing to you because you share your home with a member of Green Miles Golf Club and we'd like to tell you about several special events we are arranging to help you share your partner's enjoyment of the facilities here at Green Miles.

We're planning exciting changes, both to the running of the club and to the clubhouse itself, one of which will be a new, family room where you can come for coffee and a chat – and bring along the children. There'll also be a Green Miles Mini Course for the younger family members, a new women's club; floodlights for the driving ranges and much, much more. We'll tell you more about all the new developments in the coming weeks.

We're also organising a whole host of social activities and with summer rapidly approaching and the school holidays looming, you'll find Green Miles will have something to keep the entire family happily occupied, both on and off the course.

We'd love to hear your ideas to help make Green Miles the place to be for you and your loved ones and in a spirit of fun, we're setting up a group called, 'The Green Miles Golf Widows' Club'. We hope to organise a variety of activities such as coffee mornings, wine tastings, writing and painting classes and book groups etc. We're thinking of Murder Mystery Dinners, picnic lunches and lots more besides, so please sign up for our online newsletter if you'd like to join and get involved. You'll also be able to find us on Facebook and Twitter.

We're looking forward to seeing you at the dinner dance on Saturday when Robert Miles will be officially introduced as your new Chairman and Club President, and he'll explain his vision for the future of Green Miles but if you'd like further information about the contents of this newsletter, please feel free to contact Jenna Baker at the club.

Our aim is to make our home your home and here at Green Miles, you can be sure of a warm welcome, whatever the weather!

Best wishes,

The Team at Green Miles Golf Club

She had just stuck the stamp on the last envelope when Robert called.

'How's your afternoon been?' he said.

She was tempted to say, 'After I discovered you slept with Sherree, you mean?' but she didn't.

'Okay, thanks. How was yours?'

'Even better than I expected. I've got so much to tell you. Are you doing anything this evening?'

Jenna was so surprised by his question that she was lost for words but luckily her mobile rang at that moment and she saw it was her mother.

'Sorry Robert. May I call you back? My mum's on the other line and I'd really like to talk to her.

'Of course. Call me later. I hope it's good news.'

She hung up without saying thanks or goodbye.

'Hello Mum. Are you okay? I've been waiting for you to call all day.'

'I'm fine, thank you, darling and I told you it would be this evening when I called. Your father came home earlier than I expected actually and, as I knew he would, he's chosen us.'

'Thank God for that,' Jenna said, breathing a sigh of relief.

'I really don't know why you were so worried, darling. I told you he would. He and I have been discussing things this afternoon and it seems Green Miles isn't the only place where big changes are in the air – there may be quite a few at the Baker house too. Anyway, I just wanted to let you know everything's fine and that your father would like you to pop in later, if it's convenient.'

'Of course it's *convenient*, Mum. Any particular time?'

'No, no. Whatever suits you. We were thinking of ordering in a Chinese though. Would you like to join us, say seven-ish? If not, that's fine, we'll be here all evening.'

'I'd love to,' Jenna said. 'I can't remember the last time I had a Chinese. See you around seven. I'll bring a bottle.'

'Just bring yourself, darling. We've got plenty of bottles.'

Jenna was so relieved that her mum and dad were fine, she almost cried with joy. She started packing up for the evening and was debating whether to go home for a couple of hours, go straight to her parents or pop in to see Daisy when she remembered that Robert had called and asked her what she was doing.

She could meet him for a quick drink and hear what he had to say. Then go to her parents but she still didn't feel up to seeing him and she decided against it.

'I know,' she said out loud, 'I'll call Tom.'

It wasn't because she wanted to see him. Far from it in fact, but they were all going to meet up in the pub on Friday night and after what had happened today between her and Robert, even if that didn't go any further, it would be awkward if Tom turned up at the pub on Friday and started behaving as if they were an item. It was better to tell him now that she wasn't interested in him.

He seemed genuinely surprised to hear from her.

'I wondered if we could just have a quick chat, Tom,' she said. 'I'm going to my parents at seven and it's just gone five now. I don't know what you're up to at the moment but is there a chance of a quick coffee or a glass of wine?'

'Well, this is a coincidence, Jenna,' he said. 'I was just thinking about you. Something's come up and I'd quite like five minutes with you too. Shall I come to yours?'

'No!' Jenna said, a little too decisively, she realised. 'I mean ... why don't we meet in town? How about Claremont Casks? I don't know if you know it, it's the wine bar on the High Street. The only wine bar, really. You can't miss it.'

'I'm sure I'll find it,' he said. 'See you there at five-thirty.'

'That's great. See you.'

She hung up, took a deep breath and dialled Robert's number.

'Hi,' he said. 'I've been sitting by the phone waiting for you to call back. Not that I'm eager to see you again or anything. How are things with your mum and dad? All okay, I hope?'

She felt a knot form in her stomach. She could think of nothing she'd rather be doing than spending the evening with Robert but she couldn't – not tonight. It was too soon. She needed time to think.

'Yes thanks. They're fine. Dad's back at home. They want me to go round this evening and have dinner with them.'

'Oh.' He sounded disappointed. 'That's good news. I'm really pleased. What time are you going? Do you have time for a quick drink with me first?'

'No. Sorry. I ... I said I'd go straight there. I'm just walking out the door, actually. Oh. I've done the newsletters and I'm posting them on my way to the ... Mum and Dad's.'

'Oh. Okay. That's good about the newsletters. Thanks. It really feels as if things are starting to go in the right direction. Speaking of which, about what happened today between us. I'd really like to –'

'Sorry, Robert. My cab's here. I can't talk and get in it, holding all these letters. I'll see you tomorrow. Have a good evening. Bye.'

She hung up and quickly dialled the number for a cab. She grabbed the pile of letters from her desk and walked to the door. Well, she thought, it had been partly true. The cab would be here soon and she was now carrying a pile of letters.

159

CHAPTER FIFTEEN

Tom was already waiting for Jenna when she arrived at Claremont Casks. She didn't see him at first because he was sitting at one of the secluded tables near the back. Even though it was broad daylight outside, the dark wood, slightly concave panelling which covered the walls from the floor to the ceiling of the wine bar, made the interior quite dark. Jenna and Daisy often joked that when you went into Claremont Casks, you felt as if you'd jumped into a barrel and by the time you'd emptied the barrel, you felt as if you were on board a ship from the Elizabethan era.

'You found it then,' Jenna said, smiling.

'Yes. I remembered seeing it on my way home last night. I've bought Merlot, is that all right?'

'Fine thanks,' she said, sitting down as far away from him as the cosy little table and half barrel chairs would allow.

He poured her a glass of wine and they clinked glasses. She wasn't actually sure why but she'd noticed it was something he did last time, when they were in the pub on Tuesday.

'So,' she said, 'have you had a good day?'

'To be honest, no.'

Jenna was a little surprised. She'd come to assume that Tom was one of those people who always said they'd had a good day even if the world had come to an end. She hoped she wasn't about to make it worse.

'The thing is, Jenna,' he continued 'and I can't believe this myself, I've met someone. I hope you're not too disappointed but I'm just not the sort of guy who can go out with more than one woman at a time and I feel awful but ... well ... I think I may actually have fallen in love at first sight.'

'Wow!' Jenna exclaimed.

She realised that, as weird as it was, she did feel a little disappointed. It wasn't because he'd met someone and fallen in love, it was because, after everything she'd thought about him, Tom had turned out to be the decent guy and Robert, whom she'd put on a pedestal for so many years, had turned out to be a womanising bastard.

'I'm so sorry, Jenna. I hope you won't think too badly of me, and I hope that we can still be friends.'

'I don't think badly of you at all, Tom. In fact, you've restored my faith in men – well, some men. Is she someone I may know?'

'What? Oh. No. No, I don't think so. To be honest, I'd rather not discuss her because, as awful as this sounds, she's got a boyfriend. It's all over bar the shouting but I don't want to say anything else until she's told him. You know how easily rumours spread and get out of hand.'

'Only too well,' she said. 'Well, I'm really happy for you. I hope it works out and if so, you must bring her to the pub. We're there every Friday if she can't make this one.'

'Thanks. I'll ... er ... mention it to her. So, what did you want to talk to me about?'

'Oh. I ... do you know? I really can't remember. I must be losing my mind.'

'It's the pressure of the new job,' Tom said. 'I hear it's very ... demanding.'

Jenna wondered what he meant by that but as she didn't want to talk about her job, she changed the subject.

'Any more news about the Claremont Cliffs' proposal? How's it progressing?'

She thought she saw him flinch but she could have imagined it.

'Swimmingly,' he said. 'Absolutely swimmingly. Let me top you up.'

161

Robert was at a loose end. He'd had a really good day and he'd hoped to take Jenna out to dinner and tell her all about it. Then he'd hoped to take her home and do all the things he'd wanted to do to her this morning on the cliffs and, if he were being honest, last night, when he'd taken off her dress and shrug and tucked her up in bed. Of course, if he were being totally honest, he'd wanted to make love to her since the first day he'd set eyes on her in his office.

He tried to call his mum but all he got was her voicemail. He was beginning to get a little worried despite the fact that she'd left him a message earlier saying that she wouldn't be able to meet him after all because she was spending the day with an old friend and that she'd talk to him later.

Pacing up and down in his rented apartment, he realised he didn't have any friends he could call and go for a drink with. The only people he knew in Claremont were Jenna's friends and he could hardly call them. There was no point moping around the apartment, he thought. He may as well go to the club and get on with some work. He made his way to the car park, got in his car and headed along the High Street towards Green Miles.

He couldn't believe how slow the traffic was at six forty-five in the evening in such a small town. It moved faster in New York! Probably road works he thought, glancing around and spotting the wine bar he'd seen Sherree in last night. It didn't seem very busy. A couple were just leaving and he thought he recognised them as they got into a BMW convertible parked right outside the door.

He *did* recognise them. It was Tom – and he was with Jenna. The lying, cheating, bastard, he thought, and Jenna was clearly just as bad. He watched them drive away in the opposite direction, laughing and smiling and he felt a

162

rage building inside him like nothing he'd ever felt before.

She'd told him she was going to her parents when she was really meeting Tom. What a bitch, and after all those things she'd said yesterday. Well, they were clearly all lies too. So much for being in love with him. But why? He couldn't understand it. And then again this morning, when he'd kissed her; she had behaved as if all she wanted was him, right then, right there. Shit! Why did he always pick the wrong women? Why hadn't he learnt his lesson with Lou?

Tom dropped Jenna at her parents and drove off feeling rather fed up. He didn't have any plans and now he didn't have a woman. When Jenna had called and asked to meet this evening for a chat, he'd known what that meant because, when he'd spoken to Adam that afternoon, Adam had told him two things.

First, that he thought it very unlikely that the proposal for the development of Claremont Cliffs would go any further because he had just discovered that the council didn't own the land, even though most people working in the council offices, thought they did. He also said that he had it on good authority that the real owner would never sell.

Second, that he also thought it unlikely that Tom would get anywhere with Jenna. It now turned out that Robert wasn't gay after all and Adam felt Tom should know that Jenna had been in love with Robert for most of her life, although that wasn't public knowledge.

Once Tom had had a chance to digest both pieces of unwelcome news, he decided that, whilst there wasn't much he could do about the development, if Adam was right, there was something he could do about Jenna. There was no way on this earth that she was going to get the better of him. If anyone was going to do the dumping, it was going to be him, so he'd made up a story about falling in love with someone else.

He still needed to keep on her good side, in case Adam was wrong about the land and he needed Adam's help. Best not to ruffle too many feathers until he knew for sure, so giving her a lift to her parents was no hassle, especially as he had nothing better to do.

He didn't even have the number of that hot little piece he'd bedded last night. In fact, he couldn't even remember her name. Was it Beth or something? No, wasn't that the other one? Was it Sheila or ...? It was no good, he just couldn't remember. He hadn't really paid that much attention. After all, he'd just thought she was a one-night stand as he'd get Jenna into bed on Friday night without fail. He had meant to get her name and number in the morning though, just in case Jenna didn't come up trumps or if she just wasn't that good and he needed a backup lay, but to his astonishment, when he'd woken up late, after a night of very hot sex, the woman had gone without a trace.

Before Jenna had arrived at Claremont Casks that evening he'd asked the bar staff whether any of them could remember the woman or knew who she was but it was just his luck that none of the staff there were working last night, so they were no help at all. Maybe he'd just go back there and sit and wait. She might just come back in again tonight.

'Mum, Dad, it's me,' Jenna said, letting herself in as she always did.

'We're in the sitting room, Jenna,' Fiona called out.

She took a deep breath and strode towards the door. She wasn't sure what to expect even though her mum had said her dad had chosen them in preference to the club and that there were going to be changes at home, too. She didn't know what that meant. Would her dad be resentful; would he still be angry? She was astonished by the sight that greeted her.

164

Her mum and dad were snuggled up together on the sofa like two lovebirds. He had his legs stretched out on the footstool and his arms wrapped around Fiona and she had her legs curled up beneath her and her arms wrapped around him. Neither of them moved when Jenna walked in.

'Wow!' she said. 'I can't remember the last time I saw the two of you like this.'

They both smiled and Edward stretched out his left arm towards her. 'Come and give your foolish old dad a hug, pumpkin,' he said. 'Oh, sorry that should be Jenna, shouldn't it?'

'Pumpkin's fine,' she said, unable to stop the tears of relief from running down her cheeks. She dashed to him and knelt on the floor at his feet so that she could hug both her mum and dad at the same time. 'I'm sorry, Dad.'

'Shush,' he said, stroking her hair. 'It wasn't your fault. Your mother's right, I don't listen. I told you to take the job and your mother tells me that you've come up with a lot of really good ideas to help make it more ... family friendly ... as the boy ... I mean, Robert wants it to be. I can see that the club has to move with the times and I accept that, perhaps the days of old are gone. It's silly clinging to the past when the future can be so much better. I'm sorry for what I said to you yesterday, pumpkin and I'm sorry if you've been upset.'

'Oh Dad! I'm so pleased you feel that way. I've been really worried, ever since Roddy blew up yesterday.'

'Yes, well, I can't say that Roddy will come round quite as easily as I have, but then Roddy doesn't have a beautiful wife and an equally beautiful, daughter who love him.'

'He has Robert, Dad, and Robert does love him. He just hates and resents the club because he blames it for pushing him and his mother away. That's why he wants to make it family friendly, so that families can go there and enjoy the

165

facilities together. Surely that's a good thing?'

'I suppose so but I'm not saying that I totally approve of the boy's ... I mean ... of Robert's plans. All I'm saying is that if I have to choose between the two of you and Green Miles Golf Club, I choose you two. I'll agree that, perhaps some changes are necessary but I think the boy ... Robert should discuss them with club members rather than just steamroll ahead. I know he has the final say and the only option for members if they don't like it, is to leave but that's not the point. A little diplomacy wouldn't go amiss. Shame he didn't have the benefit of strategic battle planning, but there it is.'

Jenna couldn't help but smile. 'Then perhaps you should talk to him. You'll see he's a reasonable man, Dad ... at least as far as the club's concerned. Well, I think he is.' She wasn't sure she really knew anything about him now. 'But he is determined, and at the end of the day, the club does belong to him.'

Edward nodded. 'Well, I won't be spending so much time there in the future and I really think it's time I passed the club captaincy on to someone younger. I'll have a word with him about that but I think his first priority is to talk to Roddy. Some sort of truce must be possible, surely? I'll see if I can have a word in Roddy's ear. I can't promise anything. That man is as stubborn as a mule and twice as thick-skinned.'

'Edward!' Fiona said, 'I think that's the first time I've heard you say a bad word against him.'

'Yes, well, it's not a criticism, it's just the truth.'

Jenna was stunned. 'Are you seriously considering handing on the captaincy, Dad?'

'I certainly am. Your mother and I have decided we'd like to take up something we can enjoy together. I'll still play a round or two once a week and your mother will still paint, but we think we might take up horse riding.'

'Horse riding!' Jenna repeated, even more stunned than

before.

'Yes,' Fiona said. 'We both used to ride when we were younger and neither of us can remember why we stopped. We're hoping it's a bit like riding a bike – which we also intend to start doing again. Cycling, that is. Anyway, we hope that, once we're back in the saddle, we'll be galloping over Claremont Cliffs within no time.'

'Wow!' Jenna said again. 'You may not want to ride over the cliffs though. Tom – he's the guy I had dinner with and a friend of Adam's from uni – works for Viewmore Homes and they're hoping to get the go-ahead for a development of luxury homes running the entire length of the land. It's owned by the council and they need the money, I think. Obviously, they can't stop the public using it but most of it has always been fenced off to the general public during my lifetime at least, so there's nothing much to stop them selling that part.'

'Oh how sad!' Fiona said. 'I'd hate to see houses up there. It's so pretty. Surely something can be done to stop it?'

'Well, I think Robert is also considering buying it. He wants to extend the club to include a nine hole course. You see Dad, he's not going to destroy the club but improve it. Anyway, that would be a much better option.'

'Edward?' Fiona said. 'You're unusually quiet on the subject.'

'What? Oh. Sorry, darling. I was trying to cast my mind back to years ago. I seem to remember someone else planning to build there but it never got further than discussions and I can't remember why. I'm fairly certain it had something to do with Roddy though and Green Miles.'

'He probably got someone in the council to put a stop to it. The land borders the club land on two sides, doesn't it? He wouldn't like that,' Fiona said.

'That's it!' Edward said. 'The council doesn't own the land, it leases it – well part of it, the part with the old

167

restaurant on. I can't remember precisely but I think there used to be fairs there or cattle markets or something. They had a long lease at a peppercorn rent, I seem to recall Roddy saying.'

'So Roddy had looked into buying it too then?' Jenna said, thinking about Robert's plans.

'Roddy didn't need to buy it, pumpkin. Roddy owns it! Well, Green Miles Golf Club does, so I suppose that now means Robert does. I'm surprised he doesn't know that.'

'Robert ... owns it?' Jenna said. 'Wow! The Miles' men really did want to take over Claremont, didn't they? Perhaps he does know, now. He told me this morning that he was thinking of making an offer and when I spoke to him this evening, he said it had been a good day, so maybe he's discovered he already owns it. He'll still have to give the council something for the value of the remaining lease, won't he? I mean, if they're only paying a peppercorn rent, it's worth more to them to keep it and sell the lease on to someone else than to surrender it to him, isn't it?'

'Well, it depends on the terms of the lease and how many years are remaining. I don't know because I never asked Roddy about it. I do remember that there were restrictive covenants though, so there are things the council can't do, and I also remember it was granted long before Roddy's time, so it may not have long to run, in any event. Well, well, so the b ... Robert's actually thinking of expanding Green Miles. That might help to win Roddy over.'

'I'm starving,' Fiona said. 'As fascinating as all this is, can we please order our Chinese?'

'Hello darling. It's me. Are you busy?' Amelia said when Robert answered his phone.

'At last! I've been wondering where you were. No, I'm not busy. I'm at the club.'

Amelia chuckled. 'I'm not sure how to take that.

Doesn't the club keep you busy? Sorry darling, I'm being facetious. It's been a strange, but rather wonderful day.'

'Well, I'm glad someone's been having a good time.'

'Oh dear. Does that mean you haven't? Is something wrong? Anything I can help you with?'

'No one can help me with this, Mum. It's something I've got to deal with myself. Anyway, where are you now? Do you feel like having dinner? I could use the company, to be honest.'

'That does sound serious, darling. Er ... about dinner. I'd love to, but there's something I need to tell you first and I don't think that should be in a public place. We'll meet you at your office in say, fifteen minutes.'

Before Robert had a chance to respond, Amelia had hung up.

He slumped in his chair and wondered what his mother could possibly have to tell him that would require privacy and then he realised, she'd used the word 'we'. He already knew, from her earlier message, that she'd spent the day 'with an old friend' and something started to eat away at him but he didn't quite know what.

He didn't have to wait long to find out. Exactly fifteen minutes later, his mother limped into his office, her stick in one hand and her other hand and arm linked through the arm of none other than his father. They both had beaming smiles on their faces.

'Oh my God!' Robert said. 'No wonder you needed privacy. Don't tell me you two have spent the day together ... the entire day ... together?'

'Now look here, Robert, I think –'

'Please, Roddy. Let me,' Amelia said.

'Of course, darling,' he said, smiling lovingly at her.

'Darling!' Robert said. 'Darling! After all these –'

'Robert! That's quite enough,' Amelia said. 'Let's all sit down and talk this through. No! I don't want to hear one word from either of you. I'll start and I don't want any interruptions. Is that clear?'

Robert met his father's eyes and nodded. Roddy nodded too.

'Good,' Amelia said.

Robert was astonished to see his father help Amelia to lower herself onto the sofa. He was even more astonished to see him sit down beside her and take her hand in his.

'The past is the past and whilst all three of us feel hurt, misunderstood, mistreated and pushed aside, going over it all really won't help. We have all done things we regret – even you, Robert, and our past actions have led us to where we are today. I propose that, instead of bickering and fighting and bearing grudges and resentment, we let go of what is ultimately a sinking ship and build a new one to carry us all forward into the future.'

'Just like that,' Robert said.

'Let your mother finish,' Roddy said.

'I thought she had. It was almost profound but –'

'Robert! I'm as much to blame for all this as your father is. And … whether you like it or not, Roddy and I are in love. We always have been. We were both just too stubborn to realise it and even when we did, we were either too proud or too stupid to admit it.'

Robert was too astounded to comment. It would have been laughable if it weren't so serious, he thought.

'Now, I'm going to say this. Robert, you love your father. You may not understand him or like what he does sometimes, but you love him regardless, you just don't want to admit it. No! I'm warning you, Robert. You're not too old for me to box your ears. Or you, Roddy. Be quiet, both of you!'

They both closed their half-open mouths, their retorts remaining silent on their lips.

'And you, Roddy. Robert means more to you than I do, you just don't know how to show him that, but you could start by telling him. All those years when he thought he was in the way here, you were just trying to do what you thought was best for him but you never stopped to ask him what he wanted. So, this is how things are going to be – and I mean it or believe me, I'll get up, walk out of here and never speak to either of you again until you come to your senses.'

'Amelia!'

'Mum!'

'I mean it! You are going to shake hands – I'd say hug but let's not run before we can walk … and you are going to say sorry to one another. That's it. No recriminations, no buts, nothing. Just sorry. Well? Go on then!'

Robert and Roddy stared at Amelia and then at one another. To Robert's surprise, his father rose from the sofa and walked towards him. Robert saw his mother glower at him, so he got up and met Roddy beside the desk. Roddy held out his hand and, Robert, in a dazed state, took it in his.

'I'm sorry, Robert,' Roddy said.

Robert was stunned. He looked his father in the eye and he saw something he thought he'd seen a few times before but had dismissed. He saw it now, as clear as day and it brought a lump to his throat. Roddy Miles actually loved his son.

'I'm sorry too, Dad,' Robert said and he meant it.

Roddy immediately did two things he hadn't done since Robert was a very young boy. He hugged his son – and he wept.

'I'm so proud of you both,' Amelia said.

Robert glanced in her direction and he could see she was crying but he knew they were tears of joy. He even felt something prick at the corner of his eyes but he blinked several times and then he felt fine.

Roddy released Robert and wiped his own eyes.

'I love you, son,' he said 'and whilst it may take me some getting used to, I'll try to support you in any way I can, both in the changes you want to make to the club and ... in your personal life.'

Robert wanted to ask if this man was a visitor from outer space and what had happened to his real father but he held back the temptation.

'Thanks, Dad. In my personal life ...?'

'Yes son. I realise we can't choose whom we love and whilst I would have wanted something else entirely for you ... a wife and kids ... your choice is yours and if you're ... gay, well, then you're gay. I still love you. It's not your fault you don't like women.'

'What the ...? For God's sake, Dad. I'm not gay!'

Roddy looked confused and his eyes darted from Robert to Amelia and back to Robert.

'Roddy, Robert's as straight as you are, darling,' Amelia said.

'I don't understand,' Roddy said, looking even more bewildered. 'Then why did you tell me you were gay?'

'I didn't tell you I was. You jumped to conclusions as usual and ... well, I didn't think it would do any harm to let you think that for a few days. How wrong I was about that. It seems you told everyone.'

'What? I didn't tell everyone. I ... I told Edward, but that was because I was drunk and ... well ... shocked ... and your mother had just had her accident. So, you're telling me you're not gay but you thought it would be amusing to have me think my son preferred men!'

'Well! There's nothing wrong with it. Sometimes I think my life would be a lot less complicated if I did. Of course, we all know you'd rather I were more like you, God forbid.'

'Boys!' Amelia said in a raised voice.

'And what's that supposed to mean?'

'You know full well what that means. No one could ever accuse you of not liking women. You seem to want to *like* as many of them as possible and if they keep getting

172

younger, you'll soon find yourself in prison.'

'Robert!' Amelia shouted.

'That's enough, Robert!' Roddy boomed.

'You're right, it is,' Robert said, heading towards the door. 'Tell me, does the lovely Sherree know that she's being dumped for an older woman?'

Amelia banged her stick on the floor and screamed. Robert stopped in his tracks. Roddy raced to her side.

'Darling! Are you all right?'

'No Roddy, I'm not all right! And you, Robert. What's got into you? Can't you see how much this means to me? I really thought we'd turned a corner but in one second, we're back to the old days. Clearly, this will never work. I'm going back to the States. You two sort it out.'

She started to lift herself off the sofa and Robert could see she was genuinely upset.

'I'm sorry, Mum,' he said, striding towards the sofa. 'Dad, I apologise. I shouldn't have said those things and I shouldn't have misled you. I'm sorry about that too.'

'I'm sorry too, son. You're right, I don't listen and I have been making a complete fool of myself over young women, I'm ashamed to say. I ... I did it out of ... spite, I think. The truth is, the only woman I've ever really wanted since the first moment I saw her, was your mother.'

'I really am sorry, Mum. You're right. I'm not myself at the moment. Dad and I will work this out. Don't go.'

'Please stay, darling. Robert's right. We'll get through this.'

Amelia sighed. 'Oh well,' she said. 'Rome wasn't built in a day. I'll stay.'

Robert grinned. 'You had no intention of leaving, did you?'

'Of course not! But I am leaving now. I've just realised how hungry I am and I really need to eat. Let's go to dinner. You can tell us why you're in such a bad mood. I'm guessing it's got something to do with a certain young lady.'

Robert nodded. 'It has, and I could use some advice.' He smiled across at his father.

'Well don't look at me, son. I let the only woman I've ever really loved, run off to America. I'm the last person to turn to for advice on women. The only thing I can tell you is, if you really care about her, don't let her get away. Speaking of getting away, I suppose I'd better tell Sherree she won't be going sailing.'

'Actually Dad, I think she may have already realised that. I'm not sure I should be telling you this but ... I think she may have spent last night with someone else.'

'What?' Roddy said. 'Oh well. Good for her. At least when I tell her that Amelia and I are getting married, it won't be too big a shock.'

Robert stopped in his tracks. 'What did you just say?'

Jenna yawned. 'I've got to go home to bed,' she said. 'I'm absolutely shattered. So much has happened this week and I can't believe it's only Thursday. Oh! That reminds me. What's going to happen at the dinner dance on Saturday if Roddy doesn't ... come round? Obviously, it'll still go ahead, but I suppose Robert will have to introduce himself if Roddy won't be doing his handover speech.'

'Yes,' Edward said. 'As much as Roddy would like to think he's indispensible to the club, unfortunately for him, that's not the case. The catering was all organised months ago, as was the band. In fact, there's absolutely nothing left to do but turn up. Actually, I could formally introduce Robert, in my role as club captain. I could announce that I'll be standing down at the same time or, as you say, Robert could just introduce himself. I'll have a word with him tomorrow.'

'That's good. Right. I'm going to love you and leave you. Don't get up, I'll see myself out. Oh. I'd better call a cab first.'

'No pumpkin,' Edward said, 'I'll take you and ... Fiona, why don't you come with us? You and I can go for a moonlight stroll along the beach – like we used to.'

'Are you mad, Edward? It's May and it's gone eleven-thirty,' Fiona said, getting to her feet.

Jenna glimpsed the twinkle in her eye.

'Then it'll be a May, midnight, moonlight ... meander. It's spring, we're in love,' Edward cooed. 'It's not raining and it's time we got some romance back into our lives.' He wrapped his arms around his grinning wife and kissed her tenderly.

'God! Mum! Dad!' Jenna said 'Get a room!'

Edward slowly pulled away from his wife. 'Now

there's an idea, Fiona. Why don't we go away for a few days, maybe even a few weeks?'

Fiona laughed and walked arm in arm with him towards the car. 'Or a few months – like Roddy and Sherree.'

Jenna coughed. 'Er ... Roddy and Sherree may not be going away now.'

'Oh. Because of the club, you mean?' Edward said after they got into the car and he pulled out of the drive.

'Not just because of the club. You know you went round to Roddy's last night and he told Sherree to go out with a friend? Well, I ... I think she may have spent the night with ... someone else.'

'Yes,' Edward said as they approached the town centre. 'She called to say she was spending the night at Beth's. Why is that a problem?'

'Did she?' Jenna exclaimed. 'She clearly wasn't drunk then, to make up an excuse like that. I mean ... I think she may have spent the night with ... another man.'

'Good God! And had ... *sex* you mean?'

'Yes Dad!'

Fiona giggled. 'Oh dear. Poor Roddy. He won't like that.'

'You don't know the half of it,' Jenna said under her breath.

'What was that, darling?'

'Nothing, Mum.'

Edward turned the car into the High Street. 'Speak of the devil! Isn't that Sherree, there, standing outside Claremont Casks?'

'Ooh! Slow down, darling,' Fiona said. 'I haven't seen her. I want to see what she looks like.'

All three of them peered out the windows as Edward slowed almost to a halt.

'Well, well,' Fiona said to Jenna, 'you were right about her clothes, darling. So that's the lovely Sherree. Who's the young man she's ... oh! Kissing! That's definitely not

176

Roddy!'

Jenna looked on in amazement. 'That's not Robert either!' she mumbled. 'Oh my God! That's ... Tom!

'I'm so happy, I could cry!' Jenna yelled down the phone at Daisy at exactly seven o'clock on Friday morning.

'I'm so glad. Of course, I'm now deaf and you did ruin a really good dream I was just having as I was *fast asleep* but as long as you're happy. So, what's caused this sudden euphoria and couldn't it have waited until I'd had at least two cups of coffee?'

'Sorry, Daisy. I didn't mean to yell, or to wake you up but you're lucky I waited until now. I've been dying to call you since I figured it all out last night.'

'That's funny, I don't feel lucky. Okay, tell me.'

'I don't think Robert did have sex with Sherree. I think you were right. He saw her with someone else – not having sex, I don't mean – just kissing or something. That's what she meant about Robert telling Roddy. I should have listened to you. Then I could have spent last night with Robert!'

'You never listen to me and once again, you've lost me. Did Robert tell you he'd seen her with someone else?'

'No! Robert just said he wanted to see me but I was still angry so I said I was going straight to Mum and Dad's but I met Tom instead and –'

'Oh my God! You didn't spend the night with Tom did you?'

'What? Of course I didn't spend the night with Tom. Why would I spend the night with Tom? What's the matter with you?'

'Sleep deprivation. So what, when and who? God I need coffee. Hold on. Adam! Please may I have some coffee? Jenna's on the phone!'

'Now guess who's gone deaf. Anyway, to cut a long story short. I met Tom to tell him it was over but he told me he'd met someone and fallen in love. Then, when Dad was driving me home last night we saw Tom and Sherree kissing outside Claremont Casks. And I do mean kissing. The sort of kissing that has a big banner above it flashing the word 'sex'. You know the sort.'

'I vaguely remember. Wow! So Robert's off the hook then? Of course, she could have slept with Robert on Wednesday night then met Tom yesterday and spent last night with him ... to drown her sorrows or something.'

'Why did you say that? Why, why, why? Just when I thought it was safe to assume that Robert is a nice man, after all.'

'Sorry, it was just a thought. Forget it. You're right. Not that you really care if he's a nice man or not. We both know that you're dying to have your wicked way with him, especially now you know he's straight.'

'I'm not, actually. I'm trying to be very grown up about it and think things through. I could have met him last night but I didn't. I told you that.'

'Yes you did. Thanks darling. ... I don't mean you, Jenna, I mean Adam. He's brought me coffee. So will you be seeing him today then, at work? Robert, I mean.'

'I hope so. And I've been grown up about it and thought things through and if I get a chance today I might just grab him, push him into that incredibly comfortable chair of his and show him exactly what he was missing on Wednesday night. I must go through my wardrobe and find a sexy little dress.'

'Well, it sounds like you've got a busy day planned and I think I can see one of those banners above Adam's head. Call me later and tell me how it went.'

Jenna felt both nervous and excited. She couldn't be one hundred per cent certain that it was Tom who had slept with Sherree on both nights, or even on one of the nights come to that but the more she thought about it, the more it made sense.

Tom had tried to get Jenna into bed on Monday night even though she'd been drunk and again on Wednesday when she'd been upset about her mum and dad, whereas Robert had put her to bed and rinsed out her clothes on Wednesday. It was Tom who kept mauling her, making suggestive comments and rash statements about his sexual prowess, whereas Robert just kissed her and kept his hands to himself.

She now felt guilty for having thought so badly of Robert. He may bear a grudge against his father and he may be a little annoyed with her for telling all her friends that he was gay but he wasn't the cold, hard, deceitful womaniser she'd thought he may be and he wouldn't sleep with someone just for revenge. Well, she was almost certain he wouldn't anyway.

She was now rather looking forward to today especially as she thought she looked pretty damn good. Her long, straight, brown hair was shining and her virtually make-up free skin was glowing. She thought she looked just like one of those models in the shampoo adverts, only shorter and not quite as skinny and not quite as pretty, but fairly close.

She spotted Robert's car in the car park and even the butterflies in her stomach started seeing visions of him ... and that chair. She raced up the stairs, her floral, cotton dress swinging around her sun-kissed, bare legs and skimming the tops of her knees like the ribbons on a maypole. She knew her legs looked sun-kissed because it said so, on the spray tan she'd used that morning before she'd painted her toenails 'sexy cherry' red.

She could hear Robert's voice and her heart did a double back flip and a triple somersault that would have won full marks in a gymnastics competition. She pouted her 'cherry kiss' lips and positively bounced into Robert's office through the wide open door.

179

'Good morning,' she said melodiously. She immediately stopped dead.

Amelia was sitting at Robert's desk. Robert and Roddy were either side of her leaning over and studying what looked like an ancient map and bundles of old documents. They all looked up as she entered and they each had a different expression on their faces. Roddy smiled benignly, Amelia gave her a half-hearted smile and a questioning look and Robert, well Robert first looked stunned. Then his eyes travelled the length of her body and he ... scowled. There was no other word for it. He definitely, decidedly, scowled. Jenna's heart fell off the parallel bars, missed the safety mats and hit the wooden floor with a thud.

'Oh, there you are,' Robert said, dragging his eyes away. 'Would you get us some coffee please?' He went back to studying the map.

Amelia and Roddy at least had the decency to wish her a good morning before they did the same.

Jenna backed out of the room and went to her own office. She dumped her handbag on the desk, took several deep breaths, blinked back her tears and headed down to the kitchen. She wondered whether she had imagined the look on Robert's face but she knew she hadn't. It wasn't until she reached the kitchen door that she suddenly realised that Roddy and Amelia were with Robert in his office and they all seemed like one big happy family. How the hell had that happened? And when?

She shoved open the door and came face to face with Sherree.

'Morning Jen,' Sherree shrieked.

Her face was back to its coffee colour, matching the rest of her body, most of which was exposed, save for a small strip of black metallic lycra around her chest and an equally small strip of plain black denim around her hips. She jingled louder than she had before as she sat on the edge of one of the worktops, her long legs dangling down to the points of her ice-pick high heels.

'Good morning, Sherree. I must say, you're looking a lot happier than the last time I saw you.'

'Ooh, I know!' Sherree giggled, hunching her shoulders. 'Life is so weird, isn't it? So much has happened, I don't know if I'm coming or going. Ooh! I'm doing both I guess!'

'I'd agree with you there,' Jenna said. 'Anything exciting?' She knew she shouldn't ask but she just had to. She watched the strange face and the hunched shoulders and waited.

'Lots! You know the night your dad came round – Ooh! Is everything sorted there? Eddie is such a sweetie.'

Jenna nodded. 'Yes thanks. Just a little misunderstanding.'

'Brill. Beth and me went to the wine bar and I met this man. Ooh! He was so fit! And the things he said! It made even me blush and I've been around the block I can tell you.'

Jenna didn't doubt it although who was she to talk, she thought.

'We had such a laugh. He works for this big property development company. They were going to buy some cliff but now he's decided it's not ... I can't remember what he said … via … something.'

'Viable?' Jenna said.

Sherree smiled and hunched. 'That's it. So now they're not. We talked and talked and ... I was so naughty but his eyes and his hands and ... Ooh, just thinking about him makes me go all gooey. So ... I slept with him. I felt awful in the morning and that's why I was here, crying but then I thought about it and ... as lovely as Roddy is – and he is lovely – he is a lot older than me … and Tom – that's his name – isn't so old and I saw him again last night and ... you know … we did it again, lots of times. I was so scared

181

of telling Roddy but he was lovely and Bobbie's mum is back and I think they might get back together which would be nice because they're both old.'

She giggled, jingled, hunched and contorted her face all at once and Jenna found herself smiling at her.

'I hope you'll both be very happy,' Jenna said.

'Ooh! We're not getting married, Jen! Not yet anyway. We're just having a laugh! I was sad not to be going sailing but Tom says he'll take me on a cruise and I'll prefer that. We're going to get one that stops at the Canaries, so I can still see my dad. So, how's things with you and Bobbie?'

The question took Jenna by surprise. 'There is no me and ... Bobbie. I merely work for him.'

'That's what I meant, Jen. Ooh! I wasn't suggesting you were an item. I meant work. How's it going working for him? I don't think I could work for him. He's even fitter than Tom. I'd never get anything done!'

'Speaking of work,' Jenna said. 'He asked me to get some coffee. I'd better get it and go back. It's good to see you so happy, Sherree.'

'Thanks Jen.' She jumped down and gave Jenna a hug and a loud kiss on her cheek.

Jenna grabbed a pot of coffee, a tray of cups and saucers, a jug of milk and a bowl of sugar and headed towards the door.

'Take care of yourself, Sherree. I hope Tom looks after you,' she said and she really meant it.

Jenna knocked on the door of Robert's office even though it was still open, balancing the tray on one arm. She saw Robert glance up but he quickly looked away.

'Thanks Jenna,' Amelia said. 'Leave it on that small table, please.'

'I think it would work, Dad,' Robert said, ignoring Jenna.

'I think you're right,' Roddy said. 'Did you know I proposed to your mother on Claremont Cliffs?'

Jenna's eyes shot to Roddy's face and then to Robert's just in time to see him look away from her.

'Thank you, Jenna,' he said, studying the map again. 'Please close the door on your way out.'

She thought she saw Amelia give both her and Robert a curious look but she turned on her heels and walked briskly out, closing the door behind her with a decisive bang. She had been wrong about him yet again. He was a cold, deceitful bastard.

There was nothing else she could do. She had to call Daisy.

'I hate him!'

'Oh God! What's he done now?'

Jenna told her what had happened, including the conversation with Sherree.

'Well, that's good then,' Daisy said. 'At least you know he didn't sleep with her. I must admit, I have no idea why he's behaving like an absolute shit this morning but maybe he's embarrassed because his mum and dad are there. I say, wait and see if they go and whether he behaves differently then. If not, my advice would be to forget him. He's either deranged or he's a bastard.'

'Thanks a lot!'

'Well what else can I say? Monday, he's flirting, Tuesday, he wants to be friends, Wednesday, he puts you to bed, Thursday, he's all over you and Friday, he's treating you like the hired help. I'd say the relationship's run its course. Of course, the fact that you *are* the hired help may be a factor but I can't fathom it. Unless he hasn't forgiven you for telling everyone he's gay when he's not. I don't know. You're on your own, I'm afraid.'

'It's just so weird. He did look at me like ... well, like he thought I looked pretty when I first walked into his office. Then it was as if this shutter came down and now he's treating me like he'll catch something nasty if he just looks in my direction.'

'Wasn't there a film about that? If you looked at someone, they took your soul or something?'

'Daisy! This isn't helping! He's not worried about losing his soul if he looks at me, for God's sake.'

'No ... but there is the slightest possibility that he is worried about losing his heart. Did you think of that?'

Jenna hadn't. 'No. Not for one moment.'

'Well that, my friend, is why you call me. Hang in there, be brave and see what happens. You could even try doing some work. That might impress him. It is what he pays you for. If all else fails, or if he continues to wipe his feet on you, call me again and we'll go to the pub.'

As usual, Daisy had made Jenna feel better and Jenna told her so.

'That's my purpose in life,' Daisy said.

'You do know I love you, don't you?' Jenna said.

Daisy laughed. 'Of course I do, but I've told you a million times, I'm just not that sort of girl. Now bugger off and count golf balls or whatever it is you do all day.'

'Okay.' Jenna laughed. 'See you tonight in the pub.' Then she blew kisses down the phone before Daisy hung up.

'When you've finished exchanging your declarations of love, perhaps you would be good enough to spare me five minutes, if it's not too much to ask,' Robert stated brusquely.

Jenna shot round. She had been slouched in the chair with her back to her door and she hadn't heard him come in. She had no idea how long he'd been standing there but clearly long enough to hear her tell Daisy she loved her, although, of course, he wouldn't have known it was Daisy she was talking to. She saw his mouth form into a sneer and panic seized her. Perhaps he thought it had been a man.

'I was on the phone to –'

'I am really not interested in your personal life, Jenna,' he said and walked back to his office.

She blinked back her tears. This day was getting worse by the minute. How could she work for him if this was how things were going to be? It had been bad enough when she thought he wasn't interested in her because he was gay. To know that he just wasn't interested in her would be unbearable. And yet, only yesterday, he'd said such lovely things and he'd kissed her and –

'Jenna! Today would be good,' Robert bawled from his office.

The bastard! The absolute bastard!

She scribbled a few words in large, bold letters on a piece of Green Miles Golf Club headed paper, grabbed her bag and stormed towards his office. She was surprised to see Amelia and Roddy on their way downstairs as she hadn't heard them leave. She marched into Robert's office and almost lost her nerve. Robert was leaning back in his chair. The very chair that less than an hour ago she'd pictured pushing him down onto, climbing on top of him and –

'Shut the door,' he said.

She didn't. Instead she sashayed over to his desk and leant forward with a provocative smile on her lips, placing her fingertips on the desktop to support her. She saw something flash across his dark eyes and she leant closer. She was surprised that he remained silent.

'Whilst I appreciate I shouldn't make personal calls during office hours, that was Daisy and I called to ask her if she had any idea how a man can kiss a woman one day then treat her like dirt the next. Please accept *this* little declaration of my feelings for you.'

She tossed the note at him, turned and marched out of his office, slamming the door so hard that it sounded like an explosion. She mouthed what she had written as she did so.

I RESIGN.

FUCK OFF, YOU BASTARD.

Yours sincerely,

Jenna Baker

Robert blinked several times, unable to fully comprehend what had just happened. He was still furious that she'd lied to him about seeing Tom last night but his mother had told him that, unless he were actually dating Jenna, he couldn't expect her not to see other men. Amelia had also suggested that perhaps the reason Jenna hadn't told him was because she didn't want him to think she was playing one off against the other.

Whilst this seemed one explanation for it, he didn't really like it. Lou had shown how easy it was to lie and cheat and he would be extra careful not to fall for that again. He'd decided to play it cool and keep today on a purely business footing. He'd be out of the office for most of it again, anyway. Tonight, he'd go to the pub and see exactly how the land lay. If Tom was all over her and she seemed happy about it, Robert would back off.

If, on the other hand she kept her distance from Tom ... Robert didn't want to think of the wonderful possibilities. He had to remain cool and detached, he told himself. Cool and detached. He had repeated it several times on his way to the club this morning.

Then she'd breezed into his office, looking so incredibly beautiful ... and so, so sexy in that pretty little cotton dress, the skirt of which floated around her lovely, shapely, bare legs and the top which clung loosely to her shoulders and her pert breasts. He'd almost forgotten his parents were there because all he could think of was taking her in his arms, throwing her on his desk and making love to her until they were both exhausted. He still wasn't sure how he'd managed to remain calm and not display any visible signs of the effect she had on him.

When he'd heard her on the phone, he assumed it was Tom and he'd wanted to kill the man. Sarcasm was his safety valve. Then she'd marched in here and leant on his desk like she was offering herself to him and he'd had to grip the arms of his chair to stop himself from just grabbing her.

The thunderous slamming of the door made him come to and he glanced at the piece of paper in front of him. He read the words at least three times but they still didn't make any sense. Why was she so angry with him? Because he'd told her not to make personal calls?

Then he remembered that she'd said she was on the phone to Daisy and what she'd asked her, but that didn't make sense either. Jenna was the one who'd lied, not him. He should be calling her names and telling her to fuck off, not the other way around.

And now she was resigning. Just like that. Without even a moment's notice. Leaving him in the lurch. Leaving him ...

He was out of his chair and down the hall in less time than it would have taken a Superhero.

Jenna reached the top of the stairs before she realised what she'd done. She had just resigned from the only job she'd been offered since being made redundant, almost six weeks ago. Not only that but she's told her boss to 'fuck off' – in writing.

What the hell was the matter with her? She needed the job. She needed the money. And what was more, she'd actually enjoyed it. She'd even enjoyed learning about golf – and that was something she never thought she'd say.

She wondered whether there was the slightest possibility that she could go back and apologise but she knew there wasn't. A little part of her had even hoped that he might come running after her but she quickly realised that wasn't going to happen.

'Well done, Jenna,' she said to herself and reached into her bag for her phone so that she could call Daisy and ask her to meet her at the pub, even though it was only ten o'clock.

She didn't realise what was happening at first. She thought she heard running and as she turned to look back, someone grabbed her arm and swung her round so fast that her bag flew off her shoulder, hit the wall and landed on the floor. She saw the contents scatter across the hall, including her toothbrush and the spare pair of knickers she always had with her – not in case she got lucky, but in case she had an accident and was rushed to hospital. Her grandmother had told her more times than she could remember to always have a toothbrush and spare knickers, just in case.

She let out a startled scream as her body thudded against Robert's solid frame.

'What the hell do you mean by this?' he demanded, waving her note just inches in front of her eyes.

She tried to regain her composure and pushed her hand against his chest to distance herself from him. She could feel his heart pounding and his chest muscles tense as he held her arm in a vice-like grip. She looked up into a pair of glacial, midnight blue eyes.

She could have apologised. She could have said it was a fit of pique. She could have said it was that time of the month. She could have asked him to forgive her. She could have asked if she could take it back. She could have simply asked him to let go of her arm because he was hurting her.

Instead, she took her mother's advice, and using the full weight of her body, she kneed him in his groin.

He let go of her so suddenly that her head and shoulder smashed against the wall and a searing pain shot down her arm. Her eyes glazed over and she felt as if the ground had disappeared beneath her. The last thing she remembered as her body slid down the wall and before she landed in an unconscious heap on the floor, was seeing Robert doubled over, seemingly in more pain than she was.

CHAPTER SEVENTEEN

Jenna opened her eyes to find Robert on his knees, leaning over her. His face was drained and contorted and his dark eyes were awash with a mixture of pain and fear. He was lifting her head and placing something under it – she wasn't sure what – as he repeated her name over and over again. Amelia and Roddy were bending over him, their eyes full of concern and their faces etched with lines of worry. Jenna was sure she could hear sirens in the background, along with the 1812 overture.

'That's the ambulance,' Roddy said. He yelled, 'Send them up here.'

A few minutes later, two paramedics replaced Robert, Amelia and Roddy in her line of sight. One shone a light into her eyes whilst the other asked her for her name, where she lived and her date of birth, which she told him.

'She seems okay,' someone said, 'but we'd better get her to A&E, just in case. What happened, exactly?'

'I –' Robert began.

'I tripped!' Jenna said. 'I was running and I tripped and ... hit my head and shoulder.'

Robert gave her a concerned but appreciative smile.

'Well, I don't think anything's broken but we'll get you checked out,' the paramedic said. 'You can never be too careful with a knock to the head.'

'I'll follow in my car,' Robert said. 'I'm her ... friend.'

The paramedic didn't seem particularly bothered.

'Dad, will you call her mum and dad,' Robert continued. 'I don't want to worry them but it's best that they know. And will someone find her bloody phone! I can hear it ringing but I can't see it.'

Amelia put her hand on his shoulder. 'Calm down, Robert. I'm sure Jenna will be fine. You suffered

190

concussion once. Remember? She's awake and she's coherent. Those are very good signs.'

'Here's her phone,' Beth said. 'It says Daisy.'

Robert grabbed it from Beth as Jenna reached up for it.

'Daisy,' Jenna said. She heard Robert say the same.

'Yes. She ... she's had an accident. Nothing serious, we hope, but she's hit her head and we're going to A&E now. Yes, of course, but I can call you if – Okay, I'll see you there.' He hung up and deposited the phone in his shirt pocket. 'Daisy will meet us at the hospital,' he said to Jenna.

'I wanted to go to the pub,' Jenna said.

Robert gave her a sad sort of smile.

'No pubs for you for a few days, young lady,' the inquisitive paramedic said and turned to Robert.

Jenna could hear the paramedic asking Robert questions as he and his colleague lifted her onto a gurney, and Roddy talking on his phone, presumably to her parents. She could see Beth hovering in the background, talking to Amelia. She saw Roddy bend down and pick up some of the things that had spilt from her handbag including her toothbrush and knickers and she thought how sensible her grandmother had been. He passed them to Amelia who put them in her own handbag.

Then she saw him pick up what looked like a list and as he read the first line, his eyes shot to the back of Robert's head and his face looked like thunder. She remembered the note she'd written, resigning, which Robert had been waving in her face and assumed it was that but Roddy's eyes were reading on and on. It couldn't be the note because it didn't say that much.

She suddenly realised exactly what Roddy was reading. It was the list she and Daisy had written in the pub and it read:

Reasons for Robert having sex with Sherree - what to do now:

191

a) For revenge on his father – sensible women would avoid/possible to forgive and forget

b) He's a cold hearted, deceitful, bastard – should be avoided, if at all possible

c) He's a womaniser – see b) above

d) He fancied her – forgive and forget/everyone makes mistakes/mustn't happen again

e) Purely for the sex – see d) above

Jenna closed her eyes and wondered whether it might have been better if she hadn't woken up after all.

Having been poked and prodded, x-rayed and scanned, all Jenna wanted to do was sleep. She was wheeled into a private room and thought she either had something contagious or she was dying. You didn't get private rooms in Claremont Care Trust Hospital unless it was one of those two – or you had private medical insurance, which the Baker family definitely did not. She asked her mother, who was waiting in the room, which one it was.

Fiona laughed tearfully. 'It's neither darling. Robert insisted on it – at his expense.'

'Oh,' Jenna said, not quite sure whether that was good or bad. Being indebted to him might not be a good idea.

'What happened, pumpkin?' Edward asked, coming into the room bearing two cups of coffee and handing one to Fiona. 'Can I get you anything?'

Jenna shook her head but wished she hadn't because it hurt and she screwed up her face in pain.

'Some painkillers would be good,' she said.

'I'll get the nurse.'

He pressed the button on the cord and a few seconds later a nurse arrived. She checked the chart after speaking to Edward and asking Jenna a few questions, walked off and came back with painkillers and a fresh jug of water.

'So,' Edward said when the nurse left, 'you were going to tell us what happened.'

'Have ... have you spoken to Robert?'

'Briefly, but he wasn't making any sense. He said that he wasn't one hundred per cent sure what had happened but that he'd grabbed you and you fell and hit your head against the wall. That seems a damn silly thing to do. How did you manage that? And why was he grabbing you? To stop you falling?'

'I tripped. I was running and I tripped.'

'Why were you running?' Fiona asked.

'She was obviously in a hurry, darling. Why else would she be running?'

'I don't know,' Fiona said, 'but Robert seems to be in a little discomfort himself. Did you fall over each other or something? Did you have an argument?' She eyed her daughter curiously.

'No we ... we bumped into one another. I was running and he was coming out of one of the offices when I bumped into him. Then I tripped and fell. He ... he tried to grab me to stop me falling and ... and I think I may have kicked him or something.'

'I see,' Fiona said. 'Well, that explains the rather large bruise coming out on your arm then. I wondered how that got there as it was your other shoulder that hit the wall.'

'What's this, Mum? Considering a new career as a scene of crime officer?'

'I don't know, dear. Has a crime been committed?'

'No,' Jenna said, laughing. 'It was an accident, a silly accident. You know me. I never look where I'm going.'

'That's true,' Edward said. 'Nasty bruise though. The boy clearly doesn't know his own strength.'

'Speaking of which, he's outside with Daisy. They're both as worried as we are. Are you up to a quick 'hello'?' Fiona said.

'Yes.'

Fiona leant forward. 'He seems awfully worried about you, darling. Robert I mean, and he is even more good-looking as a man, isn't he? What a shame he's gay.'

Jenna had forgotten that she hadn't yet told her mum and dad that he wasn't.

'Robert's not gay, mum,' she proclaimed, her voice louder than she'd intended, just as Edward ushered Robert and Daisy into the room.

She saw the look of surprise on her father's face and the grin on Daisy's before she saw Robert close his eyes for a split second and let out a long, deep, martyred sigh.

'Pumpkin!' Edward said.

'Really? Fiona said.

'I see you're back to your normal self,' Daisy said, grinning at Jenna.

'I'm concussed!'

'Whilst I feel this is hardly the time or the place to discuss my sexual preferences,' Robert said, 'let me just assure you all that I'm not gay. Perhaps you would be kind enough to tell everyone you know. So, Jenna, how are you feeling? Is there anything I can get you? Good God! Did I do that to you?'

Jenna saw the horrified expression on his face as his eyes focused on the mushrooming violet shape on her arm that her mother and father had commented on. She nodded.

'Not on purpose though. You did it when you bumped into me whilst I was running down the hall and you grabbed me to try to stop me from falling but I tripped and kicked you in the ... somewhere.'

Robert raised his eyebrows. 'Did I? Well I'm so, so sorry, Jenna. I wouldn't harm you for the world. You do know that, don't you?'

She met his eyes. 'And I ... didn't mean to ... kick you.'

'So,' Daisy said, glancing from Robert to Jenna and grinning even more broadly. 'When will you be out and about and causing your usual mayhem? I take it you won't be going to the pub tonight?'

194

'Certainly not!' Edward, Fiona and Robert said simultaneously.

'No idea,' Jenna said. 'I'm just the patient. They haven't told me anything.'

'I'll go and ask,' Edward said.

'I expect they'll keep you in overnight,' Robert said. 'Possibly longer – just in case.'

'But then I'll miss the dinner dance!'

'You won't feel up to going to that anyway,' Fiona said, 'even if they do let you out tomorrow. I only go to show my face, to support your father but they can be quite good and it would have been lovely to have you there this year. Oh well, there's always next year – if you're still working at the club next year, that is.'

'I ...' Jenna glanced across at Robert and saw the corners of his mouth twitch.

'I sincerely hope Jenna will be with me for many years to come,' Robert announced. 'I know you've been having a few doubts about it, Jenna, but I'm sure there's nothing we can't straighten out if we just put our heads together.'

She thought, by the look in his eyes and the sensual smile on his lips, that he was talking about more than just work, and whilst she wasn't sure exactly where they went from here, she really hoped he was.

'I hope so,' she said.

'They're keeping you in for observation but they'll let you out tomorrow morning if you're still okay. They recommend someone stays with you for the next twenty-four hours after that, so it's probably best if you come home to us,' Edward said.

'Thanks, Dad but I'm sure I'll be fine and I'll sleep better in my own bed.'

'Let's see how you are tomorrow,' Fiona said. 'We can discuss it then. Right. I think you should get some rest. Your father and I will be outside if you need us. Come along Edward, Daisy, Robert. I think we should leave her for a while.'

'I am tired and I think I will sleep but please don't hang around here – any of you. I'll be fine. Go home, please.'

It took ten more minutes of debate before Fiona and Edward finally agreed to go home but only on the basis that they'd be back again in a couple of hours. Daisy and Robert felt the same.

'I wonder if you might explain this,' Roddy demanded, the moment Robert entered his office.

He was seated in the chair opposite Robert and he passed him the list that he'd found on the floor.

Robert could tell from his father's tone that he was not at all happy and as he read the list, he could understand why.

'Where did you get this?' he said. 'Who wrote it? I've never seen it before and I can assure you, Dad that at no time have I slept with – or even thought about sleeping with – Sherree. Not that it should actually matter to you. You've dumped her for Mum.'

'That's not the point! It must have been written before then anyway, otherwise it wouldn't say 'to get revenge on his dad', would it? Sherree told me she was staying with Beth on Wednesday. Did she sleep with you instead? It couldn't have been any other night because –'

'I just told you, I did *not* sleep with Sherree. Not on Wednesday night or any other night for that matter.'

'And I just told you, she didn't sleep with me on Wednesday night – so where was she?'

'So ... even though I've told you it wasn't me, you're still convinced it was!'

'That's what this says!' Roddy poked his finger several times at the list. 'What am I supposed to think?'

'You're supposed to listen, Dad! That's what you're supposed to do. And then, you're supposed to believe me – because I'm your son and I wouldn't lie to you.'

'Don't give me that holier than thou look! You told me you were gay and you're not! That was a lie.'

'Why the hell is everyone still going on about me being gay? I didn't lie. You didn't listen. Just like you're not listening now. I *did not* sleep with Sherree and the fact that I'm telling you that should be good enough but as it isn't, I can tell you who did. At least whom I believe did. It was Jenna's boyfriend, Tom! Happy now?'

Roddy blinked several times as Robert scowled at him across the desk.

'Oh!' How do you know that?'

Robert sighed. 'Because I saw Sherree in a wine bar with Beth earlier that evening. Then later, I saw her leaving the wine bar with Tom and believe me, if they weren't going somewhere to have sex, then I'm no judge of human nature. They were all over each other like a rash – and that was in the High Street. Of course, there's a slight chance that, after realising I'd seen her, Sherree said no but frankly, I doubt it and Beth was nowhere to be seen. Who gave you that list?'

Roddy sighed. 'Jenna's boyfriend, you say. Sherree slept with Jenna's boyfriend?'

'At last, you're listening.'

'Well, I'm sorry if I jumped to conclusions, Robert, but when I saw it like that – written in black and white, well ... I thought that ... well, you know what I thought, and this happened before your mother and I ... reconciled, of course.'

Robert nodded. 'I realise that. So you thought I did this before you and I agreed to ... bury the hatchet?'

'Yes.'

'Well I didn't. And quite honestly, if you knew me at all, you'd know I could never do something like that in any event. I mean, what sort of man would sleep with a woman just to get revenge on his father? And what sort of person would think he would, and write a list like that?

Which reminds me. You still haven't said who gave it to you.'

'No one gave it to me, son. I found it in the hall ... when I picked up everything that had fallen out of Jenna's bag. This must belong to her ... and I can only assume ... she wrote it, though Heaven alone knows why.'

'You're completely mad,' Daisy said. 'You do know that, don't you?'

Daisy had popped back to see Jenna around three in the afternoon, and Adam was meeting her there on his way home from work.

'I was angry!' Jenna replied. 'He kept barking orders at me and he was so ... cold.'

'I hate to point this out, but he is your boss. At least, he was. Bosses do tend to give orders. So, do you think he'll take you back? He did say he hoped you'd be with him for many years to come or something like that, so it sounds as if he's forgiven you.'

'Yes. But really, I'm the one who should be doing the forgiving. I mean, I've done nothing wrong.'

'Hmm. Apart from telling everyone he's gay, trying to seduce him, telling him to fuck off, and believing he slept with Sherree, you mean? No, you've done nothing wrong at all.'

'Oh my God ... Sherree!'

'What about Sherree?'

'You know that list we wrote? The reasons why Robert slept with Sherree, one. I've just remembered. It fell out of my handbag and Roddy picked it up. I saw him reading it as I was being stretchered out. Oh God! Oh God! Oh God!'

Daisy sniggered. 'Oh God is right! Although I'm not sure even He can help you. Well, I think we can safely assume that Roddy will ... mention it to Robert. Why on earth did you have it in your handbag?'

'I don't know! I forgot it was there. What am I going to do?'

'I'd suggest emigration, but then you'd just cause mayhem in another country. There's nothing you can do, except – and here's a radical notion. Apologise! Tell him you made a mistake. People make mistakes. He'll probably forgive you. Failing that, just tell him you're an idiot – at least you'd be telling the truth!'

Jenna hung her head. 'How did I get myself into this mess, Daisy?'

'You're in love. Love's a messy business. Of course, you do have one other option.'

'What? Join a convent?'

'They wouldn't have you. No, feign a relapse next time you see him. He's obviously guilt- stricken. If you pretend to be dying, he'll forget all the stupid things you've done, realise he loves you and you can get the priest to marry you and give you the last rites at the same time. Then achieve a miraculous recovery and tell Robert it was the power of his love. That way, he'll never be able to bring it up again, and you'll live happily ever after.'

'Meanwhile, back on planet earth. Don't stand there grinning like a Cheshire cat. Is that really the best you can come up with? Besides, Robert isn't even a tiny bit in love with me, so that wouldn't work.'

'Delivery for you.' A smiling nurse knocked on the half open door and walked in carrying a bouquet of a dozen yellow roses, a box of Claremont Chocolate Lovers, *Diamond Collection* chocolates, a teddy bear-shaped helium balloon and a card. 'Who's a lucky girl then?' the nurse said, handing the card over to Jenna and the chocolates and balloon to Daisy.

'Aww, thanks,' Daisy said, winking.

'I thought flowers were banned,' was the first thing Jenna could think of saying.

'Not in *this* hospital,' the nurse said, 'although we like

199

to keep them away from patients' bedsides. Shall I put them on the windowsill? They all came together so that card will tell you who they're from.'

Jenna opened the card. It was a 'Get Well Soon' card with a dancing black and white cat on the front and inside it read:

Hope you'll soon be back on your feet
Full of life, and dancing.

Beneath that was a handwritten note which read:

I'm so sorry for hurting your arm and anything else. I hope you'll be back with me very soon.

Robert x

Jenna handed the card to Daisy who grinned and said, 'You were saying ...' Then she glanced over to the nurse. 'Excuse me, but what time does the priest do his rounds?'

Robert couldn't believe it. So after thinking he was gay, Jenna now thought he'd slept with Sherree. What on earth had made her think such a thing and why write a list about it? He read the list again and the words, *For revenge on his father; cold hearted, deceitful, bastard; womaniser; he fancied her; purely for the sex,* hit him in the face like a boxing glove on a spring. Well, she certainly had a very low opinion of him.

He went over and over in his mind everything that had happened before Jenna hit her head. She'd looked so happy first thing this morning and he had to admit, he might have treated her badly. But why had she been so happy? She'd spent the evening with Tom, possibly even the night. Was that why?

He thought she'd been telling Tom on the phone that she loved him, but it had been Daisy she was talking to. That didn't mean she didn't love Tom though – that only meant she wasn't speaking to him at that moment.

Okay, Robert thought, he shouldn't have been so cold and sarcastic and he'd obviously upset her. But enough to deserve being called a bastard and told to fuck off? Enough to make her want to resign?

Then, like the fool he was, he'd run after her ...and what does she do? Knee him in the groin. He shifted slightly in his chair. And that still hurt – in more ways than one.

This list, why had she written it? Why had she thought he'd slept with Sherree – and on the same night that he'd held her hair back whilst she threw up, washed her stained clothes, put her to bed, and even kept his hands to himself in spite of her trying to seduce him? And why had she tried to seduce him? She even said she'd loved him – all her life. She was drunk, he knew that, but drunken people usually tell the truth, not lie.

And why had she let him kiss her on Thursday morning and ... kiss him back, if she thought he'd spent the previous night in bed with Sherree? His head swam and he wondered if he were suffering from concussion too. Could you get concussion from being kicked in the balls?

And why, oh why, had he just sent her those flowers, the chocolates and that balloon? Nothing says, 'I think I love you' quite as effectively as that would. And then he realised it. That was the problem. He very possibly, did.

Robert tried to stay away. He'd already made himself look like a lovesick puppy. To turn up at her bedside again just a few hours later would only make things worse. But he had to know. He had to find out exactly what game Jenna was playing.

Through the glass-partitioned wall of her hospital room, he was pleased to see that she was alone. Unfortunately, she also looked as if she were asleep. Oh well, he thought, he was here anyway. He may as well pop in and check on her and return her phone which was still in his shirt pocket. He'd only stay a minute. He had better things to do than sit by her bedside whilst she slept.

201

CHAPTER EIGHTEEN

Jenna opened her eyes and thought she must be dreaming. That was the only explanation for it. Either that or she was having hallucinations. She knew it couldn't possibly be Robert sitting by her bedside, holding her hand and staring at her so ... so ... lovingly.

A nurse was approaching with a cup of tea. Thank heavens for that, Jenna thought, I could murder a cup of tea.

'Here you go, dear,' the nurse said, apparently to Jenna's 'vision'. 'You've been sitting here for nearly an hour. I thought you'd like a nice cup of tea.'

The 'vision' that had been smiling at Jenna, turned to the nurse.

'Don't go!' Jenna said.

She saw his brows crease momentarily and then the smile returned.

'I'm not going anywhere,' he said, squeezing Jenna's hand before letting go and taking the cup from the nurse. 'Thanks for this. You must have read my mind.'

The nurse patted him on the shoulder and smiled at Jenna.

'How about you, young lady? Would you like a nice cup of tea?'

Jenna nodded. The nurse smiled again and left the room. Jenna forced herself to open and shut her eyes several times but each time she opened them, Robert was still there, although the smile was slowly fading.

'Are you okay?' he said, putting his teacup down on the bedside cabinet and standing up and leaning over her. 'Shall I call the doctor?'

Jenna stared up at him and shook her head.

'You're really here?' she asked.

He looked confused. 'Yes. I'm really here. How are you feeling?'

'Much better, thanks. Still a bit achy, but fine. I ... I thought I was dreaming when I woke up and saw you sitting there.'

Robert resumed his seat. 'Good or bad? Dream I mean.'

She smiled. 'Good. Very, very good. Oh, thank you for the flowers – and the balloon – and the chocolates.'

'It was nothing,' he said. 'I didn't know which one you'd prefer so ... I sent all three.'

Jenna noticed that the loving look had gone. His tone was now cool and businesslike.

'The card would have been enough,' she said. 'Did ... did you mean it? That you hoped I'd be back with you soon? Can ... can you forgive me for ... what I called you and for ... resigning?'

She looked into his eyes and they gazed at one another for several seconds before he reached into his pocket.

'That rather depends on this,' he said, handing her a piece of paper.

She knew what it was without even looking at it. It was the list; the list of reasons why Robert would have slept with Sherree.

'Oh,' she said.

'Oh, indeed. An explanation would be nice – if you feel up to it.'

For a split second, she wondered whether Daisy's plan to pretend she was dying might actually work, but overall, she thought Daisy's other suggestion might be preferable.

'I'm so, so sorry, Robert. Unfortunately, I have to admit, I'm an idiot.'

She saw his raised eyebrows, and the midnight blue eyes seemed to be scanning her face, but he didn't speak.

'I ... I seem to jump to all the wrong conclusions, and when I saw Sherree crying, after you'd kissed me, when I thought you were gay, but you said you weren't, and you were annoyed that we'd been discussing it, but I was so happy. Then Sherree said that you'd tell Roddy, for revenge, that she'd spent the whole night – I thought she meant with you, but she didn't. She meant Tom – that you were horrid, but Daisy said you might not be, so we wrote the list. Then I realised I didn't care because I loved you anyway, so I told Tom, who pretended to be nice, but I'm not sure he is. And I wanted to push you onto your chair and climb on top of you, but Roddy and Amelia were there, and then you *were* horrid. I was upset and angry, so I resigned and kicked you in the groin because that's what Mum told me to do, but I never meant to hurt you, really I didn't. Can you forgive me, Robert? I really am sorry.'

Robert's brows had knit tighter together and his eyes seemed to pierce her very soul. She felt a tear trickle down her cheek.

'Well,' he said, reaching over and gently wiping the tear away. 'That explains that, then.'

'So what happened next?' Daisy said.

As soon as she was alone again Jenna had called her and told her about Robert's visit.

'Nothing. Unfortunately, Mum and Dad chose that particular moment to come back and visit me. Robert said he'd 'get out of the way' but he did say that he'd see me on Saturday which is good. Then he smiled – one of those gorgeous, made me go all weak at the knees type of smiles. Then he left.'

'So ... I assume that means you've got your job back.'

'I think so. I also think, but of course I may be wrong, but you don't sit by someone's bed for an hour unless you do – that he may, actually, really like me!'

'Yes, because of course, a dozen yellow roses, a massive box of top quality chocolates and a teddy bear balloon didn't give you any indication of that at all. I've said it before and I'll say it again – Jenna Baker – you're an idiot!'

Jenna didn't have to wait until Saturday to see Robert again. To her surprise, he popped his head in, just an hour or so later, a few minutes after his mother, Amelia had arrived. Amelia was returning the toothbrush and knickers Roddy had picked up from the floor and passed to her to put in her handbag.

'I just thought I'd drop these back to you,' Amelia said, smiling. 'I forgot I had them to be honest. I meant to give them to your mother earlier. How are you feeling?'

'Much better thanks and you needn't have worried about these. I've asked Mum to bring me a few things later.'

'Hi,' Robert said. 'I'm not stopping but I just thought I'd mention that I've spoken to the doctor and he says you can go to the dinner dance tomorrow if you're feeling okay in the morning. Oh! Hi Mum. I didn't know you were here. Is Dad with you?'

Amelia nodded. 'Yes. He's chatting to Edward somewhere. We bumped into him in the corridor. It's just a flying visit. We just wanted to pop in and say hello. Right, I'll leave you then. Look after yourself Jenna and perhaps we'll see you at the dinner dance tomorrow.' She patted Jenna's hand, kissed Robert on the cheek and left.

Robert remained at a slight distance from the bed. 'You mustn't do any dancing though – or anything else energetic for a while ...'

His eyes seemed to focus on something on the bed and Jenna felt herself blushing, realising he was looking at her spare knickers, not that that should have mattered; he'd seen her in her underwear, after all.

'Your mum was just returning my knickers ... I mean ... my toothbrush ... I mean. I should explain –'

'Please don't,' he said. 'My head's still spinning from your last explanation. Well, I should leave you in peace. I

205

just wanted to ask the doctor about the dinner dance and to let you know.'

'Thanks,' she said. 'I was really looking forward to it, especially as the newsletters have gone out and we may get some feedback from some of the wives.'

'Yes,' he said, 'so was I, but not for the same reason. Actually, Jenna, there are a few things I would like to clarify.'

'Oh,' she said.

'Yes. And it would be helpful if you could just answer yes or no, for the time being.' He stepped closer towards her bed. 'Firstly, am I right in believing that you're not going out with Tom? Or anyone else? You're not dating anyone else, I mean.'

Jenna nodded. 'Yes. I mean, no. I'm not dating Tom or anyone else. I suppose I was dating Tom but I'm not now, so no.'

'Good. Not quite yes or no, but we're getting there. Secondly, may I assume that you now know for certain that I am definitely not gay and that I didn't sleep with Sherree? Also that I'm not a cold, vengeful, deceitful bastard and that you don't want me to fuck off?'

Jenna blushed and nodded. 'Yes ... I ... yes and … no, I don't.'

'Wonderful. Thirdly, that you're withdrawing your resignation and coming back to work, although, of course, not until you're fully recovered?

Jenna smiled and nodded. 'Yes, and I'll ... sorry. Yes.'

'Excellent. Fourthly ... now, what was the fourth thing I needed to know?' he said, having reached her bedside. 'Oh yes, I remember.' He sat on the edge of the bed, took her in his arms and kissed her.

Jenna was so surprised that it took her several seconds before she wrapped her arms around him and kissed him back.

When he finally eased himself away from her, his eyes

reflected the passion she knew must be burning in hers and if the room didn't have glass panels, she thought, she'd drag him onto the bed and try to seduce him for a second time.

'Well,' he said, smiling tenderly, 'I think that's all I needed to clarify. Ah! There was one other thing. Will you be my date for the dinner dance? Again, a yes or no will suffice.'

Jenna didn't answer. Instead, she grabbed his tie, pulled him towards her and kissed him in a way that she hoped would make her answer very clear.

'That's enough of that,' Adam said, laughing as he walked into the room. 'There doesn't seem to be much wrong with you, Jenna.'

Robert turned and smiled at Adam. 'I was just about to give her a thorough examination when you walked in. You can't be too careful after a knock on the head.'

'I bet you were,' Adam replied, mockingly. 'Shall I come back later or shall I just round everyone up and we can stand outside and watch?' He winked, approached the bed and gave Jenna a kiss on the cheek. 'Daisy's outside talking to your mum. We were thinking of staying here instead of going to the pub tonight but I suspect your mum would rather we didn't.'

'I expect so too and to be honest, as much as I love you all, I'm feeling really tired. I think I may go to sleep soon.'

'It's all that kissy, huggy stuff.' Adam grinned. 'It always knackers me.'

'What always knackers you?' Daisy said, strolling in. 'Oh, hello Robert.' Her eyes shot to Jenna's face. 'Are we disturbing anything?'

'You should have been here two minutes earlier,' Adam said. 'They were playing doctor and patient.'

'Really!' Daisy beamed at Jenna. 'Just as well it was you then, Adam and not Mrs Baker who is on her way as we speak.'

Robert stood up and a few seconds later, Fiona Baker walked in.

'Good heavens,' she said, grinning, 'it's like Piccadilly Circus in here. Hi darling. Well, I must say, you're looking much better than you were earlier. You've got the colour back in your cheeks.'

'Yes,' Adam said, 'Robert was just saying the same thing. Well, we'll love you and leave you then, Jenna. We'll go to the pub and drink to your good health. Fancy joining us, Robert?'

Robert glanced at Jenna and she smiled at him.

'I'd love to,' he said. 'Jenna, I'll see you tomorrow. Goodbye Mrs Baker. See you tomorrow too. It was good to meet you today even if it was under less than pleasant circumstances.'

Fiona smiled at him. 'It was lovely to meet you too, Robert. I expect I'll see you on Saturday.'

Daisy leant across to Jenna and gave her a big hug. 'Don't worry,' she whispered, 'we'll take good care of him, and I'll call you if I've got anything to report.' She turned to Jenna's mother. 'Bye Mrs Baker. See you tomorrow.'

Fiona waited until everyone had left. She smiled at Jenna and said, 'I may be wrong, but I think young Robert has a bit of a thing for you, darling.'

Jenna was given the all clear at ten o'clock on Saturday morning and told she could go home. Fiona and Edward came to collect her and the doctor confirmed that, whilst she should take things easy and get plenty of rest, he could see no harm in her going to the dinner dance provided that she didn't dance, didn't drink alcohol, went home early and had someone with her for at least, the next twenty-four hours.

Despite the doctor's reassurances, it took Jenna half an hour to get her mum and dad to agree to take her to her

208

own home and another hour to get them to accept that she was going to the dinner dance, whether they liked it or not. It was almost noon before she could finally call Robert and tell him she would be going. She was disappointed to get his voicemail.

'Hi Robert, it's Jenna. I'm just calling to let you know that I can go tonight and I've told Mum and Dad that I'll be going with you. I hope that's okay because you did ask me to be your date but you didn't say whether you'd pick me up or I should meet you there. So will you call me please and let me know, only Mum –' She stopped short as the message timed out. 'I'll have to wait until he calls back,' she said to Fiona.

'Well, I still think you should come with us. We'll be bringing you home anyway, so it seems pointless him coming to get you.'

'Er ... why will you be bringing me home?' Jenna asked. She was hoping Robert might offer to do that.

'Because we'll be staying here the night. You heard the doctor. Someone should be with you for at least twenty-four hours.'

She was rather hoping Robert might offer to do that too. 'I'll be fine, Mum!'

'So you keep saying but I'd never forgive myself if something happened to you.'

Jenna heard her phone ring and answered without looking, thinking it would be Robert.

'Oh it's you, Daisy. Hi.'

'Well don't sound so delighted. I assume you were expecting someone else.'

'Yes. Sorry. How was last night?'

'Good. Robert's really nice. He was telling us all about his hotel business. You didn't tell me he owns a hotel right in the centre of New York City! He said we can all go and stay there sometime.'

'I ... I didn't know he did. I only found out he was in

the business when his mum told me at breakfast the other day. Wow! That must be worth a few quid. I'm surprised he came to Claremont then.'

'That's what I said.'

'I suppose it was because he really wants to change the club.'

'That – and to get away from his ex. Has ... has he said anything else to you about that?'

'No. All I know about it is what I told you on Tuesday night. That she cheated, he finished it and she won't stop calling him. Why? Did he say anything to you?'

'Not really, but you know me. I asked if he'd had anyone special in New York and he said he'd been in a long-term relationship but it had ended several months ago. Naturally, I pushed for details and he said that it ended badly and that was one of the reasons he came here – to put distance between them. Apparently, she kept turning up on his doorstep at all hours of the day and night. She sounds like a bit of a nutter to me. She's seeing a therapist. Mind you, everyone has a shrink in New York, don't they, so I suppose that doesn't mean much. Even so, to keep turning up like that. I'd find that rather worrying. It's a good thing she's over there and not over here.'

'That's true, I suppose. Did he say anything else?'

'Only that he ... and this bit I didn't like and I'm not sure if you knew so I wasn't sure whether I should say anything but I think you should know, although you may already and –'

'Daisy! What? Just tell me!'

'Well, he said that he was hoping that, by the time he goes back, she'll have got the message and moved on to someone else. Did ... did you know that he's not planning on staying here? That he's going back to New York. Jenna? Jenna, are you still there?'

'I'm still here. No. I had absolutely no idea.'

Daisy's news had come as a complete surprise and Jenna's mood changed instantly. One minute she had been looking forward to the dinner dance and her 'date' with Robert with joyful anticipation of a possibly, very bright future; the next, she was seeing herself in floods of tears, waving him goodbye at the airport.

'I think I may go and lie down for a while, if you don't mind, Mum,' she said.

'Are you all right? You see, this is what I mean. You mustn't overdo things and –'

'I'm fine, Mum. I just want to have a lie down now so that I feel ... refreshed for tonight. That's all. You really don't have to stay you know I –'

'I don't want to hear another word about it, darling. We're staying. You go and get some rest and I'll bring you up a nice cup of tea in a couple of hours.'

There was no point in arguing, Jenna realised, so she made her way upstairs. Her mind was reeling as to why it hadn't even occurred to her that Robert might go back to New York.

Robert collapsed onto his chair, put his feet up on his desk and raked his hand through his hair. He was exhausted – and it was only one o'clock.

He had expected opposition from his father to the changes he was making – although he'd even underestimated how badly Roddy would take it. He accepted that if it hadn't been for Amelia's intervention, things would not be on such an amicable footing now with his Dad. He'd also expected opposition from Edward and some of the club members, but he hadn't, for one minute, expected this.

Since eight o' clock that morning he'd been lectured to, shouted at, ignored by, dragged into heated debates with, hugged by, thanked by or threatened with legal action by, nearly every member of Green Miles Golf Club – and their

211

wives.

Jenna's newsletter had been received and had clearly been the subject of a great deal of discussion over breakfast tables throughout Claremont and the surrounding countryside.

The phones had not stopped ringing. Members had stormed into the club demanding to speak to Roddy or Robert or 'this Jenna Baker' all morning. Some had brought their wives or partners, eager to find out more about the 'Golf Widows' Club' as they were all calling it, ignoring the 'Green Miles' part altogether. Some said they would never bring their wives and if it weren't for the fact that the Green Miles course was one of the best in the country, they would seriously think about terminating their membership. Some just wanted to know when the floodlights were being installed or where the children's course would be. No one, it seemed, had just read it and ignored it or even just read it and decided to wait and see how things progressed.

'Well,' Roddy said, dropping onto the chair opposite his son. 'I think you can safely say that the newsletter got a reaction.'

Robert smirked. 'Really, Dad? I hadn't noticed.'

Roddy grinned. 'Not quite what you were expecting, I take it.'

'To be honest, I wasn't really sure what I was expecting but no, I wasn't expecting to meet or talk to nearly every member, his wife, his child, his relatives – even his dog, within a space of just a few hours this morning.'

'A dog! You're not telling me someone actually had the audacity to bring a dog onto Green Miles' property, are you? That is strictly against club rules! Who was it?'

Robert sniggered. 'An offence punishable by death, no doubt. Don't worry. No one brought a dog with them but I did have to listen to one barking rather loudly throughout a five-minute conversation with someone. I'm still not sure

212

who was more upset – me, the dog or the caller, but as I've already forgotten who it was, it obviously wasn't me.'

'I thought you might need this,' Beth said, tapping on the open door and carrying in a tray of coffee and sandwiches. 'The restaurant is packed and we're closing it at two to get ready for the dinner dance tonight. Is this okay or do you want to go down and have a proper lunch?'

'No, this is perfect, Beth,' Roddy said. 'I'm not sure we could face the hordes, to be honest.' He grinned at Robert. 'This is fine with you, son, isn't it?'

'Absolutely! And thanks Beth. You're a life saver. The restaurant's packed, you say. Well, at least we're making money from all this furore then. Are you all coping okay? Do you need a hand?'

'We're fine thanks, Mr Miles. Everyone is too busy talking about the changes to worry about the fact that it's taking longer than usual to get the food orders out.'

'Please call me Robert. Tell me, Beth. What did you think about the changes when I told all the staff what we had planned?'

Beth shot a glance at Roddy.

'Don't worry about me,' he said. 'I've come to terms with them now and I must admit that some of them, I rather like.' He glanced across at Robert. 'Not all, mind you, Robert, but some.'

'Well,' Beth said. 'I feel the same ... I think. I loved things the way they were but I also like the idea of involving wives and children ... and allowing women members. My mum has always wanted to play with Dad but ... ooh! I didn't mean play with Dad, I meant, play golf with Dad.'

Beth giggled and Robert waited for his father to make some remark about Beth being 'cheeky' but he didn't.

'We know what you mean,' Robert said. 'We'll look forward to welcoming your mother as a member then.'

'Thank you,' Beth said. 'She's so excited and she's

joining the Golf Widows' Club too, even though she won't actually be a golf widow if she's a member. Oh! Can she do that? Join the golf club and join the Golf Widows' Club as well?'

'I have no idea, Beth,' Robert said. 'I assume she can. I'll have to ask Jenna. It was her brainchild. Oh! Speaking of Jenna, I haven't called her yet and I said I would. Excuse me.'

He jumped up from his chair and headed towards Jenna's office, passing Beth in the doorway and dialling Jenna's number as he went.

'Jenna's phone,' Fiona Baker said.

'Oh. Hello Mrs Baker. It's Robert, Robert Miles. How are you? Is Jenna all right?'

'Hello, Robert. I'm fine thanks and so is Jenna. She's upstairs asleep right now though. May I give her a message? She tells me you're taking her to the dinner dance tonight. I believe she was wondering whether you were going to come and pick her up, although there's really no need. Her father and I are more than happy to do so and I expect you've got a hundred and one things to be getting on with. We'll be bringing her home too because we'll be staying here, so it just seems sensible for us to take her both ways.'

Robert smiled, although he felt a little disappointed. Jenna's mother also believed in long and complicated answers, it seemed, but he was rather hoping that he'd be the one taking Jenna home ... and possibly staying the night. He hadn't planned to make mad, passionate love to her, of course; the doctor had said that Jenna mustn't do anything energetic and when they did make love for the first time, Robert hoped it would be very energetic ... for both of them. He had hoped though to spend the night kissing and cuddling and maybe just a little bit more. He coughed to bring his mind back from the images already flashing before his eyes.

'Er ... I was rather hoping to escort Jenna both to and from the dinner dance actually, if that would be okay with you, Mrs Baker. You see, I asked Jenna to be my date tonight and, well, a date's not really a date unless one calls for their date and then escorts them home again, is it?'

'Oh! Well ... um ... when you put it like that, I suppose not. But the doctor said someone should be with her for the next twenty-four hours, at least, so her father and I were planning to spend the night here anyway so ... Oh! Er ... is ... is this your first date?'

Robert grinned to himself. 'Our first real date, yes,' he said. 'But I'm more than happy to stay the night, and obviously sleep in the spare room, in the same way that you and Edward were intending to, if that meets with yours and Jenna's approval, of course. I totally agree that someone should be on hand in case there are any ... complications. Not that there will be, I'm sure. I can assure you, Mrs Baker, my intentions are honourable. I could bring along my lap top and possibly get on with some work during the ... quiet hours.'

'Er ... well ...'

'Why don't you ask Jenna to give me a call when she wakes up and we can discuss it? Obviously, if she'd rather you stayed with her then I'll be perfectly happy to just take her home and kiss her goodnight. After all, that was my intention, so it really makes no difference, as far as I'm concerned. I just thought it would be more comfortable. It is only a single bed in the spare room, I believe. Have a chat amongst yourselves and let me know. I'll fit in with whatever's most convenient to you.'

'Well, that's awfully kind of you Robert. We'll do that. I'll get Jenna to call you later. Good bye.'

Robert strolled back into his office with a grin on his face. Unless he was very much mistaken, he'd be spending the night at Jenna's. His grin broadened – he'd better take his toothbrush ... and a spare pair of underpants!

215

CHAPTER NINETEEN

Jenna was pleased with the way she looked when she checked her reflection in the full-length mirror at seven o' clock that evening. She was also pleased that, after a great deal of discussion, her parents had finally, albeit a little reluctantly, agreed that it made sense for Robert to stay the night instead of them.

Edward made a few grumbling noises about men and women alone at night, under the same roof, after a dance and that he wasn't sure it was appropriate. Jenna gently pointed out that she was thirty years old and she did have her own house, so it was just as well she had suffered concussion. At least he could be sure that Robert wouldn't try to take advantage of a vulnerable woman, whereas, if she'd been fit and well and gone to the dance as his date ... She hadn't needed to say anything further.

She called Robert to tell him but got his voicemail. Later, she had a voicemail from Robert when she'd been on the phone to Daisy so they hadn't actually spoken at all until he came to pick her up at a few minutes after seven.

'Wow!' he said when she opened the door.

Jenna could tell he was impressed. His eyes lingered for a few seconds at her bare shoulders and the embellished bust of her midnight blue chiffon evening gown which gave just a hint of her cleavage then swept down the full length of her body, travelling back up by way of the long split on the right side from the hem to just short of her hip where a fine metallic thread, lace-up detail was tied in a tiny bow.

'And I do mean, wow! he exclaimed.

'Wow yourself!' she said, relishing the sight of him in his single button, black dinner jacket, matching trousers and white dress shirt. The midnight blue and black, fine swirl patterned bow tie and matching cummerbund were almost the same colour as his eyes.

'I almost wish we could stay here,' he said, 'and that I could ... undress you and put you to bed.' He grinned wickedly at her. 'But we can't, so we'd better go before I say "to hell with it" and renege on my duties and do just that.'

'Aren't you forgetting something? I've suffered a concussion.'

'I'll be very gentle,' he said, slipping his arm around her waist and easing her towards him.

'My mother warned me that this might happen,' Jenna said, 'although I believe she thought it more likely to occur at the end of the evening, not the beginning.'

He smiled and leant forward to kiss her.

'And you do remember what happened the last time my mother warned me of something, don't you?' she said, teasingly as his mouth was just inches from hers.

His eyes held hers; he was so close that she could feel his warm breath on her skin and it sent shivers down her spine. Before she realised what was happening, he'd spun her around and pinned her to the wall with his body, her legs held firmly in place by his.

'I'm not sure I'll ever forget it,' he whispered into her ear.

His mouth kissed its way down her neck and back up again, across to her nose and her lips. His lips brushed hers before covering them with his mouth in a soft, slow, lingering kiss.

Jenna was glad he had her tenderly pinned against the wall; she was sure she would have slid down it if he hadn't because her legs felt so weak, she could hardly stand up. She wrapped her arms around his neck as an added support.

'So that's why I've been so busy all day,' Robert said

when they were driving towards the club fifteen minutes later and he was telling her about the response to her newsletter. 'It seems you can arouse strong emotions in everyone at the club – not just me.'

She blushed and then grinned at him wantonly. 'But I don't think I rouse quite the same emotions in them, or quite such strong ones,' she said, provocatively sliding her fingers across his thigh.

He tapped her fingers with his left hand, grabbed them, pulled them to his lips and kissed them. He then placed them firmly in her lap.

'Behave yourself, Miss Baker,' he said, 'at least until I get you home tonight. You seem to be forgetting that I'm the boss in this relationship.'

He winked at her and she smiled.

'And you seem to be forgetting that I've suffered a concussion.'

'So you keep saying,' he said, 'but the only thing you seemed to be suffering from a few minutes ago, was wandering hands.'

'You didn't complain at the time,' she said 'and I only offered to ... rub it better.' She glanced across at him from under her lashes.

He shifted a little in his seat and glanced round at her.

'Don't give me that innocent look, miss. You were doing a great deal more than that and you know it. If we hadn't been late already and I could have spent another five minutes, I'd have given you "rub it better" – make no mistake.'

'Only five minutes! You are going to be staying the *whole* night, aren't you? What on earth will we do for the other eight hours or so?'

His grin spread across his face. 'I don't know about you,' he said, 'but as I told your mother, I've brought along my laptop.'

'Speaking of laptops,' she said, 'I think we should

sneak up to your office and ... give your chair some attention.'

His head shot round and he looked her full in the face. 'Concussion indeed! I've a good mind to put you across my knee and give you a spanking.'

She sighed and beamed at him. 'Sorry Mr Miles ... sir ... but I'm not really into pain, I'm afraid. You're welcome to put me across your knee and do anything else though. Ah, here we are, back at the grindstone.'

Robert drove through the open gates of Green Miles Golf Course and headed up the long drive.

'I've a good mind to do exactly that – right here, right now,' he said, 'but I think your newsletter and my planned changes have given everyone here enough to talk about already. I'll just say this though. You wait until I get you home, my girl. You'll be begging me for mercy.'

He got out of the car, walked around to the passenger door, opened it and helped Jenna out but he didn't step back so she was caught in the space between Robert and the body of the car as she stood up.

Their bodies pressed against one another and she looked up into his eyes. 'Really?' she said. 'If you only take five minutes, I'll certainly be begging for something. Oh! Hi Mum and Dad.'

She waved across at her parents who had clearly arrived just minutes before them and were standing by their car.

Robert grinned at her and stepped aside. 'You'll pay for that too,' he said, gently tapping her on her bottom as she passed by.

'I think tonight went very well indeed,' Roddy said, 'all things considered.'

It was almost midnight and he was sitting at one of the tables with Amelia, Robert, Jenna, Edward and Fiona. They were drinking champagne, apart from Jenna because

219

she wasn't allowed alcohol.

'Thanks to you and Mum, and Fiona and Edward. Not forgetting Jenna, of course.' Robert said. 'When we arrived tonight, I think some of the members were still ready to have me hung, drawn and quartered for having the temerity to suggest that Green Miles needed to change. If you hadn't said what you did in your pre-dinner speech and you too, Edward, when you said you were handing over the captaincy to someone younger, I believe I might now be swinging from that ancient oak tree in the middle of the seventh fairway.'

Roddy grinned. 'They can't get to the tree, my boy. The holly bush is in the way, and believe me, no one will dare to tamper with that holly bush – not even you.'

'I do believe you. I tried once – to get to the tree I mean, when I was a young boy. I learnt my lesson. Seriously though, Dad, it was really good of you to say that you wholeheartedly support my vision for the future of the club, especially as we all know that's not completely true. Having your backing made all the naysayers think twice.'

'That's because they know that if I agree with it, there's really no point in arguing. They might have been prepared to go into battle with one Miles, but two, never. Besides, I think like me, once they'd had a chance to have a look at the rough plans you've had drawn up and realise that many of them will actually improve the club, they saw reason.'

'Personally', Fiona said, 'I think a lot of the wives and partners helped bring many of them round. All the women I've spoken to had nothing but good things to say about the changes.'

'And we've got Jenna to thank for that,' Robert said. 'Your idea of the Golf Widows' Club was brilliant, Jenna. All the wives seem really keen to get involved.'

'That's very true,' Edward said. 'And when a man's

wife is happy then the man is happy ... and speaking personally, I'm very happy.'

He smiled lovingly at Fiona. She smiled back, leant over and kissed him.

'Speaking of wives,' Roddy said, taking Amelia's hand in his, sliding his chair back and getting down on one knee. 'Will you marry me, Amelia? I know I am one of the most stubborn, pigheaded and sometimes, ridiculous, sixty-year-old men alive but if you marry me you'll also, without question, make me the proudest, happiest and luckiest one. I know we joked about it but I'm serious. I've spent the last eighteen years of my life without you by my side. I don't want to spend another day without you. Not one day. Please say yes.'

'Yes, Roddy!' Amelia said, little pearls of joyful tears rolling down her cheeks. 'Yes, yes, yes!'

She flung herself into his arms and neither of them noticed that everyone at their table and all those left in the room were cheering and clapping and raising their glasses in a toast to the happy couple.

'I can't believe how tonight ended,' Jenna said as she and Robert got into his car. 'Did you have any idea that your dad was going to propose?'

Robert shook his head. 'None at all, although he did mention they'd discussed it. And ... tonight hasn't ended ... yet,' he said, giving her a devilish smile.

'Well ... technically it's now tomorrow as it's gone midnight.'

'And my car hasn't turned into a pumpkin,' he said with a grin. 'But I do have a pumpkin in my car. I see your dad still can't stop calling you pumpkin, although you didn't seem to mind tonight.'

Jenna smiled. 'He's trying but after all these years, I feel it's probably a losing battle. To be quite honest, until this week, the only time he's called me Jenna is when he's been cross with me, or very serious about something, so I think, on the whole, I prefer pumpkin. I still can't believe so much has happened in just one week. This time last week, I had no idea you were even back in this country, let alone that I'd be working for you and ... going on a date with you.'

'And spending the night with me. Well five minutes at least. After that, I'll be searching for suppliers of laughing golf balls, on my laptop.'

Jenna glanced at him out of the corner of her eye. She had been dreaming of this night for most of her life, at some time or another but now that it was here, now that she knew she was actually going to go to bed with Robert Miles, she was more than a little terrified.

Robert seemed to sense it. 'Jenna, you do realise I'm joking, don't you? About spending the night with me, I mean. Nothing's going to happen tonight, well ... not much anyway. All I want to do is hold you and kiss you and ... talk to you.'

Jenna's head shot up and her eyes met his. She could see he was serious.

'Are you sure you're not gay?' she said, not entirely sure she was joking.

He smiled. 'Absolutely, believe me, in my head I'm doing things ... we're doing things that would rid you of that idea for ever. I'm just following doctors' orders and the doctor said "nothing energetic".'

'Doctors! What do they know? Anyone would think they did years of training to get where they are. Anyway, they're always saying exercise is good for you.'

'I'm flattered that you can't wait to have your wicked way with me, Jenna and I expect I'll have to spend most of the night under a cold shower but all joking aside, the doctor said "no" and "no" it is. I can wait if you can.'

'I've been waiting for eighteen years,' Jenna said. 'I guess I can wait for another twenty-four hours or so.'

'Eighteen years?'

'Oh! Did I just say that out loud? Maybe I am concussed.'

'You said something about that before. About my party or something. I ... I think you even said I kissed you. Is that true?'

She put her hands up to her heart in a mocking gesture. 'Yes. And I'm heartbroken that you don't remember. Don't worry, I'm joking.' She wasn't joking but she had no intention of telling him that.

'Why did I kiss you?'

'Oh, thanks very much. And there's no need to sound quite so surprised that you did.'

'Sorry,' he said and laughed. 'I think I told you I was rather drunk that day. Mum and Dad were rowing again and ... well, so tell me. How did it happen?'

She sighed deeply. 'To be honest, I'm not totally sure. One minute I was walking along looking up at the sky and the trees, and the next, I was face to face with you. Well, not face to face exactly, you were tall for your age and I ... wasn't. We just looked at each other, smiled and ... the next thing I remember is being in your arms and you kissing me.'

His head shot round. 'Really? Wow. That's like love at first sight.'

'Yes. Except it wasn't the first time we'd seen each other, and you couldn't remember a thing about it. What's more, you never so much as looked at me for the rest of the afternoon. But apart from that, it was exactly like love at first sight. Someone called you and said your mum wanted you and you let me go as quickly as you'd grabbed me and ran off. I think, to be fair, you left not long afterwards.'

'Now fate has thrown us back together,' he said.

'Yes and that would sound very romantic if you weren't grinning from ear to ear. You too, can have a

223

concussion you know. Believe me, it would be no trouble. No trouble at all.'

They arrived at Jenna's, and Robert, still grinning, took Jenna's hand in his as they walked to her door. Neither of them spoke as they entered the hall. Jenna threw her bag on the hall table nearby.

'Would you like coffee?' she asked, feeling like a schoolgirl face to face with her idol.

He nodded. 'Okay. Shall I make it? I remember where it is from the other night.'

'I don't remember you making coffee,' she said.

'You don't remember anything from that night ... so you say. I made coffee after I put you to bed. I ... wanted to hang around a bit in case ... well, in case you needed anything. I stayed for about half an hour but when I checked, you were fast asleep so I let myself out.'

'Oh. Er ... I can make it. You sit down and relax.'

'Actually,' he said, reaching out again for her hand. 'I don't want coffee, I want you.'

He pulled her gently into his arms and kissed her deeply and longingly. Finally, he took her hand in his and led her towards the stairs.

'I thought you said we couldn't,' Jenna said, every fibre of her being tingling with excitement. 'The doctor told you "nothing energetic", you said.'

'Doctors! What do they know?' He winked at her. 'Besides, he just said you mustn't do anything energetic. He didn't say I couldn't. But we're not going to anyway.'

They reached the foot of the stairs and he turned and pulled her to him.

'Oh, what are we going to do then?' she said, staring up into his eyes.

'You're not going to do anything. I am. I'm going to undress you, very, very slowly and I'm going to ease you down onto the bed and lie down beside you. Then I'm going to give you a thorough external examination, which

224

will involve kissing and caressing every inch of you and then I'm going to hold you in my arms until you're asleep. Then I'm going to go and have the longest, coldest, shower in the history of man.' He swept her up into his arms. 'Unless, of course, you'd rather I searched for laughing golf balls. It's your choice.'

'Don't ask me,' she said, 'I'm still thinking about you undressing me and kissing me and ... I think my head's already exploded.'

Jenna couldn't decide if she were in heaven or in hell. Robert was doing exactly what he said he would do – nothing more, nothing less.

The feel of his fingers loosening the metallic thread tie fastening at the back of her dress whilst he held her in his arms and kissed her; the swoosh of chiffon as her dress slid slowly to the floor followed, minutes later, by her strapless bra. The thrill of his hands gliding over her body, caressing her breasts, replaced by his mouth as he kissed and licked and stroked his way down to her tummy, then swept her up in his arms again and gently lay her on the bed. He lay down beside her and kissed her again – a long, lingering kiss. His agile fingers traced excruciatingly intricate patterns around her nipples and down the length of her torso, hovering at her black lace panties. They teased their way over the gossamer material and … slowly, so, so slowly, removed the final barrier between her and complete nakedness.

She gasped as his fingers traced their way up her quivering legs, over her tummy and fondled her breasts and his mouth teased hers with soft wet kisses. Then he eased away from her and his eyes took in all that his hands had explored.

'You're so beautiful,' he said, his voice crackling with emotion and his eyes alive with pent-up desire. 'You have no idea how much I want you, how much I want my fingers to explore every inch of you, how much I want to be inside you. I almost wish I hadn't touched you, hadn't seen you like this.'

His kiss was so deep, so passionate, so exciting it made Jenna's head spin and she moaned his name when he finally eased away from her.

'Robert, I want to see you too. I want to see what I can't have tonight. I want to touch and kiss and stroke everything my eyes take in. I want to feel your muscles tense and your heart pound. I want you to experience the agonising pleasure you're giving me.'

He watched her nimble fingers undo the buttons of his shirt and coax it off his shoulders, and closed his eyes as she unzipped his trousers, moaning her name as she slid her hand inside. He lifted his hips as she removed his trousers and pants and teased off his socks. His fingers gripped the duvet as her tongue traced a line the full length of his long leg and over his taut stomach. He groaned and caught her hair in his fingers as her mouth and tongue teased his nipples. He couldn't take any more.

He wrapped his arms around her and rolled her onto her back, his body pressed against hers.

'Stop,' he said his voice ridden with desire. 'I can't take this. There are limits to my self-restraint. I can only endure so much before I ignore what the doctor said – and we reached that the moment you touched me. I'm hanging on by a thread here and it's at breaking point.'

'I don't care what he said. I'm fine. More than fine. No headache, no memory problems and the only dizziness and blurred vision I'm having is caused by you, your fingers, your kisses. I want more. I *need* more.'

She slid her hand down his stomach but he caught it in his.

'Jenna, I'm serious. Deadly serious. I thought I could do this. I thought I could restrain myself but I can't. Not unless we stop now. Even one more kiss will send me over the edge and once I'm there, I won't be able to drag myself back. I knew it would be hard but this is agony and if we don't stop now, my head will explode, not yours.'

She smiled up at him, her heart pounding, her breath coming in short gasps of excitement.

'Speaking of hard,' she said and she raised her head and kissed him, wrapping her arms around his neck and pulling him down to her. She couldn't care less what the doctor said.

CHAPTER TWENTY

Jenna opened her eyes, stretched like a contented cat and reached out for Robert but he wasn't there. She sat bolt upright. There was no way last night wasn't real; no way she could have imagined all the wonderful, thrilling, exhilarating sensations she'd experienced over the course of several hours. Not even her imagination could conjure up images that vivid, that intense.

Her eyes frantically scanned the room. The curtains were still drawn but the sun poked through between the curtain rings and the rail, providing shards of light, one of which was clearly sent from heaven, she thought, because it shone upon what to her, was a truly heavenly sight. Her dress and underwear were draped neatly on the back of her dressing table chair, along with Robert's still crisp, white evening shirt.

Then she heard him singing. It seemed to be coming from the kitchen. She fell back against the pillow, tossed the duvet to one side exposing her naked body to the dappled sunlight and kicked her legs in excited circles in the air. Not only had she definitely *not* imagined that wonderful, magnificent, spectacular night ... but Robert was still here. She glanced at her bedside clock. It was still early.

She heard him making his way upstairs and she positioned herself seductively, she hoped, on the bed. By the look in his eyes as he came into the room – she clearly had.

'I've got to go to the club,' Robert said, some considerable time later. 'Don't look at me like that. Some of us have got work to do, Miss Baker.'

He kissed her tenderly and jumped out of bed, pulling

his clothes on and smiling wickedly.

'But it's Sunday,' she said, pouting.

He came back and kissed her on her forehead. 'I know it's Sunday but the club is open seven days a week, three hundred and sixty-five days a year. Yes, even Christmas Day. Why anyone would want to play golf on Christmas Day is beyond me but then again, people go for a walk after Christmas dinner and golf is a bit like going for a long walk. God, I'm waffling! All that sex has addled my brain ... and not just my brain.' He smiled down at her. 'I'll only be a couple of hours, I promise. Then let's go out for Sunday lunch – if you're feeling up to it.'

'Oh I'm feeling up to it,' she said, pulling him down to kiss her. 'Exercise is good for you. The doctors are right about that.'

He grinned at her. 'I'm not so sure. I'm feeling absolutely one hundred and one per cent knackered. You get some sleep, and I'll see you, definitely, no later than twelve-thirty. Bye.'

He raced to the door, took one last look at her and let out a heavy sigh. He then blew her a kiss as he dashed down the stairs and out of the door.

She rolled over and clutched the duvet to her, glancing at the clock. It was still only nine 'o clock.

'I wonder if Daisy will be up yet,' she said out loud. She shrugged, and dialled her number anyway.

Robert couldn't remember ever feeling this good. Last night had been even better than he imagined – and he'd imagined plenty. In fact, he seemed to have been unable to think of little else since he'd first laid eyes on the sensational Jenna Baker. He realised that Monday hadn't been the first time he'd laid eyes on her. They'd met before and apparently, although he still couldn't remember it, he'd pulled her into his arms and kissed her.

He smiled to himself. Perhaps fate had brought them

back together. He'd joked about it last night and he didn't really believe in that stuff – but look at his mum and dad. They'd fallen in love the moment they'd laid eyes on one another and despite circumstances conspiring to pull them apart, within minutes of seeing one another again, after eighteen years, they were in love again, possibly even more so than the first time.

He sauntered into the restaurant, humming the 1812 overture, smiling at the thought of how that had come into his head. He'd just ask Beth if he could have some toast and coffee sent up to his office where he'd get a few urgent things done and leave earlier than he'd planned. He'd go back and see if Jenna had got up by then – and part of him, sincerely hoped she hadn't.

'Good morning, Robert. You're looking pretty pleased with yourself. Good night was it?'

Robert's head shot round to the woman sitting at a table near the window and he stopped in his tracks.

'Shit!' he said, the smile draining from his face. 'What the fuck are you doing here, Lou?'

Her eyes flashed with anger. 'I was hoping for a warmer welcome but never mind. How are you, Robert? Have you missed me? I can't say I like what you've done with the place. Looks like quite a party. I'm surprised I wasn't invited.'

Robert glanced around at the remnants from the dinner dance, which were being cleared as she spoke.

'It was. You weren't. You're still not. I'm beginning to feel as if you're stalking me, Lou, and there are laws against that sort of thing, you know. I think I've been more than tolerant but this is verging on crazy and, I would strongly suggest you leave. That means right now, Lou.'

His voice was hard and cold and his eyes held a look of murder in them.

'Robert, sweetie. There's no need for all this. I've said

230

I'm sorry. How many more times do I have to say it before you take me back? I'm getting a bit tired of this game, to tell you the truth. Playing hard to get is one thing but this is getting silly.'

Robert marched over to her, yanked her to her feet and dragged her from the restaurant. Several pairs of eyes stared after them.

'Not as tired as I am, Lou, believe me. I don't know what I have to do to get through to you. I will never take you back. Never. Not even when hell freezes over, and I'm beginning to think that happened the day I met you. This has gone on for far too long. You seriously need help Lou. Serious help. Full-time professional care, for a start.'

'Ooh, Robert! You're so strong. Where are you taking me, darling?'

Robert didn't answer but Beth and the rest of the catering staff watched as he dragged the almost manically laughing woman, up the stairs towards his office.

Jenna couldn't sleep in spite of the fact that she too, was exhausted after the night she and Robert had spent together. She'd told Daisy most, but not all, of the things they'd done although not in specific detail. No matter how close your friends are, some things need to be left unsaid and some things don't need to be said anyway if your friends know you well enough, and Jenna had no doubt that Daisy knew her very well indeed.

All Jenna could think about was Robert. She glanced at the clock, saw it was still only nine-thirty and made a decision. She leapt out of bed, all thoughts of her concussion gone for good. She showered, dressed and was in a cab on her way to Green Miles Golf Club within the space of twenty minutes.

She ran up the stairs and pushed open the door to his office, only realising it had been shut when her eyes focused on the sight before them.

Robert was leaning over a scantily clad woman whom he had pinned to his chair with his hands and it appeared, one knee. His shirt was torn open and his hair dishevelled. He was clearly panting for breath and the woman, whom Jenna could see was stunningly beautiful, was laughing coquettishly up at him.

Two pairs of eyes shot to look at Jenna's face. The woman's eyes narrowed, and Robert's opened wide in horror, mirroring Jenna's expression to perfection.

'Jenna!' Robert said.

'Don't tell me she's your new little tart, Robert. I forgave you once but you can't keep cheating on me. I won't –'

'Jenna. It's not what you think,' he said. 'This –'

Jenna didn't wait for an explanation. She turned and ran, tears streaming down her face. She could hear Robert calling her name but he didn't come after her and as she ran, all she could think was that Robert was just like his father after all.

'Shit, Jenna!' were Daisy's first words when Jenna sobbed down the phone, telling her the latest episode in the drama of her love life.

'I can't believe it, Daisy! I really can't believe it. How could he?'

'I can't believe it either. I'm coming to get you, right now. Where are you? Don't tell me – you're in the woods.'

'In the woods! No, I'm not in the woods. Why would I be in the woods? I'm ...' She searched around her with her eyes. She wasn't sure where she was. 'Oh, I am in the woods! I'm heading towards the drive right this minute.'

'Okay. I'll be there in five minutes,' Daisy said.

She was there in four and a half.

'So, let me get this straight,' Daisy said as Jenna got in the car. 'He's just spent virtually the entire night – and morning – making mad, passionate love with you and then he goes to his office, pins some total stranger to his chair and is about to climb on top of her when you walk in.'

'That's right. I just can't believe it.'

'I *don't* believe it. Are you sure that is what you saw?'

'Yes! She's probably one of the golf widows and Robert intends to make the club more than just family friendly. You should have seen some of those women, Daisy. They were all over him at the dinner dance. I bet last night, he arranged to meet her there this morning. That's why he was so keen to go into the office.'

'Can you hear yourself, Jenna? Really? Is that what you think?'

Jenna shook her head. 'I don't know. Last night he seemed so ... well, almost besotted with me and yet ...'

'And yet you are an idiot. Why didn't you stay and ask for an explanation there and then. At least that way you'd know?'

'I was in a state of shock! I was hurt, upset. I ... I don't know. After everything else that's happened this week, after everything I thought about him was wrong and then this.'

'I think you may have hit the nail on the head, honey. Everything you thought about him was wrong. Are you absolutely certain you're not wrong about this too?'

'I ... well, I ...'

'Did he look as if he were enjoying himself – before he saw you, I mean? Was he laughing too, or was it just her? Was ...?

Daisy met Jenna's eyes and simultaneously they said, 'Lou!'

'It can't be,' Daisy said.

'It could be. Perhaps he was holding her down because she was trying to hurt him or something. His shirt was torn. Perhaps she was laughing because she likes violence. Some women are into that sort of thing, aren't they?'

Daisy nodded.

'Perhaps. Perhaps that's why he looked so upset. Not because I'd caught him doing something but because he *was, genuinely,* upset.'

'Well I'd be upset if I had a stalker and she was in my office, although it would be a 'he' not a 'she', if it were me being stalked, although –'

'Daisy!'

'Sorry. Anyway, I think we may just have solved this latest dilemma and without even leaving the driveway! Do you want to go to the pub and write a list of options or shall I just drop you back at the club and you can go and ask him?'

'The pub, I think. I could use a drink.'

Robert was livid. He had never hit a woman in his life but he was coming very close to it with Lou. He let her go when Jenna rushed out of his office as his instinct was to go after Jenna, not restrain Lou but Lou had jumped up and lashed out at him. It had taken all his strength to stop her causing either him, or herself, serious harm.

He had no idea what to do next so he yelled at the top of his lungs for someone to help and when a startled Beth appeared at his door, he asked her to call his father and to stay with him so that he at least had a witness in case Lou did something even crazier. It was as if she had had a complete breakdown. He'd never seen anything like it before.

Roddy and Amelia arrived just a few minutes later. They'd been on their way to the club when Beth called and were astonished when they discovered what happening.

'I know someone who can help,' Roddy said, dialling a number. 'I've only ever seen something like this once before and that was a chap in the RAF. He had a nervous breakdown. We'll get her admitted to a local rehab centre a few miles from here. The owner's a friend and an excellent doctor. He'll know just what to do.'

Roddy was right. Dr Phillips did know exactly what to do. He gave Lou a mild sedative; got the details of her doctor and therapist from Robert, called them both and told them that in his opinion she had had a breakdown and that he was admitting her to his centre. They called her parents who called Dr Phillips back and gave immediate consent, saying they would get the next flight over. Dr Phillips then led a decidedly calmer Lou out to a waiting, private ambulance.

The entire process took less than half an hour and Robert collapsed in his chair very shaken but very, very relieved.

'I can't believe what has just happened,' he said. 'One minute I was happily thinking of Jenna, the next – Jenna!' He leapt from his seat. 'I must find Jenna.'

'We saw that friend of hers picking her up half way down the drive as we were coming in,' Roddy said. 'What's the girl's name? Daisy or something? What's happened? Was Jenna caught up in all this?'

'What you need to do is sit down and get those scratches seen to, Robert,' Amelia said 'and a stiff brandy wouldn't do any harm. Roddy will get you one.'

'I'm fine,' Robert said. 'I need to find Jenna and explain. She ... she came in and saw – well, thought she saw, me, in what could have seemed like a rather compromising position. I need to find her and explain what was really happening.'

Amelia and Roddy exchanged glances.

'History repeating itself,' Amelia said without a trace of irony.

'Just calm down, son and call her. Everything will be fine, I'm sure of it. You don't know where she is so there's no point in chasing around the town trying to find her.'

'Your father's right, Robert. She could be anywhere. Sit down, take a few deep breaths then call her and tell her you need to explain. I'm sure she'll hear you out.'

Robert sneered. 'Like you heard Dad, you mean, all those years ago.'

On Thursday evening when the three of them had gone for dinner, Amelia had explained to Robert just how wrong she had been about the redhead in Roddy's lap.

'That was different, Robert. Your father and I had ... history, as we told you. Jenna, on the other hand, has no reason whatsoever to doubt you, has she?'

Robert sat in his chair and picked up the brandy Roddy had poured for him.

'No,' he said, 'she has no reason at all to doubt me.'

He smirked, remembering how she had thought he was gay, how she'd thought he'd slept with Sherree, how she'd thought he was a womaniser like his father. Then he sighed deeply and dialled her number, wondering if she'd even bother to answer the phone.

The 1812 overture sounded much louder than it usually did and when Jenna answered, her voice sounded as if she were just feet away.

'Hello Robert,' she said.

His head shot up and he couldn't believe his eyes. She was standing in the doorway of his office and, although it couldn't be said that she looked pleased, neither could it be said that she looked anywhere near as angry as he'd expected her to.

'Jenna!' he said getting to his feet and walking towards her, the phone still at his ear. 'I can explain.'

'I hope so,' Jenna said, walking slowly to meet him, her phone still at her ear.

'I think our work here is done,' Roddy said, taking Amelia's hand and leading her out, smiling at Jenna on the way.

Jenna didn't notice. Her focus was fixed firmly on

Robert's face.

'I don't know where to begin,' he said into his phone.

They were now just inches apart, their eyes locked, their breathing slow and steady.

'Daisy always says, start at the beginning but all I want to hear is the end. Was that woman, Lou, by any chance, as Daisy and I suspect it was, and were you in fact, trying to stop her from doing something to you, or herself, as we believe, rather than participating in it?' Her mouth curved into a sardonic smile. 'A yes or no will suffice – for now.'

Robert didn't say either. He took her phone from her and together with his, he tossed them onto the sofa and swept her up into his arms. He kissed her so passionately that they both thought they heard the 1812 overture – and it wasn't from Jenna's ringtone.

CHAPTER TWENTY-ONE

'I think that's a brilliant idea!' Robert said.

He and Jenna, Amelia and Roddy, Fiona and Edward and Daisy and Adam were all sitting round a table at Carluccio's one week later.

'Well, if you're going to change the club and start diversifying, you may as well make it a wedding venue too,' Roddy said.

'And don't look at me, Robert,' Amelia said. 'This is totally your father's idea. I do agree though. The house is the perfect backdrop for wedding photos and some of the gardens and woods are idyllic, too. So, we want to be the first couple to be married at 'Green Miles Weddings' or whatever you decide to call it. Jenna, I expect you can come up with something.'

'I'll try,' she said. 'It's such a shame that this isn't a house, as it once was, or a hotel even. It would make the perfect place for wedding and golf weekends combined. It could be called 'Green Miles Manor' or 'Place' or 'Park' or ... Why are you looking at me like that?'

She'd noticed that Robert, Roddy and Amelia had exchanged odd looks amongst themselves and were now looking at her with a mixture of amusement and amazement.

'Because,' Robert said, 'I was telling Mum and Dad last week that what I'd really like to do is turn this place back into part house, part country hotel and do exactly that – although I hadn't thought of the wedding bit, until now. Mum said that when she was telling you the story of poor old Eleanor and Theodore, you said something similar, about it being a hotel and having Eleanor and Theodore themed dinners. It just seems that you and I think alike.'

'Oh,' she said.

She wondered if he was thinking what she was thinking

238

at this moment, that if it was a hotel, he might want to stay and run it and wouldn't want to go back to New York. It seemed not.

'When I go back to the States,' he said, 'I'll have a word with Rick, my hotel manager and see what he thinks. So that's it then. Let's toast to Amelia and Roddy and weddings at Green Miles.'

They raised their glasses and Daisy smiled comfortingly at Jenna.

'You could always go with him,' Daisy leant over and said.

'He'd have to ask me to and let's face it, he still hasn't told me anything about it so I don't think there's much chance of that, do you? Besides, I'm not sure I could ever leave you and Adam, Mum and Dad and everyone.'

'What are you two whispering about?' Adam asked.

'New York, and how it must be such an exciting place to live' Daisy said. 'We've never been, have we Jenna?'

'You've never been to New York!' Robert exclaimed, as if going to New York were like popping down to Claremont Casks. 'Well then you must come back and stay with me for a while. I said last week that you can stay at my hotel whenever you like Daisy. All of you must come, including Gray. I've got a couple of friends there I think he might like the look of. We'll arrange something very soon.'

'Wow!' said Daisy.

'We'll all go,' Roddy said, 'if you youngsters don't mind us oldies tagging along. Fiona, Edward, you'll come won't you?'

'Well, I?' Edward said, glancing at Fiona.

'We'd love to, Roddy,' Fiona said, 'if that's okay with everyone else. Edward and I were saying only the other day that we must get away more and we haven't been to New York since our first anniversary. We went there and then up to Niagara Falls, didn't we darling?'

239

Edward was clearly too surprised to reply. He just nodded instead.

'It's fine with me,' Robert said.

'I'd love it,' Amelia said. 'We can go shopping, Fiona. There are some fabulous shops in the City.'

'I'd love that,' Fiona said.

Jenna met her father's eyes and smiled. Her mother sounded genuinely pleased. There was obviously a new friendship blossoming there but Jenna wondered what Aunt Jennifer would have to say about that. It reminded her of Lou.

Fiona and Amelia and Edward and Roddy were chatting about New York and Daisy was texting Gray to tell him he was going on a blind date in the Big Apple and she'd let him know when.

'Have you heard from Lou?' Jenna said to Robert.

'No,' he said, 'but her father called me one day in the week to say they'd got her into a private sanatorium near them. I thought I'd mentioned it to you.'

'No. You didn't. A sanatorium. That sounds grim.'

Robert smiled. 'Believe me, it's far from it. And she really does need help. I had no idea but she's apparently been taking drugs. MDMA, cocaine and others. It seems the guy she cheated on me with, is into all kinds of stuff, some of it really serious and Lou was starting down that road too. I must admit, I never could understand how she changed from being a reasonably sensible, rational woman into the volatile, one minute happy, one minute paranoid, neurotic stalker she became. I should have seen something was wrong months ago, I suppose.'

'Wow!' Jenna said, feeling she lived a very sheltered life in the small seaside town of Claremont.

'So a wedding at Green Miles,' Robert said, changing the subject to happier topics. 'Mum, Dad, have you decided on a date yet or are you going to wait and see how long it takes to get the paperwork and everything organised?'

'We thought sometime in the autumn would be nice,' Amelia said, smiling at Roddy.

'We thought, perhaps, of having it on the anniversary of our original wedding, which was the 21st of October.'

'Aw! That's so romantic,' Daisy said.

'Well, that's four and a half months away,' Robert said. 'I'm sure we'll have everything in place by then.'

'We don't want a big fuss,' Amelia said. 'We thought just a morning ceremony and a wedding luncheon. That's it. We're too old for all the party stuff, although ... I did enjoy the dinner dance last Saturday – or at least, I would have if it hadn't been for this silly foot.'

'I'm not sure how you'd feel about this,' Jenna said, 'and please say so if you think it's a terrible suggestion but ... well, Roddy, you said in your speech last Saturday that Green Miles Golf Club is 200 years old this year and that's one of the reasons you chose to hand over the reins to Robert.'

Roddy nodded. 'Yes, it is. Theodore turned Claremont Manor into a golf club in 1813.'

'I see!' Robert said. 'You're suggesting having a double celebration, aren't you? Mum and Dad's wedding and the bicentenary.'

'Yes, but it's a terrible idea. Sorry. No one wants to –'

'I love it!' Amelia and Roddy said simultaneously.

'You do? Well, it gets better then because, according to the records, the club actually opened in October 1813. Not the 21st unfortunately, but close enough.'

'That's brilliant!' Robert said. We can have your wedding in the morning and your wedding luncheon. Then we can open up the club for the evening and have a bicentennial celebratory dinner dance in the evening.'

'With a firework finale!' Daisy said.

'To music,' Fiona said.

'And I know just the music,' Robert said, grinning at

Jenna.

'The 1812 overture,' Jenna and Robert said together, laughing.

Robert sat at his desk staring out the window at the long sweep of the grounds of what was once Claremont Manor. The first tee of Green Miles Golf club now sat on what had once been quite magnificent formal gardens leading to areas of rose gardens, flower gardens, water gardens and shrubberies containing plants and shrubs from every part of the globe. He had seen sketches of the gardens and wondered what sort of a man Theodore Miles could have been to tear all that up and turn them into a golf course. A very embittered man indeed.

Robert knew the story by heart and he couldn't understand how Theodore could have loved Eleanor so much and yet hated her so much at the same time. No one would ever know if they made their peace at Eleanor's deathbed but it was a great story and one he had decided to make the most of.

'I thought you might like coffee,' Jenna said, carrying a tray of coffee and biscuits into his office.

Robert jumped up and took it from her. 'You read my mind, as usual,' he replied.

He took the tray from her and placed it on the small sofa table. Then he took her hand in his and led her to the window, standing behind her and wrapping his arms around her waist. They looked out onto the fairways basking in sunlight and the trees, standing tall and still, untroubled by even a hint of a breeze. It was early June but the weather had turned hot and sultry; the cloudless sky was so blue that it seemed to go on forever and even the birds seemed to have taken shelter from the glaring sun and were having a siesta.

'It's so beautiful,' Jenna said, 'even though it *is* a golf course.'

'You're so beautiful,' Robert replied, 'and it doesn't have to be a golf course.'

She turned to face him.

'What do you mean, "it doesn't have to be a golf course"?'

'Exactly that. I've decided to go back to New York next week –'

'So soon! Just like that. Robert! You should have told me you were planning this, you should have –'

'Whoa! Hold on. I didn't mean to stay. I simply meant for a visit. I want to see Rick, my hotel manager. I told you that the other day.'

'Oh,' she said.

'Oh indeed. Did ... did you think I was planning to run off and leave you, Jenna? *Do* you think I'm planning to do that?'

'Well. Daisy said that you said you were intending to go back to New York but you never talk about it and I ... I suppose I was too frightened to ask in case you said you were and that this has been fun but thanks and goodbye.'

He lifted her chin with his fingers. 'Is that what you think I'll do? Say thanks and goodbye?'

She nodded and shrugged her shoulders at the same time.

'And ... if I did – go back to New York I mean, would you be ... upset?'

Her eyes met his. 'Of course I'd be upset. You know I would. I've loved you all my life and just when I ...'

'Just when you ...?'

'Nothing. It doesn't matter. I realise that's where your hotel is ... and your home is. I know you're only renting here and –'

'Jenna, I think perhaps it's time I told you what my plans are. I've decided, as we were discussing the other day, to convert this clubhouse. The main part of it will be an hotel but there will also be a fairly large and I hope,

243

rather handsome, apartment. The course will be redesigned to move the first fairway from its present position and in its place, I'm going to re-establish part of the formal gardens from Claremont Manor. What do you think so far?'

'I ... I think that sounds wonderful. Is ... is that easy to do? Won't it cost a great deal of money?'

'Yes, but fortunately, Mum and Dad have decided that they would quite like to be involved in the project so they're helping out on the financial side.'

'But ... will this still be the clubhouse too?'

'No. The restaurant will remain for the new hotel, but the clubhouse and everything to do with the golf side, will move to a new clubhouse we're hoping to build between the eighteen hole course and the new nine hole course.'

'Oh. So you're going ahead with your plans for the nine hole course on Claremont Cliffs then?'

'Yes. We're in negotiations with the council and it's looking very promising. The old restaurant will be the new clubhouse and it will also have a bar and a restaurant open to all, not just members, so that people walking the cliff path – which will remain, can pop in for a coffee, a drink, or a meal.'

'Wow!' she said. 'You've thought of everything. So ... you're not going back to New York until all that's done then? Is ... is that what you're saying?'

'No. That isn't what I'm saying. Jenna, several times since I've known you, you've said that you've loved me all my life. Do you mean that or is it just a throwaway line? What I mean is, are you in love with me? Do you love me now? The reason I ask is because I know beyond any shadow of a doubt that I'm in love with you, that I love you, so it would be really good if you were.'

Jenna's eyes opened wide and she was sure her lower jaw hit her chest.

'You ... you love me?'

Robert nodded, 'Yes.'

'Really? You ... you really love me?'

'Yes. Would you like me to write a list of the reasons why? I can think of several. But you didn't answer my question. Do you love me?'

'Yes, Robert! Yes! Oh yes! I love you!'

She flung herself into his arms and kissed him. When they finally eased apart, she kept her arms around him, almost afraid that if she let him go, she'd wake up and find she'd imagined the entire conversation.

'That's answered that question,' he said. 'But there are one or two other things I'd like to clarify, if that's okay with you? First, I've decided to make my home here, at Green Miles Manor or whatever you decide we're going to call it, in the new apartment in this very building. Would that meet with your approval?'

'You're staying ... here? Honestly? You're really staying here?'

'Yes. Do you think turning part of this place back into a home is a good idea?'

'Yes, Robert, I do. Very much so.'

'Wonderful. Second, would you consider moving in here with me? Into the new apartment?'

'Moving ... in here ... with you?'

'Yes. Would you consider it?'

'Yes, Robert, I will. I mean. I'd love to move in here with you. Yes, Robert. Yes!'

'Excellent. We can draw up the plans together and decide exactly what it'll look like. Third, I know we haven't known each other long but I want you to understand that, if you do this, we are as good as engaged. I won't actually propose to you yet because that would take the shine off Mum and Dad's wedding ... not forgetting the bicentennial celebrations of course, and we all know, nothing is more important than celebrating 200 years of Green Miles Golf Club, don't we?' He grinned.

'But you do understand don't you? As far as I'm concerned, this is a lifelong commitment? Yes will suffice.'

Jenna was utterly speechless. Was Robert Miles actually proposing to her – in a very roundabout way?

'Jenna?'

'Yes!' Was all she could manage to say.

'Superb. Now what was the fourth thing?' he said pulling her tighter into his arms. 'Oh yes, I remember. Something about an office chair ... I have a few ideas but I wondered if you'd like to help me come up with a few more.'

'Yes, Robert. Yes. I'd like that very much indeed.'

'I thought you might,' he said taking her by the hand and leading her towards his chair.

One year later

'It's so beautiful here,' Jenna said.

Robert took her in his arms. 'You're so beautiful,' he replied.

She smiled up at him and looked around her at the grass-covered ground beneath her feet, the plump green leaves of the ancient trees barely rustling in a whisper of a June breeze. A chorus of birdsong serenaded them as they stood together, surrounded by a circle of sunlight filtering down from a cloudless bright blue sky. She glanced at the tree stump where she'd sat and cried more than a year ago and sighed.

'This time tomorrow,' she said. 'Are you sure you're ready for this?'

Robert laughed and tilted her chin up so that he could look into her eyes. 'I've been ready for this since the first day I met you,' he said. 'Are you sure you're ready for this? A yes or no will suffice.' He kissed the tip of her nose.

Her eyes took in the streamers of white ribbons tied to

all the trees encircling her and Robert, at the pergola erected over the tree stump and wound with white ribbon and yellow roses and at the chairs placed in a semi-circle around them. Her face glowed with pure happiness.

'I've been ready for this since I was ten years old,' she said. 'I hope it doesn't rain.'

'It won't rain,' he said.

'I wonder what Eleanor and Theodore will think.'

'Of us getting married in the woods, you mean, or of this?' He laid his fingers on the bump barely visible beneath her summer dress. 'We can ask them in six months time when they're born. Well, we may have to wait until they are old enough to talk to get an answer,' he said.

She smiled. 'I meant, calling them Eleanor and Theodore.'

'They'll love it,' he said, 'and if they don't, it'll give them something to resent their parents for. Now, Miss Baker, before you become Mrs Jenna Miles tomorrow, there's something I need to clarify. Well, not clarify, exactly, just ask, and a yes or no will suffice. First, have you ever made love in a wood?'

Jenna giggled. 'No.'

'Good. Second, would you like to make love in a wood?'

Jenna's eyes met his and she wrapped her arms around his neck.

'Oh yes, Robert. Yes. Very much so.'

'Excellent. Third. Oh, I forget what the third was,' he said, leaning closer.

He kissed her and eased her slowly and gently towards the bed of grass and moss beneath their feet.

*** THE END ***

Sailing Solo
Love's not always plain sailing

Willa Daventry knows what she wants. She's thirty-two, single and determined to take her family's travel company to the top of the 'singles holidays' charts. She has the next two years planned out and nothing's going to get in her way.

Thirty-five-year-old travel writer, Mark Thornton, believes singles holidays are a joke, but he's writing a feature about them, so feels there's no harm in having a little fun in the sun – and a sailing holiday in Greece should be a lot of fun.

Greek hotel owner, Aristaios Nikolades, and holidaying advertising executive, Harry 'Banner' Bullen, feel the same. When Harry drunkenly suggests a wager to see which of them can get a date with Willa, Mark and Aristaios both agree.

Competitive Mark is determined to win but Aristaios and Harry don't play fair. He'll have to keep divorcee, Suki Thane and sex-mad, pilates instructor, Blossom Appleyard, at bay if he is to stand a chance. Will Mark sail off into the sunset with Willa – or will Harry or Aristaios, scupper his plans?

Willa doesn't usually mix business with pleasure but the attentions of three handsome men are enough to turn any girl's head. Should she keep things professional, or risk a little romance and get what she wants into the bargain? Harry's advertising skills could prove useful; a new deal needs to be negotiated with Aristaios, and a five-star review from Mark would be a dream come true.

But when Willa learns of the bet, will she forgive the men, or will she feel she's better off sailing solo?

***

To see more of my books or to contact me, pop over to my website (link below). I'd love you to nip over to Facebook and either 'Like' my author page or send me a friend request on my personal page – or follow me on Twitter or Pinterest. You can subscribe to my newsletter via the 'Sign me up' box on my website, send me an email and/or leave me an honest review of this book on Amazon. You'll find the links below.

Thanks again, and I look forward to chatting with you soon.

Author contacts :
http://www.emilyharvale.com
http://www.twitter.com/emilyharvale
http://www.facebook.com/emilyharvale
http://www.facebook.com/emilyharvalewriter
http://www.emilyharvale.com/blog
http://www.pinterest.com/emilyharvale
http://www.amazon.co.uk/Emily-Harvale/e/B007BKQ1SW

Printed in Great Britain
by Amazon